When We Become Men

The tensions of Naomi Mitchison's new novel
spring from her setting, Bechuanaland, and
from the problems surrounding the loyalties
and loves of her characters. It is, in particu-
lar, the story of Isaac, a political refugee from
the Republic of South Africa who is granted
asylum by the chief on the other side of the
border. But the chief dies and police spies
infiltrate across the frontier. The ripples
widen, and Isaac becomes just one of the
many problems confronting the young chief
who arrives from London in time to prevent
a schism in the tribe. Both men face acute
personal danger and violence, both find
difficulties in the path of love and ultimately
have to answer opposite questions about
the new Africa in which they live: can Isaac
afford to accept the traditional benefits of a
tribe for ever or can the young chief afford
to let them disappear?

When We Become Men

Naomi Mitchison

With an introduction by
Isobel Murray

Kennedy & Boyd

Kennedy & Boyd
an imprint of
Zeticula
57 St Vincent Crescent
Glasgow
G3 8NQ
Scotland.

http://www.kennedyandboyd.co.uk
admin@kennedyandboyd.co.uk

First published by Wm Collins in 1965

This Edition first published 2009

ISBN-13 978-1-904999-23-2 Paperback
ISBN-10   1-904999-23-9 Paperback

For my friends among the Batswana
and most of all
for my dear son
Linchwe of the Bakgatla

Wild rider with hounds afoot
In the glare of African day,
And the bay reined tight,
Let him gallop, gallop, the bay!
He will not shake you off
Nor will your people shake you
When you give them a loose rein,
Your people who love and make you
Into what they cannot explain:
Who know and will never mistake you.

You are our child,
We send you out
To show us the things of the outer world:
What truth is about:
Let us not be beguiled!

You are our mother
And you our wife:
We shall have food if your hand is there,
We shall take our life
From you and no other.

You are our bull,
You lead the way
Into hope and sense for a Tribe and Country,
To a better day
And the spirit's river full.

Wild rider, bull and child,
This weight of hope on your head
Balances you as you ride:
All and nothing is said;
The world is left outside
Keeping alone for you
Your people's love and mine:
Love keep the balance true.

I would like to state most definitely that all people and situations in this book, as well as the two main towns, are entirely imaginary. The only exceptions are the real people who appear momentarily under their own names in Chapter 22.

Introduction

The last time I met Naomi Mitchison was at the launch of Jenni Calder's biography, *The Nine Lives of Naomi Mitchison*. This was at the Edinburgh Book Festival in 1997, when the biographer spoke about her subject, and I contributed a short paper on another novel, *Lobsters on the Agenda*. Everyone was thrilled at the appearance of the tiny, frail figure in a wheelchair, the centenarian herself. And despite the frailty, perhaps no one was entirely surprised when, at the end, the author asked to speak. In a surprisingly strong voice, she asked the audience whether she had done enough for Africa.

By any standards, even her own, she had. Her association with Linchwe, paramount chief designate of the Bakgatla of the British Protectorate of Bechuanaland, began in 1960, when he was a 'mature' schoolboy, and she a grandmother in her sixties.. Thereafter she had a twenty-five year association with the chief and with his tribe, of both of whom she became the adopted mother. At first, "At that time, I didn't know where Botswana was". But she soon became a member of the tribe, and for a long time spent part of every year there, helping, advising and educating, and she began to write to, for and about "her" people.

She was always a prolific writer. Between 1965 and 1980 she wrote twenty-five books, eleven of them concerning Africa. Half of these were for young people. Typical is *The Family at Ditlabeng* (1969), which describes the life, education and career opportunities for young people in this vividly realised Botswana village, and indicates the extra difficulties caused by drought, by unpredictable lack of rain, by traditional customs and new ideas. In fiction, there was an adult novel, which you are holding now, and a fine late collection of stories, mostly related to myth or tradition, *Images of Africa* (1980).

The non-fiction books for adults include a very personal and spontaneous account of Mitchison's long involvement with Africa, *Return to the Fairy Hill* (1966). Thereafter *African Heroes* (1968) offered role models for both adults and children in a world that had been wrenched out of shape by the impact of colonialism, losing a good deal of black Africa's historical and literary inheritance. It was followed by a bold attempt at the history of the whole continent, *The Africans* (1970), and lastly by *A Life for Africa: the Story of Bram Fischer* (1973). In all but the last of these you could say that education in the widest sense was the motive force; educating the people of Botswana about their past, their culture, and their prospects, and educating a British — ideally a world — audience about the lives and future opportunities of black people in a small African country.

But with *A Life for Africa* Mitchison could be said to enter the struggle herself, describing and extolling a very exceptional white man who was prepared to suffer for what he believed. A well-born Afrikaner, he came from a distinguished family, roughly comparable in status with the Haldanes of Gleneagles in Scotland. He became a freedom fighter, a Communist, and Nelson Mandela's comrade and lawyer. He played an integral role on the defence in the Treason Trial of 1956-61, where Mandela was acquitted, and led Mandela's legal defence at the Rivonia Trial of 1963-4, avoiding a death sentence for his friend.

He was himself arrested in 1964, went underground for a year and was then again arrested in 1966, when he was tried and sentenced to life imprisonment. This was the ongoing situation when Mitchison wrote her book. He was kept in prison until dying of cancer in 1975. Mitchison's title, *A Life for Africa,* is a fitting one. Nelson Mandela later said of Fischer:

> Bram was a courageous man who followed the most difficult course any person could choose to follow. He challenged his own people because he felt what they were doing was morally wrong. As an Afrikaner whose conscience forced him to reject his own heritage and be ostracised by his own people, he showed a level of courage and sacrifice that was in a class by itself.

Besides books, and as always when Mitchison was captivated by a new cause, all these themes were reflected over and over again in her journalism. No wonder she was a thorn in the side of white governments.

Jenni Calder writes:

> It was no surprise when . . . Naomi became a proscribed immigrant, in both South Africa and Southern Rhodesia. [1]

All this provides a fascinating side light on the struggle for human rights in South Africa, during years when various countries developed, or were rechristened with more African names, or continued to be governed by variously oppressive colonial administrations. If you want to know more, Chapter Seven of Jenni Calder's biography, "African Journeys", is the best short account. But all the adult volumes referred to above are worth searching out and investigating, if Africa – or Mitchison – takes a greater grip on the reader.

When We Become Men (1965) is one of her earliest books about Africa, and the only adult novel. When I asked her about it in an in depth interview in 1984, she offered a slightly different judgement on it in hindsight. Initial excitement had had decades to reach a soberer realism:

> I haven't re-read it for a very long time. I don't know how it would read now. I think I'd probably feel that it was a bit romanticised, that it was in too bright colours. I think that probably the political thing is all right, but whether anyone now would feel about the tribe I'm not sure. And it's curious that the two older people in the Bakgatla whom I knew very well were in a curious way – they had a sort of nobility that I don't see coming up among their successors. They were people who believed strongly

in the ethos of the tribe, and who were deeply kind in a gentle way. They had, I suppose, all the things that one imagines the ideal Highlander should have, and I don't know whether the next generation is going to feel at all the same way. [2]

The comparison with the ideal Highlander is telling: before Botswana, Mitchison had devoted herself wholeheartedly to Scotland for many years, and felt a sense of failure – perhaps in another country, another continent, a different stage in civilisation, she could help to construct the ideal society she had searched to find or make since she was a girl.

The novel occasionally makes hard going, only in the sense that change was integral to politics in Southern Africa in these decades: some points are so obvious to the initiated that they do not get fully explained to a later readership, even by such a mistress of exposition as Mitchison: for example that Bechuanaland was home to Linchwe's tribe, but it was not so simple:

Linchwe's tribe was divided by a political boundary, with a large part still in South Africa, and as apartheid bit deeper and resistance grew, refugees made their way across the border. Bechuanaland, Botswana from 1966, could not detach itself from events and developments in South Africa. [C:228]

So the novel begins with Isaac and Josh caught escaping from South Africa, being returned there to justice for their actions as 'freedom fighters'. Then city-born freedom fighter Isaac takes advantage of an opportunity to jump from the train and escape into an older, tribal society with very different beliefs and customs, a society he initially regards as oppressive, run by chiefs, "old tyrants and bloodsuckers" (page14).

It is always worth giving careful consideration to the titles Mitchison gives her books, and *When We Become Men* is no exception. Is it a quotation? No, not exactly. But it does echo a very well known sentence from the Bible, with very significant differences:

> When I was a child, I spake as a child, I understood as a child, I thought as a child: but when I became a man, I put away childish things. (1 Cor 13)

Paul, convinced of the truth of his mature religious belief, writes this to the Corinthians. He has become a man, and says he can distinguish between adult matters and childish affairs. In her title, Mitchison most importantly changes both the tense and the number. *When We Become Men* implies that 'we' will definitely reach maturity, the manhood that 'we' are moving toward, but that 'we' are still to some extent surrounded by childish ideas and immature notions, seeing "through a glass darkly". The change to 'we' involves both author and readers in the process, as an early Mitchison novel did with *We Have Been Warned*: the characters are not to be seen as foreign or alien; we relate to them and learn with them.

Why are they still in some sense children? The process of colonialisation, which took place across Africa in multifarious ways, can be seen to some extent to have infantilised the Africans, deprived of their history, their traditions, their tribal patterns and their very borders, their place in the world and their ability to govern themselves and exercise choice. Now, through Isaac and Josh, the city-born freedom fighters on the one hand, and Letlotse, the young and Europeanised chief designate, we are given a sympathetic understanding of their dilemmas, and their as it were adolescent appreciation of crucial ideas and words, such as freedom, democracy, independence and modernity. What should they be aiming for?

At one time Isaac and Josh (and their lost friend Amos) are sure of the answer. City-bred, they have no tribal loyalties at first, and see everything in terms of political parties fighting for freedom, and against oppressive Acts. When Isaac jumps off the train taking him back to the Republic and prison, he fears what he will find now, "in the middle of nowhere, tribal country, but he didn't even know which tribe" (p.11).

He believes that "Everything that mattered for South Africa was happening in the towns" (p. 11), and believes he sees clearly what he is fighting for:"For their rights, for freedom and democracy, against the old witch doctors and chiefs!" (p.12).

By the end of the novel, the process of becoming Man has moved on, but is not finished. Isaac has certainly matured, to a more complex vision of the tribe and its sustaining, family-like nature. He has joined a tribe and undergone life-changing experiences, and when at the end he goes back "for a time" to the freedom struggle, he leaves an established family. There is his wife Tselane, a strong and nurturing woman; there is her son by Isaac, named after Amos; there is her elder son, Kodunzwe, the result of her rape by Motswasele, the baby whom she initially rejected but came to love; and there are Jim and Moses, the innocent sons of the traitor Big Manuel, who was executed by the group, led by Tselane. It is natural for Tselane to adopt them when they arrive in search of their missing father, as she tells Isaac:

"Those two children as much refugees from the Republic as you and Josh. . . My children, now, Isaac. I have said. . . . Your children, Isaac."(p.151)

Josh is a less central character. He joined the tribe before Isaac and was first to learn the new loyalty to the tribe, but he too will return to the struggle in time. But it is emphasised at the end that neither is to be a terrorist in the modern sense: like Mandela and his colleagues, they believe in making an impact by sabotage, by destroying man-made objects, not killing men:

"Tselane my wife, I do not go to kill. I go to make things difficult for them. Only difficult. So that slowly they may begin to know that their days of easiness are over. That they must come to terms if it is not too late. Perhaps even that some of them may become ashamed. That is why many people have to do this work." (p. 254)

Has Isaac become a man? He says to Tselane as he is leaving, "I am an altogether different person because of you and because of the Bamatsieng. There are things I am not afraid of any longer." The journey toward manhood has at least begun.

So: Isaac came from the struggle, and after consolidating his life with the tribe and his family, he returns to it for a time. What of Letlotse? For a long time he is an unknown quantity, sent far away for his education. This was clearly done with the best of intentions, and at some sacrifice, but it is inevitably going to be a difficult experience for the young man – learning a different culture and different ways, and being taught in an alien education system: he will need a very mature head on young shoulders to achieve instant African maturity out of it all. He does not return to Ditlabeng until more than half way through the book. But just as Isaac's progress is marked throughout by the discussions he has, primarily with Josh and Tselane, we have two early glimpses of Letlotse in Chapters 6 and 10. We can measure his progress in the novel if he grows from the positions he takes here. In chapter 6 we see Letlotse meeting his sister Seneo in a London café, and get first impressions of both. She is the elder and more composed; she seems more at ease in this foreign environment, and she teases her little brother affectionately. He objects:

"You must not scold me, I will not be scolded by a woman!"

"You are a savage, my little brother", said Seneo.
"Let us eat some more ice-cream, you shall pay for
it. (p. 70)

It is Seneo who raises the shadow of their father's illness, and his response is instant. If he goes back under bad circumstances, the first thing he will have to do is raise a regiment, a *mophato*.

It will be such a bore. I cannot think how I would
manage at all. Running after animals and learning all
those stupid songs and the old men hitting me if I get
a word wrong!" (p. 71-2)

When Seneo raises the possibility of Motswasele as Regent, he counters with his adolescent dream of politics:

Supposing I went home not as chief but as leader
of a whole political party? For the whole of the
country. The whole of Bechuanaland. Not just our
own little reserve. For it is little. Think how much
less than those of the Bamangwato, the Bakwena, the
Bakgatla, even, why should I be stuck there? (p. 73)

She counters his grandiose notion drily, "It is your own pond, frog."

He goes on to outline his aims with big words, Progress, Unity, Industry, Education. When Seneo warns him to count his enemies, "he had the proud look of a boy on a sand castle" – hardly a secure foundation. When she calls him "my beautiful leopard", we are the more aware of his boyishness. When the conversation moves to Motswasele, Seneo immediately remembers his undefended rape of Tselane, and he says carelessly: "Oh, Tselane. I expect she wanted it." (p. 76)

This is a million miles from the scene in chapter 20 where Seneo tells her brother about herself being raped by Motswasele, and he is "some way torn with pity". (p. 213) Clearly at this early stage Letlotse's maturity has not been reached.

In Chapter 10 we encounter him again, still in London. He is aware now of his father's death and the urgent necessity for him to return, and goes to talk with his Indian friend Kumar. Inside himself, he is feeling increasingly grown up:

> He remembered the time when he had been frightened of the Underground, especially the moving staircase. A long time back. He remembered how he had thought they were colour-barring him because they put up their newspapers in front of them but it was only to read; now he did the same. He used to have plenty of silly notions, but he had been proud, perhaps prouder than he was now. Thought he could carry the world in front of him! He had been altogether too young. But now, looking back even a couple of months, he felt he was changed, more grown up. (p. 105)

Two months, he believes, have changed him so much! He and Kumar discuss Letlotse's ambitions not just for the tribe, but for the whole country, and he speaks with some confidence, although progress would surely involve uncertain relations with the Americans or the Russians. But when Letlotse feels that the Colonial Office suspects him of being pro-Communist, after a recent undergraduate visit to Russia, he immediately, unthinkingly and angrily accuses Kumar of treachery. He is going to have to learn more measured ways. Only after some time does he wonder if it was the Regent Motswasele who smeared his reputation. The patient Kumar asks what he would do if he knew for sure, and Letlotse replies with a laugh: "There is nothing like a good old assegai". This has an ironic ring, if we remember the old chief's words about his former authority at Isaac's first meeting with the tribal authorities:

There was an assegai lying on pegs above the door. The chief pointed at it.

That used to be for justice. Or against the disobedient. It has been taken from me. Perhaps that is right. It is not, what do you say, Motswasele, modern. Modern is napalm, is bombs dropping on people you do not see. But I say in the name of the tribe, that it shall protect these men. And you" – he turned to the younger man – "if you bargain with them it shall be pointed at you. (p. 23)

There is still a lot of "tribal justice" in the book, with a fairly shocking amount of killing in secret of traitors and rapists, and in the end Motswasele does die in this way, not by a chief's assegai but by an old woman's smothering, followed by all present holding the cushion down "so that we should share what had to be done"(p. 210). Seneo regretfully relates this after her rape:

I had thought he might struggle but he did not. It was like killing a dead man. It was a pity we could not hurt him.

As often elsewhere, here the women are strong and firm of purpose, as when Tselane tortures and kills the traitor Big Manuel. But the impact of this is lessened by most of it taking place "off-stage", and being reported more briefly in the novel.

In general, it seems the chief sometimes exerts less power than the people, when it comes to the point: the two men responsible for poisoning Letlotse and Isaac are doomed by the tribe while Letlotse is still fighting for his life, and his choice is to let them die quickly or slowly, and whether to make their children suffer too: a more mature Letlotse has them shot at once, and their sons spared.

But earlier, when Letlotse returns to Botswana he still has much to learn. Seneo warns Tselane of his foolish ideas, learned abroad:

Tselane, he thinks he can talk reason to Motswasele, and to Motswasele's creature Dikgang, the one who told the new D.C. he was a Communist! Oh yes, I know. Poor me, only a woman. Letlotse is the man, the leopard, thinks he can talk reason to everyone. Sees himself as head of a Batswana National Political Party. Programme: reason, sweet reason! Oh, he is crazy." (p. 154)

She goes on, more sympathetically, less of the elder sister:

Letlotse will have to be very careful. I do not know how many people can be entirely trusted. Many can be half trusted, but that is not enough. And Letlotse has not learned to be careful yet.

Although Tselane is shocked at this criticism, she gets a rather similar impression:

To Tselane he seemed even more different than he had been other times, but also not grown up, a half-formed man still not thickened out, a big and clever boy (p. 156)

The author never attempts to sum up what changes Letlotse, but it has to be some kind of combination of raising his *mophato* and becoming chief, learning of Motswasele's evil and the several deaths, surviving septicaemia and protecting Isaac from dying, learning of Seneo's rape and his conversations with Isaac in the later chapters. After five tough days of the *mophato,* he was already feeling "marvellously alive and well". Things were coming together, and he naturally turned to Isaac, "the only one who was likely to share his knowledge and his questions" (p. 186).

But the all-but-fatal experience of deliberate poisoning dramatically cuts into this: he is much weakened, and Isaac near death, when Letlotse seems to draw upon some ancient tribal power to call him back from death. Here, tribal wisdom triumphs, but only after the illicit use of western penicillin; throughout the book, western medicine is the only western thing that seems to attract no criticism. After this, some of the older men are certain that the bad medicine had been conquered, and so certain they were also of the power and strengthening which God and his ancestors had given the chief.

(p. 198)

Letlotse knows something definitive has happened: "I shall never forget what I have learned, my fathers, nor I think will my comrades" (p. 200).

But he still experiences internal division, a "divided self":

> And with one part of him he was thinking that in changing Isaac's name he would also break any black magic which was still holding on to him, and also tie him into the Bamatsieng and in a sense into his own possession, and with the other part of his mind he was thinking what nonsense it all was, but in a friendly way since nothing but good was being done. (p. 201)

At least for Letlotse there is not now an angry conflict between the parts. Isaac goes from secular politician to belonging – since Letlotse saved him, he belongs – "I'm his, Josh." But Josh reminds him:

> You belong to Africa, not to any one man, even your chief, even the head of your regiment. Even this Letlotse. Africa, Isaac, Africa, all this that we haven't seen but we know it's there once we get free. Africa. . . . I think all the same our Letlotse is a part of Africa that we never knew, we in the Republic, we city guys. We're lucky to have him for our new chief, but me, I didn't think he'd turn out like that. Seems he's changed in eight days. (p. 207)

Things and people have changed, and will go on changing, and Letlotse and Isaac will both have to square the values of the old life of the tribe with the new. Letlotse must accept the rites of his installation, although his other half wants to be civilised. Isaac is persuasive:

> You would have lost the common purpose which
> is in the heart. Which is happiness. The thing which
> is in the Bamatsieng now. Listen, Letlotse, for I think
> I have it! Most kinds of society are too big for this.
> It is only for war that they come together. Never for
> anything good. (p. 227)

They come to a shared hope, that if the Batswana unite in one country, while keeping the warmth of the separate tribes, then they can improve the country. But they know, there was a time, when to be seen as a man, a man must have killed, and "It is difficult to move from that kind of order into another." (p. 228)

They have not come to an end, but to a recognition of the direction in which they want to go, and some of the difficulties. Isaac cannot yet settle as a teacher:

> Not while Amos is still in. Not till we're all free. All
> Africa, Rhodesia, Angola, Mozambique, the South
> West, our neighbours. (p. 235)

As in Mitchison's first novel, *The Conquered*, (1923), tribal loyalties and questions of allegiance must be settled. In a way all of Mitchison's novels come to understanding loyalties and seeing that they do not conflict. In 1984 she said to us:

I'm sure that one of the most interesting things that happen to anyone, is this business of loyalties and how to reconcile them. One's got a loyalty presumably to one's family to begin with, and then it widens out to one's village, one's town, one's country. Perhaps to being a European, and finally, I suppose, to being a human being. But one feels that *that* loyalty is the one that's got to be cultivated, because at the moment we are all threatened, whatever our colour or race or anything. [I: 73]

Notes

1 See Jenni Calder, *The Nine Lives of Naomi Mitchison,* London, 1997, p 240. Further page numbers will be given in brackets in the text, as [C:000.]

2 See Isobel Murray, Editor, *Scottish Writers Talking 2*, East Linton, 2002, p 103. Further page numbers will be given in brackets in the text, as [I:000]

Chapter I

ONE OF THEM was asleep—was he? Isaac reached out a hand and touched him like a fly on his red knee. Nothing moved. The other was standing just outside in the corridor. But there was a woman in a dressing-gown, a horrible, a distasteful woman with thin yellowish hair wisps and dry skin. And the guard was edging up to her and both were laughing. If he could slip past. Thank God they hadn't put the cuffs on him. That would be done—at the border. Was there room? If they saw him, he would say he had to pee. Not that he had anything to pee with; the guards drank tea when the steward came round, and one of them had flicked a hot drop in his face, but naturally there'd been no cup for the prisoner.

The train, never very fast, was slower at night, bumping and swinging like an ox cart almost. Nothing to show where they'd got to, stopping at every little station, and then the guards would sit up and look fierce. But Isaac didn't know where they were, only that it was a long time since they'd left Francistown behind. These names of the little stations didn't mean a thing. Except that most of them had been Englished out of Tswana. Or else the train would stop in a siding while a freight train went by, rattle rattle bump, going the other way, back

9

towards Rhodesia. How long till they got to the border? He didn't know. They'd taken his watch. Taken his money. His shoes. His pass. Everything. And where was Josh? Where, where, was Amos? On the same train? Or not? You couldn't even dare to ask in case one of them had got away when they all ran. Just possibly the guards mightn't know there had been three of them.

And if they got to the border. Into the Republic of South Africa. God. If—he could stand a good deal of pain, he'd stood it already. But they had some new tricks. He tried to feel all over what it was like, not yet being hurt; it only made him thirstier.

Slowly, slowly he got to his feet in the jolting carriage in the half dark. He edged past the sleeper easily, not touching. It was hot. He could smell the one in the corridor, smelt his sweat dripping down his neck, sweating more because of the woman, the animal smell of whites. He flattened himself, snaked through the doorway and down the corridor, past backs that swayed, dark, sleepy. He could tell by their smell whose they were. But not, for certain, that another African, perhaps out of clumsiness or fear or stupidity, would not betray him.

The train was slowing a little. Was it? But he mustn't wait for a station. Better a broken leg in the bush than to be caught in a station. If only the others—no use thinking of that now. He pressed on the handle of the outer door. He could see ground rushing in the half light. Try to fall soft. No noise. He was on the step, the single track below him. He jumped, shielding his head, rolled over and over, felt thorns, felt stones. The dim lights of the train flowed over him as though he was an old bundle, something dead and still.

He got up shakily, felt himself. Blood here and there, but nothing broken or sprained. So now? He must be in the middle of nowhere, tribal country, but he didn't even know which tribe. That wasn't the kind of thing they'd ever thought about. Everything that mattered for Africa was happening in the towns. Some of his friends had said that these tribal people were against them, hated them, would give them up to the Special Branch, being well paid for it. They were poor, of course, desperately poor since the drought. Almost starving. If you are poor enough you do anything so that your kids get food. Or if they thought about it at all, they'd think these refugees from South Africa would bring them trouble, maybe take any miserable little jobs they had. God!

The train was out of sight now, a slinking beast of dim lights. He picked his way, feeling little trickles of blood running down here or there. He came on a fence, on a dust road, wondered whether to take it. Something moved among the bushes. Buck? Or a lion? There were lions here still. Or a snake. He wished he had his shoes. Maybe it was only cattle.

All he knew was, he must walk the other way from the train. And fast. No use trying to walk in the bush, you'd trip yourself up every second step, but he could dodge back if he saw traffic coming. Yes, there was a late lorry. He stepped back and was lost. Yet they might have been friends! Or at least given him a lift and no questions. A lift to somewhere he would perhaps be able to get water. What wouldn't he have given for a beer, a cool beer! He began to think of that as he walked, and the dust got everywhere. Even so late at night it was still warm under his feet. Maybe he should have got on the lorry. Sooner or later he'd have to trust someone. Though that was how they'd been caught. Christ!

One of the cuts was damned sore, oozing blood. But made, not by people, but by a natural thorn jagging across as he fell. He thought and thought of bathing it. The train would be across the border by now. And they'd know. Could they possibly think of driving back to see if they could pick him up? He'd better get a move on. But as he walked faster the blood oozed faster, another cut started up. Besides, he had done too much town walking in shoes, wasn't used to going the old way.

You couldn't tell what was on either side of the road, only a great swing of stars, cool looking above the hot ground, the hot dust-choky air. Something ran across the road, scuttling. He jumped and stopped, then went on, driving himself, his legs aching. Too late for traffic.

What should he do? He couldn't make up his mind. He felt dead scared of these tribal people who didn't know that, in the end, he was fighting for them. For their rights, for freedom and democracy, against the old witch doctors and chiefs! They'd know by his voice, by the remains of his clothes, even, that he was a stranger, and so someone to be got rid of. They didn't know the meaning of the word freedom: his word. How could they know, tied down the way they were, tied down by their own wish, worse than being bossed over by whites!

He felt himself inside hating them. And yet they were his only chance. He'd need the hell of a lot of luck.

Then there were car lights coming and his fear switched. Could it be—them? Looking for him! No, they were coming too slow, and the lights not the strong frightening police lights. He'd signal: safe enough. If it was a white he'd drive on. But an African might stop. Might. As Isaac stopped walking he knew how dead tired he was. He stood forward into the lights of an old Land-Rover and signalled. The car stopped. Yes, yes, they were black faces. He asked would they take him a piece along the road. His voice was low and husky with dust. He bundled into the back of the Land-Rover and tiredness came over him as he doubled up. There were two or three people there already, and someone handed him a half-full Coca-Cola bottle. He drank it in one gulp and dropped asleep, his head on his knees, feeling nothing.

Then there was a hand on his shoulder and he jumped awake. But it was a friendly hand. They were saying that they turned off here—he didn't catch the name of the place. Did he want to get out? One of them was shining a torch on him. He got to his feet and suddenly the cut opened again and bled sharply in the light of the torch. At once the driver was questioning him—had he fallen off a lorry, had a fight? Isaac stumbled over his answer, and as he did, realised that the man at the wheel was youngish, a big chap with a clean shirt and a good jacket on the back of the seat. Where was he bound? Isaac didn't know where to say that would seem right, then said Francistown, though it was the last place he really wanted to get to. He added for good measure

13

that he was a building worker. It would make sense, a mason or a carpenter travelling. If they believed him. Two or three of them began talking at once, saying the chief could use him. God, he was among the tribals! An elderly man on the front seat turned to the driver and began a long story of some man whom his grandfather had picked up on the road starving, and put into the back of an ox cart, and he had turned out to be a great craftsman, had made this and that which they all knew. Isaac wished he'd said he mended radios, that was something he did know about. If they expected him to build for them—Christ, he'd need a bit of luck! No, he'd get out—but the Land-Rover had started off with a jerk and hands were holding him, not cruelly, but hard, the thin, sinewy tribal fingers! He sank back, and the pain from the cut receded as he slept again past all the jolting and talking. And then the Rover stopped. In the headlights he saw a huge kraal of grey, close-set, sinister branches, over head height, with the shapes of cattle behind them; then with the switch-off, all went dark again. He knew he would need every bit of his luck.

They put him into a rondavel and barred the door. Someone unbarred it, threw in a couple of sacks, then put down on the floor a cracked cup of water and some rags. With the door barred again and his eyes accustoming to the dark, Isaac groped for the cup, careful not to knock it over, and began to bathe his cuts. There was no window, but a little starlight filtered in between wall top and thatch. Where and in what shape would he have been if the train had taken him on? But again he slept, the sacks between him and the earth floor, and only

14

woke when the door was unbarred and an old woman came in, bringing him a bowl of *mabele* porridge and a cup of water; she put some ointment on that stung, and a rough kind of bandage, the ragged end of an old shirt, on to the worst cut. The sour porridge, that he thought of as Kaffir-corn because he was so used to things out of packets, gave him disturbing thoughts of his childhood, which he did not want to have.

He tried to find out from the old woman where he was, but the place names meant nothing, and her accent made it difficult for him to make her out. In the end he asked what was to be done with him. She said he was to be taken to the chief.

So that was it. And if this chief found out who he was, he would sell him. Because, naturally, if any chief encouraged the refugees, or even turned a blind eye, that would mean trouble for them. And freedom—what did that mean to the chiefs? A gang of old tyrants and bloodsuckers! Well, he must not let them know who he was. Better not give his name even; it might be something they'd heard of. Could well be. They'd done a job in the Republic, the three of them. Some would call them terrorists. Others would say they were a resistance group: depending which way you looked at it. But the job had come off. They couldn't risk staying. Come back later on maybe under other names. Meanwhile get away. To Dar.

That meant going through Rhodesia, had to. No other way. They thought they'd got their papers all right, but even before they got to the Rhodesian frontier—well, that was Inter Pol, or whatever devilish thing they called it. The police heads of all countries getting together to suppress crime! To keep order. Their kind of order. Amos had spotted what was happening, knew they must scatter and hide. But it was he himself who'd made the decision to tell the man in the café, the man who'd seemed friendly. Not enough time to judge. A risk that had to be taken. And had gone wrong.

Amos had said no, they mustn't trust him. But just then they had to trust someone! They might have had a bit of luck. But once they had spoken to that man the trap was sprung. So it was his fault. His own fault. Amos. Josh. In the dim light he thought passionately about his friends and what they had tried to do together: what they had risked their lives for. But how few people cared! How few of their own people. How few Africans. He could have cried.

Later in the morning the door was unbarred again, and he was taken out by two of the men. He looked round quickly. He seemed to be in the middle of a big flat village of thatched houses in smooth and fairly tidy compounds with mud plastered walls, shaped and crenellated. He could say he worked in reinforced concrete: that would fox them! They took him to a large, old-fashioned, tin-roofed house with a flight of steps up to it, and a few old mango and citrus trees, badly looked after, beside it. Nobody held him, but he knew that they would if he was not obedient.

They brought him into a room with a worn lion skin carpet over lino, and a heavy-looking desk with some law books on it. A big, middle-aged man was writing there; he looked worried and tired, and his shirt sleeves had

16

cigarette burns on them, but it was apparent from the way the men spoke and behaved that this was the chief. Isaac acted stupid and scared, and stuck to the reinforced concrete story, also that he'd fallen off a lorry. The chief questioned him crossly, sometimes hitting the desk with his fist, and then the young man who had driven the Land-Rover came in and sat down beside him; Isaac wondered if he was some relation to the chief, cousin or nephew. He spoke suddenly in English: "Tell the truth, man, what were you doing?" But Isaac hunched himself up, deaf and dumb; he wasn't going to be caught.

The young man signed with a head slant to the two who had brought him in; they went out. Then he whispered to the chief, looking at Isaac. And then they brought in Josh with his hands loosely tied behind him. Isaac looked at him urgently, blankly, willing him not to speak. But Josh had gulped and made a movement which his tied hands jerked to a standstill. "You know one another!" said the young man, again in English. Neither of them answered; he looked furious. "Lock them in the store! I'll make them talk."

They were taken out, roughly, shoved into a small room with light only from a grating: hot, too. Isaac shook his head ever so slightly at Josh and pursed his lips. It was highly possible that they were being listened to. Josh was good all right, but not so quick as he was. But how was the young man going to make them talk? An old-fashioned sjambok most likely. Well, he thought, they could stand that. Good old Josh, it was grand to see him again. He was younger than Isaac, bigger built, and in easier days, he had laughed more easily. But not now.

Then Isaac realised that they could hear through the wooden partition what was going on in the room they had left: an argument between the chief and the younger man, who was insisting that they were not what they said. Perhaps they were thieves or murderers, more likely they were refugees. It must and could be found out; then they could decide on the most useful thing to do. The older man was uncertain, worried, finally said he'd sent a note over to the District Commissioner, at which the younger one made a scornful noise. Isaac was squatting, leaning his ear against the partition wall, but with his eyes shut and mouth open, acting stupid again in case they came in suddenly. Josh was leaning on the wall, listening too. If only they could speak to one another, ask—— And Amos? It was unbearable not to know. At last it was too much and they whispered. Josh had got away right at the beginning when they scattered and ran, but knew it was no good trying for the Rhodesian frontier, not yet anyway. He got a lift on a lorry as far as Craigs. Then thought the best thing would be to get lost, maybe hide, steal a little, let time go by. But he'd been picked up by the tribals who suspected him at once of—well, something.

Then another voice came into the talk in the other room. Isaac couldn't make it out when they all spoke at once, but now they were speaking English, and the new one, yes, he had a softer, thicker voice from lower down the throat than an Afrikaner, he must be a pure Englishman. He began to listen intently. The man was saying: "I know how you feel, Chief, you have to think of your people. But haven't you got to think of your conscience

18

too? We had refugees coming to the U.K. from Nazi Germany; some of them had certainly done something illegal there. There were people who said we shouldn't encourage them, it would only make trouble. But my father and mother had their house full of them."

"And did it make trouble?" This was the chief speaking, heavily.

Then the Englishman: "There would have been trouble anyway. You just can't help that. But if people are going to be killed or tortured or put into concentration camps, you have to help them. The right of political asylum has always been upheld."

"But if this means they shut their markets against us —put an embargo on our cattle from the abbatoir—we are not rich—if they stop our men going to work in the mines—I have to think of the tribe."

"We have to think of the whole country. We can't afford this—nonsense. These people saying they're refugees, trying to get special treatment." This was the younger man's voice, and it gave Isaac a shock. If the younger ones were thinking that way—it was worse than tribal, it was African against African.

"There is such a thing as honour," said the Englishman. Isaac began to imagine him as tall and lean, like a certain priest he had known once, with white hair and dark eyebrows.

"Certainly there is honour"—this was the chief—"but we do not even know. There was this radio message early this morning. And that police car. Wanting us to— co-operate. But perhaps these two are only strangers and thieves." Then all three spoke at once and Isaac could not make it out; and then the door was suddenly unlocked so that he had only time to take his listening ear from the partition and look stupid again.

Both of them were taken through. But how to act? A radio message and a police car! While he was thinking, he was being questioned in English and played dumb; so did Josh. He was taken aback because the Englishman was not like he had imagined, but a rather small, fair man, who looked as if he might easily become ill. Once the younger man, exasperated, slapped him across the face. He hated this man who had driven the car and brought him into this trap, him and Josh. At last the Englishman said: "Well, perhaps you are right. They may after all be thieves, or worse. Perhaps you should deal with them, Chief."

And then Isaac did something he had not intended to do, but it was as though a spring had been touched deep inside him. He took a step towards the small Englishman and said, "I am what you thought. And I ask for your protection." He told his full name, and saw them glance at one another. He noticed that his voice was shaking. And then Josh whispered his own name.

"I told you so!" said the younger man.

The Englishman made a small gesture towards him, a hint of protection. Then looked across him: "It's up to you, Chief."

The chief was making thick bundles of lines on a bit of paper with the point of his pen; he cross-hatched them, saying nothing. It all depended, then, on this man who, Isaac thought, was the one for whom he had felt most hatred and distrust, the man who, by being what he was,

made the tribal people what they were, ignorant, un-
free, who cut them off from the world of cities, his world.
But what was he like really? Isaac looked at him silently
and avidly, taking everything in, the lines of worry
and responsibility, the deep-set eyes and the bitten
fingernails. What could be expected of him? In the
moment of not knowing, Isaac felt the ground being cut
from under him, the meetings, the streets, the defiance,
the intense comradeship of cities, newspapers, jazz, the
back-room printing press, knowledge of how to make
things work, freedom because of knowledge—where was
it all running away to? He had asked for protection. If
he got it—what was it like here in the tribe? What could
it be like?

At last the chief turned heavily in his chair and spoke
to the District Commissioner: "You advise me to protect
them?"

"That is my personal advice," said the Englishman.

"But from the Government?" The Englishman smiled
and said nothing.

The younger man said furiously: "These men are
wanted by the police as terrorists. Do you mean to say
you are on their side?"

The Englishman said: "Terrorists, terrorists? These
are words which are used politically, not with accurate
meanings. There are too many words like that these
days. The crime of which they're accused would probably
carry the death penalty. It is normal to shelter such
people who have fled from one country to another." He
did not look straight at Isaac when he said this and Isaac
found himself thinking how odd it was that there were

two separate things, the words "carry the death penalty" and being choked to death after whatever the police had done to one.

The chief said slowly: "But perhaps they would make it difficult for us. If it was said that we were mixed up in politics. How do I know?"

The younger man followed up quickly, clearly trying to get the chief on to his side. "If refugees come here they take jobs our people could have. We can't encourage that. Besides, too many people know. It wouldn't be safe to do anything but give them up." Then when the chief did not answer: "They have no right to ask: they're rebels. They would do you no good, Uncle!"

"How many people know?" said the chief. "I can stop my own men from talking. You English have taken most of my powers, haven't you, but at least I can do that! and you, Motswasele"—he spoke to the younger man—"you keep yours quiet! Or I'll think you're a baby still. Whether I give them protection or not, they have a right to ask it."

The man called Motswasele glared. "You aren't thinking of the tribe, Uncle, only of what the English want! And not the ones at the top, only *him*. He gets round you talking about honour. That's not modern. They've taken all your powers and now they twist you! We could make a good bargain with these two. The police would thank us. Thank us—materially, my Uncle. Many things could be done for the tribe and ourselves with this thanks from the police."

Isaac and Josh stayed very still. It seemed to them that of the three, the younger man had the strongest will.

22

He perhaps was the real force in the tribe. The one who thought things out, got what he wanted. He was the kind they would have wanted in their movement. Strong. And now he was against them! This was, somehow, difficult to believe.

The chief got up and began to pace about. And he, now, was their only hope. If he decided against them, gave them up to this Motswasele, they were as good as dead. Is there anything I can say, thought Isaac, no, better keep quiet. He knows.

There was an assegai lying on pegs above the door. The chief pointed at it. "That used to be for justice. Or against the disobedient. It has been taken from me. Perhaps that is right. It is not, what do you say, Motswasele, modern. Modern is napalm, is bombs dropping on people you do not see. But I say in the name of the tribe, that it shall protect these men. And you"— he turned to the younger man—"if you bargain with them it shall be pointed at you."

And then, surprisingly, this Motswasele got up and made a clicking noise at the back of his throat and a kind of surly bow to his uncle. "If the Leopard says so," he muttered. Suddenly he had lost his force. It had been absorbed by the older man. Isaac thought, I have seen this before. In a political struggle. And we are safe.

The Englishman said: "If they say they are tradesmen, you can give them work, Chief, and it will look sensible to everyone. They will need to stay—some time."

Isaac all at once felt a terrible need to be truthful:

23

"Building I don't know. I was lying. But I can mend radios——"

"Just what we need!" said the D.C. He and the chief both laughed; it seemed to be an old joke between them. There was a radio at the back of the desk, under an enlarged photograph of a man in uniform; it had a set of crochet mats on top of it. Was it that? If only I can get the spares, Isaac thought, it might be a valve, but often it's just the wiring—and dust—if only I can do it for them!

The the chief spoke gravely, sitting square behind his desk: "Men, you have my protection. I take you into my people." So it came to both Isaac and Josh that they should kneel on the floor, on the lion skin, and give thanks to their chief with due respect. Almost with love.

Chapter II

"IMAGINE—no pliers!" Isaac said, wrinkling his face with effort. He and Josh were sitting on the steps of their house, one of the thatched rondavels, and the inside of a radio spread round them, the little bits glittering in the sun. It wasn't a valve, that was one thing; they were O.K. And plenty of power in the batteries; but it looked like some goof had tried to put it right and hadn't a clue on the wiring. But think of having to work with a couple of old knives and an enormous screwdriver! Suddenly Josh threw back his head and laughed. "What's killing you, man?" said Isaac.

"I like this place," said Josh.

"I don't," said Isaac, "but I'll bloody well fix this radio."

A couple of young women in short cotton frocks that ended half-way up their hefty thighs walked by, carrying pails of water on their heads, and giggled at the two. Josh got up and pretended to chase them; they fled more or less, but without spilling a drop of the precious stuff that they'd got from the bore-hole in which their family had a share.

Carefully Isaac began to put everything back in place;

he had small neat fingers that seemed able to go round corners. He was small boned every way, with a neat head, only marred where one ear had been torn in a fight.

"I'd like a chicken dinner," he said, "and as many bottles of beer as I could see, and all the newspapers back for a month."

"If only old Amos would just walk in the way he used, not caring a cent for anybody, the old squeeze box under his arm, the papers under his shirt."

"But he won't. Not if he was on the train. He's dead, see. We can't think what they did to him. Not me, anyhow. Can't just think about it!" He turned the knobs cautiously, tuning in. Yes, that was better. But old Ham-hand the chief would probably want a big noise; it must have been him who pulled the tuning knob half off, cross with it no doubt. He'd need to get it fixed so that it couldn't come loose again. And yet, thinking of old Ham-hand, he thought with more respect than he'd ever had for anyone: even the head of the group whose name they never even knew. Isaac hadn't really respected him, though Josh and the rest had. For Isaac he was just another cat. Isaac used to argue with him, quoting Marx and Strachey until all was blue. He hadn't got a bump of respect. But old Ham-hand was different. Somehow Isaac didn't mind respecting him. He tightened a connection, almost splitting his fingernail; there, that was better.

The rondavel had blankets, a cooking pot and a box to use as a table. Neither of them had any money, but they were given meal for porridge, sometimes milk, a

26

bit of goat now and then, and an egg or an onion or a couple of squashy tomatoes. There'd been odd cigarettes, too, and once a candle end. You could get by. Isaac's cuts had healed cleanly. He tuned in to Springbok Radio, endless birthday wishes and choices of records— always the same old ones! "If Joycie looks behind the pot of ferns she will find a birthday gift from Auntie." God, what a drag! And then there was a bit of news; he listened intently, so did Josh. Of course they'd missed what it was referring to—plot—which plot? Christ, a police shooting. Ten natives. The dirty sods. Ten natives. Not people. People with names. People with homes. Wives. Girl friends. Just natives you could get more of if you shook the next tree! As likely as not it would be—no, what was the use of teasing oneself. He listened quietly to the sports news. "She'll do," he said. "Give me a hand."

They picked the radio up and began to carry it along so the chief's house, the dust hot on their feet. People tmiled and spoke to them, if no more than a friendly 'mela. An old woman said something mocking about the radio. Everyone wore bits and patches of European clothes, but in an unwestern way, so that they draped instead of going in planes and creases. Little girls wore fragments of string kilts that showed their charming neat behinds, little boys even less. The round or square thatched houses of Ditlabeng looked pleasant in the sun. You heard the sound of ox bells and goats bleating and almost always somewhere laughter. You smelled wood smoke and the clean sharp smell of the tribe better than the smells of Lady Selborne township, at Pretoria, where

27

they'd both been brought up. Even Isaac thought so. The grey-green shade trees rose among the houses and cattle kraals; there was always room. From the school came the sound of children practising a hymn; the words, which on the whole the children didn't understand, made a nice pattern of sounds. And when Christmas came and the Mission dressed itself up, they would be praised.

As Isaac and Josh were going on, they heard the Land-Rover and both, without a word, dodged between two house walls and took a back path. Neither of them wanted to meet Motswasele, the nephew. When he looked at them they felt scared and helpless and useless; he took the guts out of them. Maybe if they kept out of sight for a long time he might forget.

The chief was pleased with the mended radio. He offered them money, which Josh was going to take, but Isaac nudged him and said no. However they were sent through to the kitchen and got a good meal of meat and potatoes and white bread and two tins of beer, and they begged a couple of candle ends and a piece of pig-fat soap. One of the women who seemed to be in charge, probably a relation of the chief, told them they could come back once in a while for another meal.

They hung about a bit, asking questions. They wanted to know about the chief's family. They knew his wife was dead and there was a daughter away, taking a nursing course. What was a surprise was when someone mentioned casually the son who was at a university in England. Isaac was struck by a pain of pure jealousy. How he'd have liked that chance, what he'd have done with it! Physics. Mathematics. Letlotse they called this son and inside himself he mocked at him, leopard! Crazy savages, calling a man leopard. Aloud he grumbled about it in English which would not be understood, as they walked back through Ditlabeng. "Me, I think leopard is a good name," said Josh. "Leopard is strong, beautiful. If I could change my own name to leopard, I would."

"You, you are a savage," said Isaac amiably. "And think what that boy gets in England. All for being the chief's son. That is exploitation! That is class."

"Who pays?"

"I suppose the Bamatsieng pays. And look at them. Poor as little mice. If no rain they starve. It is they who have to keep this Leopard at English University. Women and wine!"

"Golden curly women," said Josh. They stood aside while an ox team went past slowly pulling a sledge of firewood.

"I spit on golden curly women!" said Isaac. "Not alive, them."

"I know, I know," said Josh, who had heard this one before, and then, "why did you not take the money, Isaac?"

"You'll see, man," said Isaac.

True enough, within the next week, several people brought radios into them in various states of disrepair. Some were clearly hopeless. "No good. Dead," said Isaac, and they argued or sighed. But here and there one could be dealt with and now they were paid. Not much, but enough for a packet of tea and some sugar, a pack of cigarettes, a candle. Other things were brought in, once a sewing machine and luckily this was a simple job of adjustment, but more often there were things for which spares, or for that matter, tools, were needed. The hell of it was, Ditlabeng was a long way from the railway, twenty, thirty miles, they weren't too sure. Isaac went along to the trader's and poked about, bought some wire while Josh stole a few nails. It was wonderful what could be done. But valves, now. That was different.

By now they had a couple of radios in the hut which they couldn't do anything with, but which the owners insisted were not yet dead. Next thing, they had in a record player, an old model. It was the spring. Not much to be done with that. Isaac was poking at it when a tall girl in a red-spotted cotton dress came by. She had a gilt necklace and bracelets and carried her head well; Ditlabeng girls were either dead shy or saucy gigglers. This one looked you straight in the eyes, so straight, thought Isaac, that you couldn't look her in the breasts where you'd like. She leant over the wall and said in English: "Seems you're stuck."

Isaac nodded. "I'd like to make a go of this. Least if I'd the records to go with it!"

"You like music, man?"

"Do I like music!"

"American music? African music?"

"Just anything good." He hummed a tune.

She hummed back another, moving her shoulders a little. Then she said: "And the radios, how do they go?"

"I'm stuck for valves. Don't see a chance to get them. Wouldn't like to get me some spares, sweetheart?"

She laughed, leaning over the wall, her red dress cut low but not low enough. "Spares you'll get at Lobatsi or Francistown, I don't know which is farthest. Maybe at Craigs."

"We'll run you over one day in our little red sports car," said Josh, and they all laughed.

Suddenly she said: "It's true, is it, what's said—about you?"

Isaac froze. So something had got out. No, stick to the old story. "True I fell off a lorry. True my friend got into trouble. True we know radios and that."

The girl looked him through with her great shining eyes. "Motswasele told me something else," she said. "Didn't know I'd be interested. Just showing off, him. Wanting to get me where he wants me. I was interested, see? Not the way he is. Your way."

Isaac got up and came over to the wall, but stood along it a bit, for there were plenty of eyes in Ditlabeng. "You any relation of his?" he asked.

"Cousin," said the girl, "just cousin. Far out cousin. Not rich cousin! But I got a record player and a few records. Did you hear me say I was interested?"

"What in? Music? Me?"

"Politics," said the girl very softly.

"I see," said Isaac and then, "suppose we come and play your records one evening? How's that, honey?"

"That goes," she said. "But mind, no funny business. I'm through with that. I'm Agnes Mookodi and if you follow past the bore-hole and then turn left at the witch

31

tree past Small Snakes Rock, I live in the square house with my mother."

"I get it, Agnes," said Isaac. "Can I call you Agnes?"

"No," she said. "You can call me Tselane. I don't like Agnes, not much." And then she turned and was gone.

"Going to risk it?" asked Josh.

Isaac shrugged his shoulders. "Looks very like I'm going to risk it."

"Because of the chick?"

"Not altogether."

"Because of the records?"

"Not that either. Got to find out. Man, I wish I'd a clean shirt!"

"Well, neither of us have. Do I come with you?"

"I think you should, Josh, yes, I think you should."

They went off at the beginning of the evening when the ox teams moved into Ditlabeng among dust and bells, and the yokes and riems dropped to the ground until to-morrow. As the sun set, roofs and trees were outlined against clear pale gold, but before they came to the dark hump of Small Snakes Rock, the first stars were out. They could tell the house, though, by the sounds that were coming, real top-class jazz, a long player surely. They stood at the opening to the courtyard and coughed and talked loud. By and by the girl Agnes or Tselane came out. "So you came," she said, and motioned them in. It was a small, square, thatched house, two rooms. Her mother sat on a chair, sniffing sometimes, looking as if she were stuffed, and there was a baby asleep in a nest of blankets, grey and pink. "Nice kid," said Josh.

32

Tselane half grinned and half scowled. "Your kid?" he asked.

She nodded. "But for that I'd have been a teacher." And then she said violently, "Motswasele!"

"Nice kid all the same," said Isaac.

Chapter III

THAT WAS THE FIRST EVENING. In a way they all went much the same. First of all they'd play a record; they sat drinking it in, moving a little with its movements. She had a lot of records. At first Isaac and Josh wondered how she got them and the batteries, then one day Josh was talking about a new one he'd heard just before—before they left. A real gas! She scribbled the name on a scrap of paper. "You going to get it, Tselane?" said Josh. "How you get it?"

"What you think?" she said.

He shook his head. But Isaac guessed. "Motswasele," he said under his breath; she nodded and her mouth twitched.

After the record her mother would shuffle off and make tea; it would be strong tea with milk and sugar and bread to go with it, real shop bread and jam or sauce to spread on it. Once or twice there were slices of tinned meat or beetroot. Good! There were a couple of stools, blankets and karosses tidily rolled, a shelf with plates and cups and a few tattered books. The baby slept. The lamp made a pool of light on the table and then they talked, sometimes in Tswana, but sometimes in English; she liked that; it took her back to her teacher time. At first it was only about what could almost have been in the papers. But Tselane had both of them puzzled. Was it possible that she was sent as a decoy, that Motswasele was using her to get things out of them? If so, she would get no more than he would find out anyway. Neither of them needed to warn the other to say nothing about Amos.

She asked. She wanted them to tell about things that happened. Back there across the border in the Republic. To tell so that she could see for herself. "And what then?" she would say. "What then?" But they clammed up. Then one evening she said abruptly, "You think I tell what you say to Motswasele."

"We think nothing," Isaac said.

"You do think that. It is not true. Look, men, he wants me, but not for his wife; he is thinking big, him. Bigger than me. I am only his cousin and my father is dead. My uncle paid my education until I had this baby. Now he does not care. Motswasele will give no cattle for me!"

"But you go with him still?" Josh asked, interested; women were curious creatures; he wanted to know.

"What do you think?" She looked from him to Isaac. And Isaac said: "No."

Tselane said: "I belong to the People's Party. Because it is against Motswasele."

"What else is it against?" Isaac said.

"It says Independence, Independence," Tselane said. "I suppose it is against the British."

"You don't know when you're well off," said Josh. "These British, they give you things you are too poor to

35

get for yourself. Best, you can get a passport. A big British passport. Have any British persons hurt you?"

"No," said Tselane doubtfully. "They seem to smile mostly. But you cannot tell what they're like inside."

"You should go to Jo'burg," said Isaac, "or Pretoria. You should go in the wrong entrance to the post office. You should be on the pavement when one of them wants it all. You should have your wrong coat so your pass is not in the pocket. After that you might even like the British."

"You should be there on December the sixteenth," said Josh. "That you see, is Dingaan's Day."

"Ah, Dingaane!" said Tselane.

"That is the day we have to hide if we can," said Josh. "Because we are dogs, jackals. Because *they* did nothing wrong in that war. Because *they* did not steal our cattle and our beautiful women. Everything wrong was done by us. They do not let us forget it." His eyes narrowed as though he was seeing something—something that happened once to him or to a friend, and there was no redress.

"And when you get this Independence, what then?" Isaac asked.

"I don't know," Tselane said. "They don't say."

"Perhaps they have never thought. It is easy to open one's mouth and say Independence, Independence. But you ask, Independence what for? And there is no answer."

"We want freedom," said Tselane.

"They will give you freedom. Perhaps you will get it before you want. And no more money out of big London! We in the Republic, we want freedom and it will never be given to us. Never. It is as simple as that."

36

"What shall I do then?"

"Oh, go on with your party. It might give you a scholarship, who knows? You might get to Dar or to Ghana. Is there another party?"

"Yes, yes: but the other party is for the chiefs."

"Well, you cannot join that one, Tselane. Not that I have anything against your chief, he saved our lives."

"He is a good man. But they say he is not well. Seneo, his daughter, she used to be my friend. Now—I cannot tell. Costs too much, writing. Besides——"

"And the son?"

"Oh, Letlotse! He is away. He is becoming different. When he comes back we do not know him."

"I see," said Isaac. "I see."

Or again they would speak of how to organise an opposition, what to do when a party was declared illegal, of vain attempts which had been made by one group or another of Africans in the Republic, to show the Afrikaners that it was wrong to treat all people with a different skin colour as though they were dirt. Of churches which had tried to help. But usually without success. Of the Treason Trials. Of trying to get the *tsotsis* to be interested in politics, instead of knifing one another. Of a concert to which Isaac had not been able to go, though so often artists from Europe insisted on one performance for an African audience. Yes, even when it made them difficulties. "I'm not saying there is anything wrong with a white skin," Isaac said, and then he gave a long slow glance at Tselane. "Though it's not so nice to look at. It's dry. It's hairy. It gets lines. It hasn't the beautiful shining look of some skins."

37

"All the same," said Josh, "if you do get a white friend why, well, why it's like having a pet giraffe. You're proud, man, you're proud, though it can be difficult taking a giraffe about with you. It knocks its head, see, and people look!"

They found out a lot talking with Tselane there in the pool of lamplight. About the tribe and its relationships and customs. Ditlabeng was the centre. There were the small villages and the people at the edge. All the time the younger men were away. Mostly over the border in the mines, sometimes nearly half of them. In the old days they used to be away in the slack time of the year, but now it was mostly on nine-month contracts which would, in practice, stretch out to a year. That made farming precarious. They weren't waiting to pounce on the ground the moment there had been a drop of October or November rain, the way a whole-time farmer might do. But the whole-time farming was mostly on the land near the rivers, the land that could have water brought to it. And, naturally, the best of that land belonged to whites. As ever. It had happened before their time; now it was just another thing that had to be accepted. On poor land, far from rivers, it worked out that if you lost the moment you lost the crop. And the men who stayed and farmed were mostly now the older ones. The boys were away herding at the cattle posts. Everyone started school late if they did start it at all. There were two primary schools in Ditlabeng, one in a square, tin-roofed building, very hot in summer, with such small windows that the packed children could hardly see the blackboard, the other quite simply under a shady tree,

38

but the children sat in orderly rows and smoothed the
dust in front of them to write, or answered the teacher's
questions in chorus. Their parents had paid for them to
go to the school, and something might come of it. But
the drought was bad this year, bad. "Perhaps they will
go to the hole," said Tselane one day, talking about
it. It had been extra hot that day, not the ghost of a
cloud.

"What hole?" asked Isaac.

But she laughed. "It will be nothing to do with you."

There were several bore-holes in Ditlabeng, and all
the girls, including Tselane, went there for their water
with pails and tins in long patient lines, faded pinks and
reds, turquoises and yellows, moving slowly to the water,
then away, upright, with the weight on their heads.
It was said that there used to be a clear stream, so clear,
that flowed all the year round, but that was long ago.
It was said, too, that in the old days the rains were certain,
so that there was always some kind of crop. It was made
certain in various ways by things which were done or
organised by the chiefs. But Tselane was not willing to
say what things; perhaps she did not know.

As there was no man in the house, she got the firewood,
carrying a big branch easily on her head. Then she
chopped it with an axe, but now sometimes, Isaac or
Josh came over and helped her. A cousin had done her
ploughing, but she and her mother hoed the crop.
Sometimes in the evening she embroidered a cushion
cover with a pattern which the Mission had given her:
she wondered what the names of the flowers were. There
were always flowers in the English books she had read at

school. It was as though they ate them, they were so important in English. Perhaps these flowers on the cushion cover could be eaten.

When the baby cried it was usually the grandmother who looked after him. Tselane had suckled him, but not for very long since she had not entirely wanted him to live and had left him much to her mother, so her breasts were not spoiled; they would still feel good in the hand like plunging one's fingers into corn. She made clothes for him against the winter, knitting angrily. Isaac and Josh both played with Kodunzwe, the baby, and when she saw him in Isaac's arms, Tselane made a face of derision that was also a little tender.

One day as a change from records they started singing hymns, the old mother joining in. "You should come to church one Sunday," said Tselane.

"You give me a shirt and shoes," said Isaac. "I'll come!"

"The Mission might give you that," said Tselane, "why not ask?"

"No," said Isaac. "That could be danger, besides I don't like taking things from missions. I'm no charity boy!"

"I thought you said we must take from the British!" Tselane laughed at him. "Which church you like anyway?"

"All the same to me, if the singing's good. But I can't like Dutch Reform. There was a Mission at Pretoria. I liked that. You got a feeling—well, there was something behind it. Maybe it was nothing all the same. I don't know. I used to think about the Mission people some-

40

times. The Englishman here—maybe Motswasele told
you——"

"Yes," said Tselane quietly. "He hates him."

"Well, he saved our lives I think. He and the chief
together. The way he spoke, that made me think about
that Mission. Maybe though it's all nonsense. Big white
God in the sky. All that."

"God is not white," said Tselane definitely.

Once or twice she gave him useful things, needles, an
old pair of scissors, bits of tin that could be used and
bent. After a bit Josh made a lamp of a kind. From
time to time they made enough money to get oil. Sometimes they'd get hold of a newspaper, not new, but not
too old. They would read it carefully whether in English
or Tswana, trying to find a line that would tell them—
anything. Anything at all that they needed to know!
One night Isaac dreamt about Amos. He thought they
were in a police cell. In the distance they could hear
someone screaming. That was the beginning; it was part
of something he had known and tried to forget. Through
the bars of the cell there came lights and people moving.
Or were they people? Perhaps they were animals or
thinkings or parts of speech. Perhaps they were not alive.
But they had mouths. There was something that had to
be found. In the dream Amos said I will find it and he
walked through the bars. But Isaac could not follow him.
He gripped and tore at the bars and screamed for Amos.
But Amos had gone into the mouths. When he woke he
was sweating from head to foot, scrabbling and tearing at
the floor of the hut. He suddenly thought he must tell

Tselane about Amos. "If I could tell her now," he thought.

He went to the door and saw the stars clear overhead, the great sweep of the Milky Way, the Southern Cross far down. There was a small slip of moon, bright silver, enough to throw moonlight and moon shadow sharper and less diffused than starglow. He breathed deep but it was scarcely cool. He felt the warmth of the thousand sleepers of Ditlabeng all round him, stifling him. He felt the warmth of the oxen in the kraals rising at him, the heat of fidgeting horses sucked by ticks, even the heat of the dogs. In the distance one barked, then another, then many, until all died down. What time was it? He did not miss his watch in the day-time. One knew when it was light, one woke to the sound of inspanning, of goats' bleating, of cocks' crowing and the pleasant chirrups of little birds that went to sleep again in the heat of the day. One woke to voices, laughter, the smell of smoke. One was hungry. One made porridge. One worked. Before the day was dark the come-to-supper star showed her small bright face above the pointed tops of the houses and the round tops of the trees and if there was supper one cooked and ate it. If there was none, not. In the evening one could not work any longer. Except when they went over to Tselane's house they mostly went to sleep early. Once or twice they went round to the other men, sat outside the trader's, or hung around on the edge of Kgotla trying to pick up whatever news there was. But they had no money for drinking; besides, the men of the Bamatsieng had their own things that they were interested in, their own complaints, their own proverbs and sayings. You couldn't talk to them. Not really talk. Isaac wondered if the Englishman knew they were still in Ditlabeng. Perhaps he would rather not know. So what time was it now?

Hot. Hot. Hot. And Amos had gone into the mouths. He twisted up his face but the tears ran down. They had killed Amos, battered him to death in a police cell, in the way that had happened before. In the way that he had prayed it would not happen to him. Because of the time when one breaks, when a man starts to scream. He hated them so much that he felt a ball of fire in his chest, heating up the tears. He groped his way by starlight into the street of dust between low walls, the dark hot channel. And then he was hating the tribe who did not know about Amos, who would not care if they did know. Because they did not know they were Africans as he and Amos and Josh knew they were Africans, who only knew they were the Bamatsieng.

It was odd the way his feet knew their way to Tselane's house. But then? How did he know she would feel about Amos the way he wanted her to feel? What was he to say? What would she expect he meant? He heard the baby cry out suddenly as babies do in the night and then he heard Tselane grumbling to it. "Hush, little bad thing! Hush or I call the devils!" And then as it still cried he heard the scratchings of a match and there was a candle light in the small house. He moved into her courtyard feeling the smooth floor pleasant underfoot; it was only days since she had given it a new washover of cow dung. He went on one knee so as to be completely hidden in the dark shadow of the wall, the moon-shadow.

43

He moved very softly but she must have heard. She raised her voice and said: "Go away." He had never heard her voice like this. What had he done to make her so angry? He stayed quite still hardly breathing. She came to the door; he could see by her shape against the candle-light that she was only wearing a strip of cloth around her hips. "Out!" she said. "Out! Or I throw your get at you."

Then he knew who she thought he was. He whispered so that it would carry only to her. "It is not Motswasele. It is Isaac." She did not move. Then she took a step back and the candle was out. The child had stopped crying, was only whimpering a little. What was she going to do? If she shut the door on him he could not bear it.

And then she was across the starglow and into the moon-shadow of the wall beside him. "What is it?" she whispered. "Why have you come?"

"I had a friend," said Isaac, "he was called Amos. There were three of us——"

And then he felt her hand on his mouth. "Hush!" she whispered, "hush up now! Motswasele told me there were three of you and I was to find out about the other. I don't want to find out."

"He is dead," said Isaac not heeding. "He was killed by the Afrikaners. My friend is dead."

"How do you know?" she whispered back; she was closer to him than she had ever been; suddenly he began to feel it.

"I know," he said. "I dreamed it. Amos was the best of us and now they have killed him."

44

"You dreamed it," said Tselane, "is that all?"

"That is plenty," Isaac whispered back. "Tselane, I have wept from my heart."

"Was that what you came to tell me?" Tselane whispered. "For me to comfort you, my Isaac?" And then he felt her arms going round him, pulling him down to the smooth floor close under the wall, close and dark. He felt the breasts, the corn, the rain, the honey. He felt the knot of the cloth loosened from her hips.

Chapter IV

THERE HAD BEEN A LITTLE RAIN early on in November and the beginning of December, but not enough. Some people had ploughed, but there was no follow-up rain. The crops looked dead. The mealies were dying off, tasselled at the top, but the ears not forming or not properly swelled. Kaffir-corn was better but not good, stunted. There were few vegetables. Tselane had given up hoeing her field: not even the weeds grew. The grass was shrivelling and dying; those who could, sold off their cattle, but the quota at the abattoir was usually full. Water was short at some of the cattle posts and the beasts churned everything up with their heavy, eager hoofs for hundreds of yards round. There was far less game than usual; eland and wildebeeste had moved. You hardly saw a buck in a day's walk. Only the ostriches stood and glared sometimes from across the bushes. The chief was worried; he met the headmen who all complained bitterly but finished by saying that of course they were his people so they were not complaining.

He knew what they wanted him to do, some of them anyhow. He also knew that if he did it nobody was going to keep it a secret. Out it would come and he

46

would see the look on the D.C.'s face when he knew. He compromised and asked the Mission to pray for rain. They said they would do so gladly and the chief and everyone else came to the church. So all turned up in their best suits and best dresses, hats sometimes; some even brought umbrellas in case anything came of it. Besides the umbrellas were smart.

Tselane and her mother came, leaving the baby with a neighbour. She was after all one of the royals, although in a small way and barely recognised now. She sat at the back, Motswasele was up at the front next to the chief. Tselane was feeling happy inside herself, happy in her womb, but she tried to make little spears of hate and throw them at Motswasele. Isaac and Josh stood outside with the crowd of the tribe, the ones who had not proper church clothes but who came out of respect for their chief, and the hope that this might possibly work. Josh had quite a few friends now among the men; they joked and talked; he could speak in proverbs now as well as any of them. Isaac found this difficult; he had never been one for joking. He kept on wishing he could somehow get to speak to them about real things. About how to raise themselves, to get free, to stop being exploited, to become a country. If only they could want it! The People's Party sometimes talked this way but did they really think about it, what it meant? The local secretary was as tribal as the rest when it came to being a real opposition. But somehow Josh didn't see it like that.

There was no rain. The sun was too hot, went on being too hot. Everything dried. The headmen came to

47

see the chief again. He agreed reluctantly. He had been having pains in his stomach; sometimes they were so bad he could neither sleep nor think. But he must not be the one to show it. He was the chief. He wished he could speak to Letlotse or to Seneo. But Letlotse and Seneo were both in England. Seneo was learning to be a nurse in a London hospital. Perhaps if she came home she would be able to help him to make this pain go. Or perhaps not. He could bear it. And Letlotse—how was he doing? He wrote those letters about a life one couldn't understand. He seemed interested in things which a prince shouldn't be interested in. Books, yes, he should be interested in books; he had been sent to England for his education, to make him a better chief. But all these societies and clubs—what were they? It was time Letlotse made his own *mophato*, gathered his initiation comrades and took them out in the bush as he had done himself—how long ago now? The pain gripped him again and he held on to the edge of his desk, gritting his teeth.

No, he must not tell Letlotse, he must not interrupt his studies, he had these examinations still to do. But now he had said he would travel to Europe, perhaps go to Scandinavia—where was that? Did that help a man to become a man, to become a chief? He didn't know. But the tribe had decided to send Letlotse, to make him better able to lead them, since nowadays one must have an educated chief as other tribes had.

They brought him meat but he could not eat it, he chewed a little and spat it out. It is bad when a man cannot want to eat meat. He wondered if he had been bewitched. Who by? He thought of his nephew, Motswasele. He should speak to the elders. Tell them by no means to let Motswasele get the Regency if—if the time came for himself to join the Older Ones. He took out a photograph which Letlotse had sent him. He was in the middle with two white friends, one on each side. They had been playing some game together. What did it mean—half blue? He thought back lovingly and intently to Letlotse as a boy, a young boy herding cattle with the rest, galloping along the narrow trails between thorn bushes, his face alight with pleasure. How he lit up, the boy, how white his teeth were, his eyes like jewels! And he, his father, had taught him that he was born to be chief, and that meant that any man of the Bamatsieng could come to him for justice or help, that he must be friendly to all, despising none, for they were all his brothers, but most the men of his own *mophato*, his age class. Not that initiation was what it used to be You were sore enough for a while in those days.

He looked out of a window. The headmen were beginning to come, as he had supposed they would. They could not make him—yes, they could. They were the Bamatsieng.

Isaac had spent all morning dismantling and oiling a sewing machine. If people just didn't look after things!— Well, that was fine for the producers, not so hot for the consumers. And these consumers just couldn't afford to give an extra cent to the shareholders. That was economics. That was plain sense. The sewing machine was a bit better now. Maybe if he asked them to come

49 D

back in six months he could oil it again. They would be pleased anyway to have it working smoother. He gave it a bit of a polish; you'd think at least they'd do that. No. But if once he could get some spares, then he'd make the dead radios in the hut work. Their owners came and asked for them hopefully now and then. It could be safe enough in Francistown now. Surely? Or in Craigs? The police would have stopped looking for him. Thought he'd got away to Ghana or Tanganyika. Instead of here. Ghana. He'd have been back in the middle of it all, maybe learning how to use—well, better not think about that. Learning about the African personality. If that meant anything beyond old Nkrumah on the West Coast always keeping the lead! Lucky devils there with no Boers, no settlers, only the English who walked out, and all that money. Even the gold mines in Ghana having to listen to what Nkrumah told them! Tanganyika, maybe he'd have seen Nyerere. One of the big ones, the real big ones. And he could have learnt more economics. He didn't feel too happy with what he knew. There were words, even, that twisted him. He could master them if he had the books. But not just by thinking.

Francistown. He could get a lift in a lorry to the station. But there was the fare and he'd need ten *rands'* worth of spares and tools. Easy. And you couldn't go in a store without shoes. Not the kind of store that has radio valves. He looked in the tin, not that he needed to look; he knew to the last cent. And they had not had meat for a week. Yet he didn't think he could charge more. There were no millionaires in Ditlabeng.

50

He whistled to himself softly as he polished the metal parts of the sewing machine; it would have been nice to have some music. But the music was all with Tselane. As every other kind of thing that made him happy was with Tselane. In the starlit midnight of Tselane. And he had nothing to give her. Nothing. Except himself.

Then Josh came in. "You lazy bastard, Josh man," he said. "Where you been?" For Josh looked pleased and excited. Had he found a woman? But no, it could not be a woman like Tselane.

"Me?" said Josh. "You asking me? Why you not there yourself, Isaac?"

"Nobody told me. I been working."

"Told you! You should know. You think too much about you know who. Not looking where you're going. That's you, Isaac."

"Well, then, where you were? Tell true, man!"

"With the tribe. We been making rain."

"Don't talk cuckoo. You, Josh, you a freedom fighter, you go making rain! But look—there's no rain, it's hot as hell."

"There will be rain," said Josh confidently.

"Come off it, man! You can't think so. You're not a savage. Or are you?"

Josh sat down suddenly on the step of the hut. "Maybe I am," he said. "Maybe I am."

Isaac took his hand and swung it affectionately. "Go on," he said, "tell me. O.K. you've been rain making. That's fine by me. Who else? The whole of the tribe, was it? All except old Isaac?"

51

"Just about," said John.

"And old Ham-hand at the head. Now, Josh, don't you look like that, you know I wouldn't call him that to anyone but you. Come on, what did Kgosi do?"

"He went to the hole," said Josh. "I was far in back of the rocks with the rest. How do I know what he did? Maybe he made some kind of offering. To the ones who are away. The ancestors."

"Just as much sense as praying for rain in the church," said Isaac.

"Then the little girls got given pots, got sent out to the fields. Little small girls."

"I see, I see. And then, you think, rain follows little girls with pots?"

"Well, maybe it does. So what?"

Isaac thought it out, picking his teeth. "The Christians, they go to this hole?"

"The Bamatsieng go. All want rain."

"The church choir? The lot? The Mission, what does it say about this?"

"Maybe they don't know."

"Maybe they do! One man keeps a secret, two men, twenty men even. Not a thousand men."

"More than that."

"And the Englishman, the D.C.—what about him?"

Josh shrugged his shoulders; he was watching up behind the tree a dark edge of cloud, still a long way off. "If we get rain, does it matter how?" he said. And then: "I've been thinking. Next year we could ask for a piece of land."

Isaac scratched his head. "Next year, you say! What

about our work, man? Are you deserting? Think, think. The fight against Apartheid, against the Immorality Act, the Education Act, Suppression of Communism, Unlawful Organisations, Sabotage Act—everything. Man, there's not enough of us, we can't leave the others to fight it alone!"

"I see that with part of me," said Josh. "But the other part is seeing something else."

"New spectacles you need!"

"And you, Isaac," said Josh. "You mean to leave Tselane?"

"No," said Isaac. "Tselane I don't leave. I take her."

"And if she says I won't go?"

"There's an old story in Kgosi's family. It goes back to the time of troubles, to the war with Mzillikazi of the Matabeles. It is the story of a young wife who stayed with her man through all kinds of hardships; who crouched behind rocks in hiding with him, the baby squeezed tight to her breast in case it cried. Who tied up his wounds, found him water, hunted meat for him, marched with him, carrying the baby on her back and his war-axe in her hand."

"Who is getting tribal now?" said Josh. "And what happened to that baby?"

"That baby," said Isaac, "was the great-grandfather of Kgosi and also of Tselane."

That evening it rained. There was the sharp crack of lightning, an ox whip across the sky; there was the thunder rolling all round and then the smell of rain. First the smell from a mile off and then a coolness suddenly in the air. Then the first drops in the dust. Then

53

the full downpour, men and women running in blankets but looking up gladly. *Pula, pula!* It seemed to be a lot of rain, but it was not enough, and the mealies were dead. It helped the grass a little; it saved some of the Kaffir-corn. The cattle drank at the rain pools until all too quickly they dried up.

If only we had a dam, the chief thought, that would keep back the water. I should have made a dam. In the old days I would have forced people to build a big dam for me. But now they all go off to the mines and my dam is not built. And then he thought, perhaps Letlotse will build a dam. He will have his *mophato*. At least we should have stone dykes on the slope down to stop the run-off from the rain. I must see about this. Yes, I must see. Perhaps next time a *mophato* is formed. There could be one before Letlotse comes back. I will speak to the elders. He thought of his sister's son, Mookami, who was mostly called James. He had shown signs of growing strong. He had passed his G.C.E. and perhaps he should have stayed on at school, but he felt he was too old. He had not started schooling until he was nearly twelve. Ought we to send all our sons to the cattle posts, the chief said to himself, but if we do not send how are the cattle to be herded? And we cannot keep back our own sons when the rest of the tribe go. He shook his head. Besides, they learn much there; they learn to be strong and cunning and they learn many stories and songs and proverbs. It is good they should go. At school they are herded; better then that they herd.

If there had been no rain perhaps the Mission would not have heard about it, nor yet the District Commissioner.

But as there had been rain it would be too much to hope that there would not be boasting. The Mission heard and the heads of the Mission came to see the chief. He sat behind his desk trying to see only the law books while they lectured him on his lapse into paganism. But if it had brought the rain? They are jealous, he said to himself. The Lord God is a jealous God. That is what it says. I too have read my Bible. Jealous like a woman, a head wife. His eyes lifted from the law books to the assegai above the door. In the old days they would not have come into his house and scolded him like a child! Preached, yes, they had a right to preach in their own church and he had the right not to go there. He was beginning to have the pain again, the thing gnawing at the bottom of his ribs, the pain. He said that he was sorry they took it this way; he had only followed an old custom for the sake of the tribe and the headmen—let the Mission go lecture them! But it was no good. They went on at him, demanding that he make public repentance.

It was almost a relief when a message came that the D.C. was here. "Let him come!" said the chief. The Mission heads were less pleased and least pleased when the D.C. disagreed with them politely over the little matter of public repentance. "I think we should not insist," the D.C. said pleasantly, "after all nothing repugnant has been happening."

"Repugnant!" said the head of the Mission. "Possibly not to you. But to me everything savouring of paganism is utterly repugnant."

"But surely," said the D.C. in his most reasonable

55

voice, "you would see the difference between this little ceremony and, say, a human sacrifice?"

They began to argue among themselves and the chief was glad to sit back and be out of it. To sit back and let the pain subside. At the end the Mission withdrew still demanding public repentance but with less conviction. He thought it could be avoided. It was clear both to him and to the Mission that the D.C. was staying; he leant across and offered the chief a cigarette. "Well, old friend," he said, "I think I've got you out of that! But I'd advise you to slip a note into the collection next time."

The chief dropped his head in his hand. "I have to thank you," he said.

"Don't thank me. It's my job to keep the balances true. You're sitting in one of them, you know. But should you have done it, Chief?"

"It was the headmen——"

"Yes, I know. The keepers of Custom. Just as much churchmen as you and me, eh? Well, it's over."

"And we did get some rain."

"Not enough. I'm afraid rain is a natural phenomenon which we can't influence this way. Perhaps one day we will be able to spray the rain clouds with something scientific out of aeroplanes."

"That would be a fine thing and get us out of much trouble. And now the rain has washed away too much good soil on the big slope."

"If there could be dykes——"

"That was the way I was thinking. The way exactly. Four low dykes in a curve."

56

"Yes, yes."

"You know my nephew that is called James, my sister's son?" The D.C. nodded. "I had thought that if he was to take out a regiment they could make the dykes first."

"Good show, Chief. Now that's what I call being a statesman. Could that be managed soon?"

"I think so, we will talk it over in Kgotla. There was another thing I wanted to speak about." A jab caught him across the stomach and he had difficulty in controlling his face and voice. He could see the D.C. watching him almost too kindly. "It is this. Letlotse is still away. I want him to finish his education. It could be that I shall join the Old Ones before he comes back. I do not want Motswasele as Regent. Do you understand that?"

"I understand. Indeed I understand very well. But what makes you speak of this? Do you feel yourself ill, Chief?"

"A little. A little. Perhaps it was the Mission coming. So you will remember that?"

"I will. By the way, Chief, how are the refugees doing? They are still here?"

"They are here. They have been mending this and that. Sometimes I give them a good meal."

"Do they mean to stay?"

"One of them at least; I think he wants to become one of the Bamatsieng. Perhaps James will take him in his regiment."

"They haven't been running around with politics?"

"I think not. We keep them too hungry. They cannot get to the railway. But I have nothing to complain of."

57

"That's good then. You were justified. But you took a risk, Chief. Yes, you took a risk to be merciful. That's as good Christianity as they teach at the Mission. But if you feel ill you should see the doctor. Will you do that, Chief?"

"Perhaps. Perhaps. But I expect it is nothing."

Chapter V

IT SEEMED TO BE HOTTER THAN EVER. And at the moment not much work coming in. Isaac didn't want to touch their savings. But they went hungry oftener than they liked. And there was never money for a beer and a man doesn't feel himself a man without a beer now and then. Not that most of the Bamatsieng were much better off that year. OXFAM had sent fortified meal for the children at school. The bags were piled up at the tribal office, then distributed to the schools. But milk was short. There were a few more cases of malnutrition every week at the clinic and they made a break from eternal bilharzia, tuberculosis, V.D., pneumonias, and sore eyes. People got well easily; they reacted quickly to antibiotics. If they came out of hospital with a leg or an arm off that was something which must be suffered. It was wonderful how people managed to survive, even enjoy what life they had left. But everyone would have someone to take care of them a little. Nobody was quite without a family.

The Mission continued to be disapproving. Although the public apology had not been insisted on nor was the chief spoken of by name, there were sermons about the danger of a lapse into paganism, the slippery slopes, the hell flames waiting. Nobody had any doubt what

59

it was about and almost all families were involved. Isaac was one of the few who, in fact, had been completely out of it, but he did not propose to take advantage of his privilege; it was not as if the Mission even knew of his existence; he was just one of the anonymous bare-foot crowd.

Then gradually the weather cooled down with April and the beginning of winter; in another month there was a real nip at night. Tselane gave them each a blanket. Isaac suspected that they had once belonged to Motswasele but that didn't matter. They smelt now of Tselane and he could sleep with his nose warmly tucked into her smell. Then one day Isaac and Josh were sent for to the chief's house. The man who came for them was a cheerful type called Murphy after a trader who had come to Ditlabeng once and made himself popular. Like so many people around Kgosi he was some kind of far out relation. When they asked him what it was about, at first he said nothing, as he had been instructed, shook his head and grinned, but finally came out that two strangers had turned up, it was thought from the Republic and that they had asked for help. Isaac and Josh were to see them and tell the chief who and what kind they were. "God," said Isaac, "God—supposing . . ." and both of them had the same thought. Amos.

They were taken straight through to the chief; each bent a knee and waited. He was sitting at his desk; one of the women brought him a cup of tea. He glanced at the two, then signed that they should each have a cup; they were glad of it, having eaten nothing that day, and there was a sweet biscuit in each saucer.

60

Then the chief began to tell them what had happened. The two men had been found some way from the railway line, lost and hungry. They had said that the police from the Republic were after them but that they were innocent; his own tribal police had brought them in and now he wanted to find out about them. "Men," he said, "I showed mercy to you and I have not had to regret it. I promise nothing, but if these ones are the same as yourselves I will think over what I should do." And then he said with the tiniest hint of a smile in his eyes: "Motswasele does not know—yet."

"Kgosi," they murmured. "Kgosi."

"I want you to go in separately, first one, then the other. You are to find out. And when it is done you are to look at my radio. The knob that makes it louder has come off." Then he signed to Isaac to go through. And Isaac took a deep breath and followed Murphy; he wondered if the two men had been put into the little store-room where they had been put when they were prisoners. But most of all he wondered if—Amos. Amos.

But that was not to happen. The two men were in another room, guarded by one of the tribal policemen with a rifle rather casually across his knees, loaded no doubt. Isaac looked at them carefully before he spoke. He knew neither of them but they looked as if they might be from the Republic; they had good shoes, socks even, and their clothes were town clothes; one of them was wearing a belted raincoat. "Well, man," said Isaac in English, "you just talk. Don't you mind about *him*——" he slanted his head at the policeman. "He is just taking care of you, see?" And indeed it was clear that

61

beyond the words of command this policeman knew little English.

The two men began pouring it out and Isaac listened carefully. They claimed they had been Congress members and had been jailed for their convictions, got out, lost their jobs——

"What was your job, men?"

"All kinds of jobs," said one of the men, "garage hand, radio fitter," and then began again on how he'd always worked for freedom, heard that there were folks in Bechuanaland who believed in freedom and would give him a break, get him away from the police, put him on the road to Ghana—after a while Isaac mentioned a couple of names and a phrase that should have meant something if the story was true. Nothing seemed to come of it, only more words, and the words seemed to mean less and less. As they were beginning to dry up, Isaac said: "You give me a hand with something, man," and walked out. "Can I have the radio for a minute, Kgosi?" he asked. "It's for a test." He and Josh carried it in and while they carried it he whispered to Josh that there was something he didn't like about these two. They put the radio on the table and Isaac brought out his screwdriver. "Check her out, would you?" he said.

After a minute or two Isaac held up his hand: "That's enough," he said. And he saw that the man who had been fumbling with the screwdriver was suddenly afraid. "It's a different make," he said.

"Don't know what you worked at, man," said Isaac. "But it wasn't radios."

"Ah, have a heart," said the man. "You know how

62

it is. Victimised, that's me. For my convictions. Every time."

"You don't need to let your boss know your convictions," said Isaac quietly; it was something he knew about. Then he and Josh carried the radio out. "Kgosi," he said, "I'm not sure of these men. They have not eaten. Could you give them a strong drink?"

"If that will help," the chief said. He ordered his men to put a strong slug of whisky into beer glasses for them. Josh and the policeman were to have plain beer: "See, the glasses with the chips out of them?"

Isaac waited and while he did, squatted on the floor and fixed the volume control knob. He said nothing but he knew the chief was watching him. Then Josh beckoned to him from the door; he got up, clicking in the back of his throat as a salute to Kgosi. Josh drew him out on to the veranda. "Man, they're not politicals. I got them talking, made them think they were safe. They'd been in a gang fight, one of them's knifed a guy, had to quit. I tell you, man, they're laughing about it now. And thinking we're with them because——"

"Josh man, you never told them about *us*?"

"No, no, just drinking. Cracks about the police. I got them to thinking I'd had it for rape."

"What do we do then? If you're dead certain they aren't politicals, I am too. What do we do?"

"I hate like hell giving a man up to the police. Those police."

"So do I. A man of my own colour. But—it's for the tribe, see."

"You say that, man! You think that counts?"

63

Isaac saw Josh looking at him curiously and was suddenly angry: "I *do* say it! We have to think of the tribe. And old Ham-hand. God knows I'm not one of them, I'm a city guy and I've not given up any one thing I believed in. But—listen, Josh, if Kgosi turns them in, co-operates with the police, all that, see how much better if anyone real were to come? One day. It might be. This would give him a good name. And the tribe: law abiding: to be trusted. Helping the whites!"

"I hate like hell to help the whites!"

"Ah, come on, Josh, this is different. They lied to us, thought we were innocents. You a bloody innocent, Josh?"

"*Ga ke nko*," said Josh and laughed.

They went back to the room and knelt in front of the chief. "Kgosi," said Isaac, "these men are not refugees but criminals. We are both sure of that."

"And so?" said the chief heavily, half to himself. Neither spoke. It was not for them. Then he said: "Go to the kitchen. There will be food for you."

A few days later someone dropped a parcel wrapped in newspaper into the hut. In it were two pairs of shoes and socks. Not too worn. They looked at one another. Then Isaac said: "I'd like to have me a pair of shoes. But not that man's."

"Nor me," said Josh, "maybe we could change them." And so they did, getting the worst of the bargain: tyre-soled sandals but better than going with nothing in winter. But nobody likes to wear a murderer's shoes unless, that is, he murders for conscience' sake. Isaac

64

had another terrible dream after that, in which he was talking to the men again and one of them turned into Amos. And all the same they had to be given up to the police. The dream stayed with him all the next day.

When Isaac managed to mend the big clock in the house of his ward headman, he was really pleased with himself. The clock did not go long or well, but the hands moved. On a good day it would not lose more than an hour. Several people brought clocks or watches but all needed more repairs than he could manage. He did a little with lorries, working with others; there were several men who were fairly good mechanics and the man who was in charge of the bore-hole pump knew his Lister engine as though it was his wife. It began to seem to Isaac that here in the tribe were people who could probably tackle any kind of problem if they had the education and the tools. And that was what he had always thought about his fellow Africans. And was also what he had heard so often derided and denied. He remembered some of the things whites had said in his hearing, deliberately sometimes, and he never to be able to answer back, what they put in their newspapers and believed in their hearts.

Or did they believe it? No, not any longer. Dutch Reform could go on preaching about children of Ham, but Verwoerd and Vorster believed in their hearts that Africans could do anything that whites could do and that was why they made law after law to stop them being able to. And surely, Isaac thought, that is worse wickedness than believing simply, as their grandfathers did, that

65   E

we are born slaves? And some way, somehow, we must show them, show the world. And before we can be equal we must, one day, come out on top.

Josh came back one evening and said to Isaac: "You know James Mookami, he is going to take out a *mophato*. They have asked me to go with them."

Isaac stood back and laughed: "You, Josh, tribalising! First you make rain, only not enough. Now you go for initiation. What do you think they do to you?"

"I don't just know yet. Not all. Not for sure. I think we stay out, live on game, sleep little, learn songs."

"Bet they circumcise you, Josh. Then what's Chrissie going to say, what Peggy, what Lolo?"

"Could be I'll never see one of them again," said Josh. "Anyway, I don't see it matters."

"They'll make you squeal!" said Isaac and laughed aloud. Funniest thing he'd heard for a long time, and yet he was half jealous. The Bamatsieng had wanted Josh, not him. Well, fair enough, he thought, I hated them like poison; and he remembered the first day and his fear of tribal country, how he only wanted to get away. Anywhere so long as it wasn't the police. And now? Yes, of course he was going back, back to the Republic and danger; he hadn't given up one small snippet of his ideas and principles. But it just wasn't possible at the moment. He wondered if he were to go to Kgosi and ask in so many words would he be let go. Would he even be given money? He might be, you never knew. And then—well, then there was Tselane. He remembered a girl called Letty, nice girl, educated, worked as a stenographer; they'd been going steady.

66

Going to church together. Going to houses where maybe there'd be some good records and a bit of talk. She went on about getting married and he kind of half said yes, but he'd thought at the back of his mind you can't get married, man, not with what you're doing. He'd thought this while they were listening to jazz, twisting, while he was petting her up. He hoped she'd found her a nice guy. But not him. Tselane was different.

Josh was taken off to help make the erosion dykes across the slope. Every *mophato*, every regiment as they called them when they spoke in English, must help with some bit of public work. It was called work for the chief, but it was work for the community, for the tribe, of which they were now to become full adult members. They grumbled about it of course and argued where the stones were to go, who was to work with the ox team and the big red-wheeled wagon, and who was to unload and lay. They broke off work and argued and laughed but as there was no rain in sight there was no great hurry about the erosion dykes. At the time Josh had most of his meals with the friends he was making, but if there was a chance he would save something for Isaac. Not that most of them were eating well, but some were farmers who had enough to carry on with in spite of crop failure. Others were in the Public Works Department, or driving lorries; a few would come into Ditlabeng from outside jobs and no doubt they had just walked out on employers who never knew what was happening, or perhaps they had said that there was a wedding or a funeral. There was even a small group back from the mines—that had definitely been a family bereavement—yes, a messenger

67

had come, baas, here he was. They had lost wages but gained—what?

One of the older *maphato* was their father group and from time to time they turned up and joined in the arguments about the erosion dykes. Some were headmen, several were relations of the chief in his generation or the one before. One of them, an oldish man, his hair grey, his face scarred, called Ramodimo, gave Josh a hunting knife, old and sharp, the blade worn down to a good point, in a leather sheath sewn with copper wire. That was altogether a nice thing to have. Many of the others had rifles. Josh had been afraid he might be the only one unarmed. Isaac, looking at it, saw it as a useful tool for getting at small parts. But Josh was already killing lions with it in his mind.

Chapter VI

A YOUNG MAN AND A YOUNG WOMAN looked for one another in Lyons Corner House and found one another all the more easily because everyone else was white or at least a kind of grey-pink colour. Each thought the other looked a good deal smarter than the rest of the crowd. They sat down at a small table. Both of them started off with two Wimpeys and lots of tomato sauce and followed them with big ice-cream sundaes, but Letlotse's was yellow and Seneo's was pink. It was her day off from the hospital and she wore a gay summer outfit, Marks and Spencer frills, light and pretty, ice-cream coloured against her skin. They talked a mixture of English and Tswana according to what the conversation was about, and they laughed a lot but low. Nobody paid much attention to them, though a few were vaguely uneasy, looking at the slightly different set of forehead and nose and lips, monkeyish, wasn't it? But most didn't notice; they had their own escorts to worry about.

Seneo was teasing Letlotse about a girl. It seemed that this girl had been very fond of Letlotse but suddenly her parents found out and objected, especially her father, since Letlotse was a nigger: "And you tell me he is some kind of clerk!" said Seneo and tossed her head.

"Well," said Letlotse, "a clerk is all right, you and I have cousins who are clerks in P.W.D."

"Ah, but not here!" said Seneo. "Listen to me—I know. You don't understand, it is different here, it is not for instance grand to be a nurse, although I thought it was going to be before I came. And a clerk is nothing. Not compared with a chief." She punched Letlotse lightly in the chest.

"All that would have made no difference to Patsy's father," said Letlotse, "but none of it matters."

"You should go higher," said Seneo. "Surely there are girls at this university of yours?"

"But not so pretty," said Letlotse.

"That is nothing, nothing," said Seneo. "What matters is class, class, class!" She knocked with her spoon on the table.

"You must not scold me, I will not be scolded by a woman!"

"You are a savage, my little brother," said Seneo. "Let us eat some more ice-cream, you shall pay for it. Why do not the other kind of girls fall in love with you, Letlotse?"

"It is just as bad," said Letlotse and grinned reminiscently, "if you are not loved because of the colour bar and all that or too much loved because of it. Pitied, perhaps. Do I know? Anyway not thought of as myself. That is not what a man likes. That is something not straight."

"Love is never straight," said Seneo.

Letlotse leaned back; where his wrists stuck out from

the white Western shirt cuff it could have been seen that he had light, delicately made wrist bones and the muscles moved clear and hard under the skin. He was straight-nosed and full-lipped and both of them had the same clear jewelled eyes, dark agates. She had been having her hair straightened and patted it nervously when he looked at it. "They are stupid," she said. "All except my patients in the hospital who just think of me as a nurse. And they are needing my help. Tell me, Letlotse, are you really going to Russia?"

"Yes, I have friends going on this tour."

"White friends?"

"Some. And an Indian."

"Do you talk to him more easily?"

Letlotse nodded. "I think it will be very educational. I have been to Stockholm and Paris and Berlin. After my exams perhaps I shall never come back to Europe."

"There is a thing I believe we must think about, you and I," said Seneo and dug her spoon in and out of the ice. "It has been seeming to me that our father is not so well."

Letlotse did not answer for a moment; the same thought had been with him but he had not liked it. He did not wish it to come out of hiding. "You do not get letters from him?" he asked.

"No, or scarcely, mostly from my Aunt Sarah. She says by the way that James is making a regiment."

"If I go back that is what I will have to do, I suppose. It will be such a bore. I cannot think how I would manage at all. Running after animals and learning all those stupid songs and the old men hitting me if I got a word wrong!"

"Nonsense," said his sister. "That is only how one feels here. The songs could be stupid in London. They are not stupid in Ditlabeng. When I raise my regiment I shall learn them faster than any of the others who will go out with me. Because I am educated. I have learnt to learn." She stuck her chin out at him.

He wriggled and screwed up his face. "But really I hate it. I shall hate it so much if I have to do it! I hate even that you should do it, my sister. I think it is all mixed up with witchcraft. People say there are no witch doctors any longer. But I know myself that there are. Anyhow why should the regiment have secrets unless they are bad?"

"It may be," said Seneo, "that when we know the secret we shall know that too. It is possible also that things may look bad, at least uncivilised, but are not underneath. Anyway, Letlotse, you have a long time. If James is raising his regiment now yours will be after you go back. If all is going well our father will not press you. It will be after you have taken your exam and looked about you. You need not think of it now, even."

"I cannot help thinking of it. I think of it when I wake in the middle of the night, and do not sleep."

"And how often is that?" asked Seneo unbelievingly.

"Well, perhaps not very often. So it will be a long time yet. Is that what you say?"

"If all goes well, but you must think about what else may happen. If . . ."

He moved uneasily. "Perhaps our father will live for a long time. I want to pass my exam."

"And I mine. If I pass my exams here in England I might even be made a Sister at home instead of some little white girl just coming out! But there is this other thing which is something which must be faced."

They had dropped their voices and were speaking now in Tswana.

"If our father died and you were here and if some of the old men think you are too young, Motswasele will be Regent."

"He would wake things up in some ways."

"I do not think he would give it up easily."

Letlotse looked across at her. "Listen, Seneo. Would that be altogether a bad thing? Here am I born to be chief but have you ever thought that I might like to get out of it?"

"Not to go home?"

"There are other ways. Supposing I went home not as chief but as leader of a political party? For the whole of the country. The whole of Bechuanaland. Not just our own little reserve. For it is little. Think how much less than those of the Bamangwato, the Bakwena, the Bakgatla even, why should I be stuck there?"

"It is your own pond, frog."

"Well, that is what I have been thinking. To be a politician."

"It is more modern, certainly," said Seneo in a flat voice.

"Our country will have to be like other countries. With a political party or perhaps, to start with, two."

"And which would you lead, Letlotse?"

"Well, mine would be for progress. Unity. Industry. Education. We would not be a Protectorate any longer: that has no dignity. But we would have to have a special protected status, oh, I have thought about it——"

"And how would our own Legco member like it if you stole his politics?"

"Oh, Dikgang! He is a fool. He is only there because Motswasele lent him money, and now he can repay Motswasele by doing what he wants in Legco. Or anywhere else. It is clever of Motswasele to have someone like that. But I do not count him."

Seneo looked at her brother over her cup of coffee, smiled and shook her head: "One should always count one's enemies, Letlotse."

But Letlotse's lip curled; he had the proud look of a boy on a sand castle: "He is not an enemy. I despise him."

"Well, you have to think if you can always be so proud, my beautiful leopard. Tell me more about your party. I suppose it will be for Independence?"

"I told you, Seneo, it will be for a special status. Until we are strong enough."

"And that will be a long time. I think we shall not have enough money for pop-guns."

"But of course I shall say Independence in my speeches——"

"Louder than the others? And of course you will be against the chiefs?" She licked the end of her spoon.

He looked at her, noticed she was not entirely serious.

He had said the same thing to Kumar, his Indian friend, and had a long argument which he only half remembered. Looking back what he really remembered most was that he and the Indian had gravitated together across a room full of whites. Kumar and he had talked to one another naturally, and agreed that there must be a great Afro-Asian Confederation which would sooner or later be against the Western world, and which was bound to win, so strong it must be, so many millions in it! They had talked in terms of exploitation, of the death of Imperialism and so on; perhaps these words were not very accurate; what mattered was the warm feeling between him and the Indian. And the thought that he must be modern, as modern as the Indian Congress party; more modern in fact. He was glad this Indian was coming to Moscow in the party. Not that he did not also look forward to being there with his British friends. But it was not quite the same. One thing he hoped was that through one of them he might get some industry into the country. Perhaps to Craigs, which was the nearest town. He had been to see one of the English new towns—oh, it was modern! Factories like little palaces, he could see a row of them at home all along the railway line, pink and blue and green. And this man's father made something, shoes perhaps, or typewriters, or cement, if he could be made to have the same vision of factories all along the line near Craigs! His sister kicked him mildly on the shin.

"Answer, Letlotse! When you make this party of your own, will it be against the chiefs?"

"That would look well," said Letlotse honestly.

"If it were to be against Motswasele I would even join it myself," said Seneo. "But I do not think the People's Party has much sense."

"Why are you so against him, Seneo? He is young still and a strong man. He might be as good as anyone at dealing with the tribe."

"One reason I am against him," said Seneo, "is that if he were to become Regent he would want to marry me. And the Council would be entirely with him; they would say it was right."

"Why would you not want to marry him? He is handsome. He is free-handed. He would give you children. If I become a politician your son could become chief."

"I know he thinks he is handsome. I know he can make children. Agnes had five minutes of him one night when nobody chose to hear her crying out."

"Agnes? Oh, Tselane. I expect she wanted it."

"That's what you men say always. When I go home I shall take a hypodermic and this and that to go in it. I am not taking five minutes of Motswasele. And I think you are wrong, Letlotse, wrong to think that you can back out of your obligations. You were born to be chief. It is a burden but it is your burden. It is harder to be a good chief than to be a successful politician, because you can have no holidays, and I do not think you have worked hard. Not work as I have worked."

"I tell you, Seneo, I will not be scolded!" said Letlotse. "And I have worked. I work for this exam. I worked when I was a herd boy."

"Riding about on your backside and shouting! It

76

would have been better for you to go to school. I have worked long and hard hours under discipline. I have had to take responsibility. So will you."

"But let us hope that our father lives many years."

"I hope so too," said Seneo. "I hope so very much." She ate a cream horn quickly and neatly.

Letlotse thought he would like to go back to the beginning and have another Wimpey. After all a man must eat meat. But perhaps they would laugh, the whites. The waitress brushed by and he pulled his arm away and wrinkled his nose. "I do not like their smell unless they wear scent," he said. "Without it they smell of cats. Let us go."

They walked out together; such people as noticed them perhaps thought they were Africans or at any rate West Indians, it all comes to the same thing, doesn't it? But nobody knew that they came from the Bamatsieng. Nobody perhaps knew where Bechuanaland was or who it belonged to. If anyone had said it was a British Protectorate and their responsibility, something on which their money was spent, hardly anyone in Lyons Corner House would have thought of anything except how to get rid of it. It was out of date, Kiplingish, to have all these blacks. As Letlotse might have said, not modern.

Two people, though, did notice; they were a middle-aged Argyllshire man and his wife. They had been down for their son's wedding and now the wife was trying to induce her husband to have a nice hot cup of strong tea. "Ah," he said, "I mind of yon café in Sicily and there was some o' thae South Africans, and here, didn't one of the brown boys come in, fighting in our war, but thae

77

bloody South Africans set on him and beat him up. And didn't we knock them all to hell for it!"

"Aye," said his wife, "There were plenty political arguments settled in the cafés of Sicily." But she too regarded Letlotse and Seneo with a certain sympathy.

Chapter VII

BUT THE CHIEF DIED. He kept on not wanting to see the doctor from the Mission; he knew what the doctor was going to say and he did not want to hear it. In the end he collapsed over his desk and dark-coloured blood came out of his mouth. He regarded it curiously for a time. He thought about other blood that he had seen spread about, blood of animals and men. And gradually everything became wavering in his mind and more blood came and he did not even know that he had been taken to the Mission Hospital to die, and did not hear the head of the Mission urging him to final repentance, or the prayers of those of his people who had followed him in.

His sister Sarah, weeping, sent off two telegrams. One to Seneo and one to Letlotse. But Letlotse was in Moscow with an Intourist group, being taken round and —he couldn't help feeling—stared at more than he liked. Then they went on to Kharkov. And the telegram had to be forwarded and reforwarded, so that it was a long time before it got to him.

So what? There was no disagreement among the tribe. Letlotse was the heir. Everyone knew that. But he was not married. He had not made a regiment. He was still being educated. Above all, he was not there.

79

That meant there must be a Regent. And quick. For a tribe can no more live without its head than a beast or a person can. When the deep grave in the great kraal had been dug and filled in, there was nobody. That was intolerable, a pain. The Mission had said the burial service; it meant little. The Bamatsieng knew otherwise about death.

A secret meeting of headmen was called at once, and then immediately afterwards a full tribal meeting. Runners went out to the villages and men came pouring in, no need to force them to come. There was a remarkable number of rifles, about twice as many, the D.C. said to himself, as there were licences taken out for. But he only thought that for a moment with half his mind, not caring much; he was like everyone else, all he was really thinking was who would be the one to be shown to the meeting. He had said and done what he could, but he was not sure whether he had been listened to: Dikgang had appeared to be taking it in, nodding wisely as befitted the Legco member, but what did he really think?

In general the men got together in their initiation groups, closing up, wanting to feel near one another. The older men sat on the Kgotla benches, Dikgang among them, wearing a hat and a rather loud sports coat. The younger ones were standing close, body to body, behind them. Opposite was the chief's house, empty, dead. Between it and them another bench where those who must speak to the meeting would sit. It too was empty, still empty. There were a good many women milling round outside, occasionally pushing at the men, being hit back, talking, talking, even when the men were silent. Josh was with his *mophato*, close to a friend he had made during the initiation period, a man called Kuate, a lorry driver with a broad, smiling face. But Isaac was on the edge of the group; he was shivering a great deal. He had not believed it when Tselane had said the chief was ill; he had not wanted to believe it; now he had to. There was Kgosi suffering and bearing it for the sake of them all, and he and Josh had called him old Ham-hand and wondered how they could get another meal out of him—Come off it, man, said Isaac to himself, what was he after all, only a savage, won't rate a paragraph in the *Star*—and then inside himself he heard the chief's voice telling them they had protection; and felt again whatever it was he had felt then, gratitude, love— ah, come off it! He edged nearer Josh into the closeness of the men of James Mookami's *mophato*, which was called Magwasa. They made room for him, feeling that he wanted to be near his friend.

There was a good deal of whispering. It looked as though the question of the Regency must boil down to three people. Of the chief's father's generation there was only one left, a younger brother, but quite old by now and never a man of much account. He would probably not want to take the responsibility, though his relatives might try to push him into it. There was the chief's own youngest brother Letlamma, who was well liked but not a heavy-weight; he had made money somehow and had a small red racing car or almost a racing car. He had friends among the whites, was perhaps too well liked in some of the bars of Craigs and Francistown or Gaberones.

He was called into the Council when he was about at Ditlabeng and he had some sense; but he was not always there. Some people said he had another wife, somewhere up the line. Again he had a following; if you were part of a chief's household and friends other things were added. There were plenty to encourage him. And then there was Motswasele.

People asked themselves, who had the chief wanted? The chief had wanted to live until Letlotse the heir, the young leopard, came back fully educated, fully accepted. But that had not happened.

The men of the Magwasa *mophato* would have had Sarah, James Mookami's mother. Some of them were saying so. There had been women Regents before, rarely enough, but it did happen sometimes, in other tribes. No question but she was senior to Motswasele's father. And if she was Regent then their James Mookami would move up in the order of importance. They knew that. And the chief had liked and trusted him. But they could not name his mother as Regent. That was in the hands of the headmen and elders and the tribe itself.

It was said that the D.C. favoured the old uncle, thinking he could carry on with the formal duties of the chief until Letlotse came back. Until the telegram from Letlotse arrived. But there was still no answer to their telegram, though there had been an answer from Seneo who was coming just as soon as she could.

And the rest? Motswasele was powerful. He had many friends. He would act as chief. With strength. The one thing that most people thought they wanted was to be ruled strongly. Isaac, feeling this, was more scared than

82

he had ever been. Motswasele's *mophato* looked confident; they were two senior to James's, youngish men in good positions, men with cattle and bearing wives. They had formed up opposite the bench which would be the centre of the meeting; that looked bad for a start. They were very well armed, some with rifles, others with kerries and axes; that looked none too good either.

A whisper came through the Magwasa and landed with Kuate who turned to Josh, gripping him by the elbow: 'Ramodimo says you must stay with us well inside, you and Isaac too."

Josh knew better than to question. This was his regiment; Ramodimo was his father. He would do what was said. So by God would Isaac.

And then the whispering died down and all were watching the empty bench. Motswasele came out of the chief's house with several of the senior headmen, one or two royals among them. It had been decided then, unless the tribe wanted very strongly otherwise. He walked slowly with his head up, a man not afraid. He looked to them already like a chief. He sat down on the bench and looked round on the meeting, his eyes sweeping across it like a lion's eyes. Kuate shoved himself in front of Josh and another man did the same for Isaac. Then Motswasele's *mophato* began to shout and fire their rifles and swing their axes, and gradually the shouting began to spread although it was half-hearted in some places, and especially from Magwasa, until after a moment James Mookami shouted and looked round at his men; it was the only safe thing to do. Any other less

83

enthusiastic groups joined in too; noise hung like dust over the meeting.

A man detached himself from the edge of the meeting and ran to tell the D.C., who was standing a little apart. He was one of the clerks and he knew the D.C.'s face in the same way as he knew the book in which he made his entries, closely, carefully. After a minute he said: "Sir, we should go back to the office."

The D.C. seemed to come to with a jerk. "Why?" he asked.

"Sir, they would not come there."

"I see. Let's go."

Back at the office the D.C. looked round, there was only himself and the clerk: "Everyone agrees, then, that Motswasele shall be Regent?"

"It was the headmen. They killed the lion for him. We heard that. I think—I think he is too strong." The clerk waited and watched for a minute then he said: "Sir, the funeral service—the Mission—they were not pleased with the chief, they were not pleased with his soul. Can they hurt him?"

"No. Nobody can hurt him now."

"They did not want us to keep guard. We did that. I think they did not want him buried in the great kraal. But it was his own wish."

"It was right to bury him where he wanted."

"Sir, at the funeral I could not pray for my chief with the Mission angry."

The D.C. looked at the door of the office. "We will pray for him now. Both of us will pray. But there is no need to be anxious. He is in some good place for he

84

was a just man and merciful." Both of them leant over the table, covering their eyes. After the noise of the meeting the office was very quiet.

But now it sank down to whispering again. A chair was brought out of the house and put in front of the bench a few yards nearer to the crowd—yes, it was *his* chair thought Josh, Kgosi's own chair—and a leopard skin was laid on it. Motswasele rose and was led to the chair by two of the headmen; he walked in a strangely blind way as though he were elsewhere. Then nothing happened for a little as he sat there staring. Everyone began to get rather frightened. It began to be whispered that there had been a quarrel as to who should present the weapons. In the end it seemed that the older man, Motswasele's great-uncle, was the one to do it; this would signify that he had renounced any ambitions himself; it would mean a safer and easier life for him and his household.

He came out of the house carrying the weapons; he looked older than his age. Motswasele did not turn round but sat there in his dark suit with his black tie and black shoes. The great-uncle came up from behind him and bowed and handed him assegai, kerrie and axe. Motswasele took them, the wide grip of his hand held them at chest height. He looked extraordinarily dangerous, much more so than if he had been armed with a rifle or even a machine-gun. All round the men ducked and murmured. It was even thought that he might assume the great leopard skin cloak of a full chief. No one would have felt themselves able to stop him. But

85

he did not do that. He stayed within custom. He was Regent. That was enough.

One after another the older headmen and counsellors came and spoke to him of the duties of a chief. Not everyone could hear what was said. Perhaps he did not hear himself; his eyes went on staring; he made no answer to what was said nor did the weapons move even a little in his hand. Tselane watched from among the women, keeping a grip on herself, saying over and over again, that she was a member of the People's Party and so totally against the leopard-throned. But she could see the local secretary of the party staring goggle-eyed as any of the rest. And Isaac—were the two of them going to be safe? Had Motswasele forgotten? He was not one to forget things which might be to his advantage. But how to find out? No, said Tselane to herself, no! no!

Chapter VIII

CERTAINLY IT FELT SAFE to be in the big rondavel with the other men tucked behind bodies and
weapons. James's house was on the far side of
Ditlabeng with a small kopje behind it, enormous stones
always about to topple, never toppling, thorn bushes
and pink-flowered spiky aloes, rock rabbits that chittered
at night. Kuate had gone straight over to their old
house and fetched their things, the box of tools and usable
bits, the blankets and cooking pot, the tin with the
money. And they ate more regularly, in fact there was
almost always one decent meal a day for James Mookami's
men. Most of the others went out and joined in the
feasting to the new acting-chief, the Regent, who had duly
slaughtered cattle. It was out of no loyalty to him,
but because one should never miss a good eating of meat.
They said that Motswasele had done something which
had not been done for a long time, the doctoring of
weapons. A rifle dealt with in this way would not miss,
unless the user had done something wrong which would
break the strengthening which had gone into both barrel
and aim. All Motswasele's own *mophato* had brought in
their rifles, but not the Magwasa nor indeed some of the
others.

Of the old chief's household and retainers some

scattered, though those with houses of their own stayed in them. Some switched and became very attentive to the Regent, bowing and my-lording whenever they saw Motswasele. He had bought a new car, an American Pontiac, big and flashy, lots of chrome plate; there was always somebody polishing it and half a dozen others looking at it. But Murphy came over to James Mookami and established himself in the men's rondavel. He also brought a message for Isaac from Tselane saying that everything would be all right, but he must not try to see her. This worried Isaac a great deal, all the more as he had had very little to do at first except odd jobs like mending furniture. But he had plenty of time to listen and think about what he was hearing. The whole structure of the tribe looked rather different from here.

He began to see it as a power struggle in a way it had never seemed in old Ham-hand's day. Yet perhaps it had been the same thing underneath. Now a great deal had come to the surface, some of it none too pretty. The old man, the great-uncle, did not matter so much, though he had his relations and followers, some with ambition. But Letlamma, who lived most of the time in a village of his own, was certainly a power. Perhaps, thought Isaac, I was right in the way I thought about the tribals first; that they are worse off than the rest of us Africans because they have tied the burden on to their own backs: chiefs and sub-chiefs and headmen, all of them born to it, never an election, nothing that democracy could start from. If the chief was a good man that was all right. Or was it? No, people should run their own lives. He began to ache again for politics, for persuasion, for finding

88

the right words to wake and fire people. And getting the word about. In the beginning was the word. That was always so. Freedom. Democracy. He knew now how much he longed to talk about it with Tselane, almost as much as he longed to lie with her.

And beyond the Bamatsieng. Was it the same? Did some people think truly about the whole country, this big bit that was called Bechuanaland on the white maps, the land and people, the Batswana? That came through in fainter echoes to the men's rondavel. Rumours of what had been said or done in the African Council or the semi-elected Legislative Council. The new Constitution and beyond it, rumours about the other Protectorates, Basutoland and Swaziland.

Sometimes Motswasele talked grandly about the whole country, and this was always spoken about, talked over among the men. At these times Isaac felt uncomfortably that this was more right, above all more modern, than talking about the tribe. If anyone but Motswasele had been saying it! Josh took things more as they came. Josh and his old hunting knife! And he wouldn't hear anything against James Mookami. Though he was as much out for power as the rest. Or wasn't he? And would this Letlotse, his cousin, be the same?

Isaac lay awake wondering, trying still to get the smell of Tselane out of snuffling in his blanket, but only getting the smoky smell of the other men. He wondered if he and Josh were really in any danger. What use would it be to Motswasele to kill them? Or did he still think he could sell them to the Republic? Probably not at this stage. How could he explain not having done it before? Still.

Better keep out of the way. Ramodimo no doubt had some reason for making them do what they had done. He had heard rumours that the District Commissioner was being frozen out. Could be. That was up to him. A nice guy. But white. Maybe he couldn't handle Motswasele.

He should at least have approved of Motswasele's tax drive. The old chief had let things go during the last year. The headmen had retired into their villages and sent in the smallest possible contributions. The tribal treasury could only just pay the essentials for the office and the schools. Now the Regent was going through tax lists and where there were defaulters he sent out not the tribal police, but his own men armed with the doctored rifles, so that there was no trouble at all in bringing in taxes and arrears of taxes for years back. Whether all those grubby *rand* notes went into the treasury was not so certain; some said this, some that. However, there had been a man from the British Government, an important man, a big car and a big frown—but it was a big smile and handshake for Motswasele—and he had come specially to give big congratulations to the Regent and he was over the D.C. Everyone knew that. Letlamma had tried to impress this one and had unwisely offered him brandy: a stupid thing with this kind of Englishman. James Mookami kept rather quiet, though his mother had been officially condoled with: did this white man even know that many had wanted her for Regent? The D.C. probably did by now, but it was too late.

It was after this that he came to see James, making it seem as if by accident. Everyone wanted to know

what had been spoken of, but James only said they had
talked about Letlotse. Which might, of course, have been
true.

Josh and Isaac had been helping to fix a bit of corru-
gated iron that had come off the roof. While they were
about it they cleaned out a nest of bats from underneath;
nobody minds about bats which in any case eat the
insects, but a certain weight of bat droppings begins
after the years to pull down a plaster board ceiling.
Murphy came over and called to Isaac who came down
the ladder; they went into the men's rondavel together.
In a little, Murphy came out and shouted up to Josh.
When Josh came off the roof Murphy said: "I think
you should go in, look at your friend."

"Why? What did you tell him, Murphy?"

"I tell him Motswasele got to have a woman now.
Got to have Tselane. He goes to her house. Soon
maybe she has her house moved. To make a little wife
for Motswasele."

"Does she say Yes?"

"What does it matter what she says? He is great chief
now. Josh, I think Isaac in there tries to kill himself."
And Murphy laughed uncomfortably.

Josh was into the rondavel in two bounds. Isaac
was down on the floor beating his head on it. His forehead was bleeding. Josh pulled him up, "Isaac, Isaac
man, stop it! You won't help Tselane this way."

Isaac looked at him with crazy eyes. "Motswasele gets
her. I can't stand it. No, Josh. I'd rather be dead."

"You got to stand it. She got to stand it.. One day we
get out. All of us. I tell you, Isaac man, that's so.

That's sure." He held Isaac's hands, gripped them hard, willed Isaac into quiet and reason.

Murphy came to the door and looked in anxiously. "I take her a message, shall I? I could do that. Nobody thinks we're mixed up, you and me. I'll take care. Shall I, Isaac?"

"No, no!" said Isaac, throwing himself about.

"Yes," said Josh. "But wait till he sobers up."

Several of the other men came in and looked on, laughing not from amusement but from embarrassment and discomfort, for Isaac was sobbing over Josh's knees, sometimes beating his fists and feet on the floor, though Josh would not let him beat his head. Kuate said: "We get you Tselane, Isaac. We get her on to the kopje. Maybe to-night."

Isaac suddenly became stiff and straight. "If we do that," said Murphy, "you are not to hurt Tselane. It is no doing of hers."

"I will not hurt her," said Isaac, his face to the floor.

That was in the afternoon. Evening came. Night. Nobody slept. Ramodimo came in with his younger half-brother Dithapo. They had rifles, Murphy had a rifle and so had Kuate, but they had gone away about the time of the moon-setting, quietly. Murphy came back and nodded at Ramodimo. "Come," said Ramodimo to Isaac. Josh would have come too, but Ramodimo said: "No, not you."

Then Josh shoved his hunting knife into Isaac's hand. Isaac looked at it and shook his head, but put it into his belt. He followed the others out through the narrow opening in the wall at the back of the courtyard. They

92

each put a hand on his shoulder, carrying their rifles sloped. He had a tear in his shirt and he felt Dithapo's hard hand on his bare skin. Tselane might have mended it. But perhaps the shirt was too far gone. She had said once that she would knit him a jersey, but she had never been able to get the wool. He shivered in the cold night and the stars seemed to shiver and grow brighter. Nobody spoke.

They came to the beginning of a kind of path. "Up," whispered Ramodimo and then he and his brother sank back behind rocks. You could not even see the tips of their rifles.

Isaac went on and up, touching rocks at each side, hard, rounded granite that the path wound between. At a corner he was uncertain but Kuate whispered to him to turn right and he heard the faint chink of a gun barrel on stone. He looked back. Ditlabeng lay below but there was no light in any house. He went on and suddenly felt utterly alone. Nothing was real. Nothing until he felt a hand close on his ankle and all reality flowed back and he was down in the dust beside Tselane.

They lay very quietly in one another's arms, not making love, only intensely aware of one another again. Isaac rubbed his head into the hollow of her neck and she felt the delicate tight brush of his hair and the shape of his nose and lips unchanged. He had thought that this pain in his heart was anger against her, but it was not, it was only sorrow for her and now it melted away and he was full of the smell of her skin and ears and the taste of her mouth. At last he whispered: "Did it have to happen—*that*?"

"There was nothing I could do to stop it," she whispered back, "if I had I think he would have killed you, even at James's house." She did not say what exceedingly detailed threats Motswasele had used—not directly but repeated to her by one of his men. They were meant to frighten her and they had. Though perhaps they might not have been carried out. Isaac's eyes were wet against the skin of her shoulder as he snuggled against her, a light loved weight; she thought with curious hatred of the violent weight of Motswasele.

He said: "It might have been better to kill me."

"No," she said, "no!" And her arms knotted round him.

"If we had been married," he said, "would he have taken you all the same?"

"I don't know," she said. "Perhaps not. But now he wants to move my house. I do not like to think of that."

"Ah, God, Tselane," he said, "he will start a baby in you and then——" he was shuddering against her, feeling as a man does when he is arrested, when he is utterly in the power of the police.

"He will not do that," said Tselane. "There is one already. Yours."

He said nothing for a moment, then: "But how? We were careful. Too careful, me!"

She stroked his head and back. "Difficult to be careful always, Isaac, you and me. I was not meaning to say."

"Why not, Tselane?"

"You must be free, Isaac. Freedom. Democracy. All that. Not tied to the Bamatsieng."

"I am tied to you, I am your ox, Tselane. Is it true? Sure true? My baby?"

"Sure true, Isaac."

"Then—he will not hurt it, he in you?"

"I will not let your baby be hurt, Isaac."

"Tselane, does he—make you feel good?" Isaac couldn't help asking that, risking an extra pain. For a moment his hand was on Josh's knife.

She answered, whispering close: "He makes me feel bad. Most especially if—ah, hush up, my Isaac! Let us not think of it for this hour when your friends guard us."

"But if he makes you go to his house——"

"I know. I know. But maybe Seneo will come."

"And if she does?"

"The elders will make her marry him. It would be thought right. Then he might eat her and not me."

"If we could marry——"

"You are not one of the tribe. And you have nothing to give. I would go with you. Even to the Republic I would go. But I cannot see it. Let us not think any more. I want you. Your baby and I, we want you to strengthen us. Come."

The stars moved over the quiet night. She lay in the dust under the edge of the great granite rock, half asleep. The first cock crowed down in Ditlabeng. Very gently he woke her. "Before the stars pale, Tselane, you must go."

She sat up, shook herself, "We will think of something," she said. They went down.

Murphy and Kuate were suddenly beside them.

95

Murphy pushed Isaac gently back. "Best if she goes alone. We follow her close. Wait a little."

She put his hand to her cheek, then dropped it and went on. The other two followed behind her. Isaac waited patiently until another cock crowed, then a third. He came down himself and found Ramodimo: "How can I get married to Tselane?" he said, "for she carries my son."

"We thought this might come," said Ramodimo. "Our father was brother to Tselane's grandmother. It is a pity you are not one of us."

"If there is anything I can do——" said Isaac and then dropped silent. There was no answer. Perhaps they were thinking about it.

Chapter IX

AND THEN SENEO CAME BACK. She sent a telegram to her Aunt Sarah, and James drove into the station to meet the train. But the post office had of course let Motswasele the Regent know. If they had not done so there might have been trouble for them. So Motswasele had driven in too, in the Pontiac, and his men had picked up Seneo's suitcases. But Seneo had said firmly that it would not be right for her to go to any home but her Aunt Sarah's and she would drive there with James. Motswasele had the luggage and it gave him an excuse to come straight to the house. Luckily, thought Seneo, I have strong locks on my cases. Not that they will probably interfere, but it could happen.

Everyone had come to the front courtyard to welcome Seneo. But when Motswasele drove up in the Pontiac in a swirl of dust, Isaac and Josh ran for it into the rondavel followed by Murphy, and meanwhile Seneo, sitting beside James, heard a good deal of what was happening. Everyone was very polite to Motswasele and Seneo used the most formal terms in addressing him. She kept her gloves on so that he did not touch her hand. He left, angry but concealing it. Seneo said to her Aunt Sarah, "I do not like him any better than I used."

"I know," said her aunt. "But that will not have much influence on the elders and the headmen."

"You mean——?" said Seneo.

"Yes," said Sarah. "They will say that you must marry him. It would be the expected thing."

"I would rather marry James," said Seneo, "but I do not intend to marry, not yet. I want to start a new clinic here. I suppose the old one is more crowded than ever?"

"That is so," said Sarah. "And more since the drought. Even with the food that is sent, many people go hungry."

"And the schools? Still only one with a roof? Letlotse will have to build a secondary school. I could teach hygiene."

"That would be fine. Tell me, Seneo, did you get that dress in London? Was it very expensive?"

"It was not expensive at all. I am stock size. In London I shopped mostly at Marks & Spencer, where all intelligent people shop."

"But not the lords and ladies?"

"Some of them, I expect. Marks & Spencer is not class."

"I remember other names of other shops in London. When I was there thirty years ago. Dickins & Jones, Debenham & Freebody, Army & Navy, Marshall & Snelgrove. They are singing names."

"They are more expensive shops. When people are hungry here I do not go to these shops."

"You are a chief's daughter."

"I was a nurse at Thomas's. I did not think of myself as a chief's daughter. But now—perhaps I do. I am not going to be forced into marrying Motswasele."

98

"How not?" She and her aunt looked at one another across the table; they were rather alike except that Sarah had grown big and heavy, no longer stock size about the hips and bust. Seneo took off her travelling hat, a little bit of straw and veil. She had decided not to have her hair straightened again, so her splendid head shape stood clear and clean above the ruffles of her shirt. She cupped her chin on her hands and smiled. James had come in and stood beside them waiting for her answer.

"For one thing," she said, "I shall say I cannot marry until I have raised my regiment. They cannot say anything against that."

"No," said James, "that would be according to custom. You would raise a woman's regiment Magwasa."

"That is the name of yours, James?" He nodded. "Well, then, it is quite clear that I cannot do this until I have stopped mourning. I shall mourn for a long time. I shall put on a black dress and then we shall go to my father's kraal."

"Should you go to the Mission?" asked James nervously.

"Yes," she said. "I think so. I think that would be good politics. I am not afraid of Missions, James! Whether or not you are."

"I wish Letlotse would come!" said James violently.

"You cannot wish it more than I do. I waited as long as I could. He seems to be still in Russia and he has been stupid about his addresses. Or they have been stupid about getting the telegram to him. Perhaps they cannot spell our name in Russian! But it may be, that as he has not come yet, he had better wait."

99

"How long till his exam?" James asked.

"Nearly a year. Too long perhaps. It depends. I shall write to him."

"If you do that," said James, "I will take your letter into Craigs and post it there. If you post here, well—I am not sure."

"Ah! So Motswasele is being a real old-fashioned chief!"

Isaac and Josh having made a good job of one bit of the roof, were put on to another corner. It was well for Isaac that he had something to do, which kept him from worrying all the time. There was a dusty wind blowing now, dust all over everything, people, animals, trees, dust off the Kalahari Desert, blowing prickles and leaves into the houses and *lapas*, blowing girls' skirts up round their legs. Seneo, visiting round, going for instance to see her old friend Agnes Mookodi, felt herself constantly irritated by this winter dust which she had partly forgotten. The two friends stayed talking for a long time; on both sides, everything was said.

One day Kuate had been to Gaberones with his lorry; the new town was going up and some of the men from Ditlabeng were working on a contract; they came back at the week-end. There were some good shops in Gaberones. Kuate shouted up to Isaac: "Come, see what I have." He unwrapped two handkerchiefs. "You like them, Isaac?"

Isaac could not be sure—was it? No, why should it be! He stroked with one finger very tentatively the rich blue and orange. "Beautiful," he said.

"One for her and one for her mother," said Kuate.

So that was what it was! Isaac looked Kuate in the smiling eyes: "This—this is the first present? But Kuate, what did these cost? They are beautiful, too beautiful for me!"

"Never mind what they cost, Isaac," said Kuate. "You are not paying for them, Isaac, you will want all your money; this is from me. But I give them from you. I am Josh's friend, but your friend too." And he danced a little on his feet, liking to see Isaac so happy.

The next morning early Ramodimo and Dithapo came in and sent for Isaac and Josh, who came and stood in front of them. James was there too, for the moment saying nothing. Ramodimo started. "You want to marry Tselane. As she will have a child by you that is right. But you have no cattle for her. Worse, you will have to take her away because of Motswasele, and she is our daughter. Will you be good to her?"

"Yes," said Isaac, "always."

"We do not think you can have a Mission wedding or make promises, you must marry by custom. But as you cannot give cattle you must give yourself and we will count that for cows. You must promise that when the danger is over you will come back and be one of the Bamatsieng as your brother Josh is."

"Yes," said Isaac very low, "I promise." He knew he had to say yes quickly in case he thought of other things.

Dithapo said: "You will join Letlotse's *mophato* when he comes back. That will be an honour. Now that his father is dead and he is to be chief he will have to make it before time. When that is done I shall be one of your fathers, as my brother is Josh's father. Meanwhile count me as father; I will help you to go."

"Where should we go then, my father? I cannot take her back to Pretoria. If my mother had still been living at Lady Selborne she could have gone there, but all of us were turned out of our houses and homes by the Afrikaners——"

"I know. I have heard," said Dithapo. "It is now what they call a white area. No, you must stay in our country, but you must go to Craigs. I think the D.C. will give you recommendation to the Public Works Department."

"Will Tselane be safe?"

"We think so. It will become known that there could be big trouble if she is hurt. Or you. And he will not do with a married woman the evil that he would do with one that is not married."

Josh said to Ramodimo: "My father, should I go with him? We have been together for a long time. Perhaps I could protect them."

"No," said Ramodimo. "You must stay here. It will look less well if both of you who are refugees leave together. It might be something for which Motswasele could speak to the police."

James agreed. "We must give him no excuse. If he murders you, Isaac, it will be clear that it is for Tselane and that will look bad with the British so he will not do it. Now, Isaac, I think we must see Tselane and get her consent." He went out of the room and came back with Tselane and Seneo, hand in hand. Seneo was wearing mourning, but Tselane was wearing one of the kerchiefs which Kuate had brought. Suddenly Isaac knew he was trapped and was glad he was trapped.

Ramodimo said, "Daughter, we have arranged your marriage by custom. Do you consent?"

"I consent," said Tselane low, and hung on to Seneo's hand. "Where does he take me?"

"To Craigs. You will work for him and bear his child and when things are otherwise you will come back to Ditlabeng. You are still our daughter."

Seneo had a pretty white plastic handbag with a gilt chain. She took ten *rands* out of it and handed them to Isaac. "Give this as a gift to Tselane for her house-keeping." He gave it to Tselane and his hand shook. "That is right," said Seneo. "So you are this Isaac. Tselane has told me. Indeed she told me much. I am one for women's rights."

"I too," said Isaac and suddenly both of them laughed a little and then the older men laughed and James.

Only Josh was not laughing: he said, "And your mother? And the baby? Do they go too?"

"No," said Tselane lifting her head, "I go alone with my husband."

"I will take care of them then," said Josh.

It all had to happen very quickly; that would stop any action by Motswasele. Kuate brought round the lorry. Dithapo put a letter into Isaac's hand; it was a recommendation from the D.C. "You will have to get a new shirt before you work for Public Works Department," said Dithapo. Tselane had a bundle and her cooking pot, but Isaac left everything with Josh, the tools, the spares, all, except his blanket. As the job was almost sure he left the tin of money for Josh too. He was moving in a daze with no time to say good-bye as it should be said. But a Freedom Fighter must learn to say good-bye lightly. Was he a Freedom Fighter any longer? Maybe not. Maybe not. And yet he believed in the same things he had believed in before! "I wish you were coming," he said to Josh.

"I wish like hell I was coming. We've been together, Isaac. A long time now. Isaac, don't trust anyone! Not whatever they say. Remember that was the way we got caught."

"I've been thinking to say the same thing to you, Josh. You going to get on without old Isaac?"

"I'll get on," said Josh soberly.

"Stay a city guy? Not go all tribal?"

"*You* say that, Isaac!"

"Remember what we worked for, freedom, democracy, our own Africa——"

"Come," said Kuate, leaning down from the cab of the lorry and racing the engine. "I will keep Josh safe."

"Come," said Tselane from the middle of the front seat, her feet pulled back from the gear levers. "Come, my husband."

"Go safe," said Josh, taking Isaac's hands for a moment, then letting go and half shoving him into the lorry beside Tselane.

"Stay safe," said those who went. And the lorry crashed into gear and the dust flew up and the goats and hens scattered out of the way and they were leaving Ditlabeng.

Chapter X

LETLOTSE COUNTED THE STATIONS he had to go in the Underground. Yes, he would have time to read Seneo's letter again: he took it out of his pocket and frowned over it. Good that she was keeping Motswasele at arm's length, if that was what she wanted. Bad that she would not be able to for much longer. Seneo raising a regiment! Would he really have to do that himself? He couldn't see himself being whacked or for that matter learning all the nonsense secrets. As if he didn't know about girls already! Another station. He remembered the time when he had been frightened of the Underground, especially the moving staircase. A long time back. He remembered how he had thought they were colour-barring him because they put up their newspapers in front of them, but it was only to read; now he did the same. He used to have plenty of silly notions, but he had been proud, perhaps prouder than he was now. Thought he could carry the world in front of him! He had been altogether too young. But now, looking back even a couple of months, he felt he was changed, more grown up. Perhaps Russia did that. Not that he believed everything he was told in the Soviet Union, but—well it had been worth it, even if they had been so stupid with the telegram and got his name mixed up.

He changed at Charing Cross and watched the faces of the hurrying, worried, unsmiling whites, sympathising with them and sorry for them, but wishing that just one or two would look a little cheerful. He got out at the Temple and walked along. Still this worry on the faces! Why? They had so much, houses, money in their pockets, food, a Welfare State to look after them. No South Africa on their borders. What was there to make them so anxious?

The plane trees along the Embankment were still heavily green, the Temple gardens full of coloured flowers whose names he did not know. Kumar was reading for the Bar. He wished now he had taken law himself. Or perhaps science. It was stupid to take history, though perhaps it helped one to decide about politics.

He found Kumar and they sat on a bench in the Temple gardens—"So what have you decided?" Kumar said.

"I have not decided," said Letlotse. "Only I am wondering if I shall be able to stay for my exam. I could go out during the Christmas vac, but if I went out——"

"Would you come back?"

"That is it, Kumar. You see the tribe would support me against my cousin the Regent. If that was needed. But I don't know if I want them to. I mean—can you see me as chief of a tribe in the middle of nowhere?"

"Oh, I can see you quite well, Letlotse! You might be able to turn it into something quite different. After all, we in India had some rather curious places not so long ago. Snake gods, magic, murders. And now the

106

maharajahs are all good boys. Or almost all. You could be a good boy too, Letlotse. You could become the Chairman of your County Council, yes?"

Letlotse wriggled: "That doesn't sound so good. I want—I must do something for the whole country. You agree, Kumar?"

"Yes. But it is difficult to be sure when one is doing good to a lot of people. One can be more sure of doing good for a few people."

"One can at least be sure if one can make them richer. Less poor. Look, Kumar, we have nothing but our cattle. And there are hardly any minerals, there is only some poor coal. Above all there is not enough water. Especially not in the tribal reserves. Where there is water there are white farmers: it is a pity for us. We have not even the money to pay half-good salaries to our tribal staffs—not one tribe has enough money for that. Not even the Bamangwato. We need more tax money; but can our people pay it? We have to look at these things as a whole. Even the Colonial Office does that, I think. Even, sometimes, our own Legco member, who does not at all like thinking!"

"But you do want Independence?"

"Yes, yes, of course. But I would like to see first what happens in the Republic and Southern Rhodesia. Things are difficult for us just now. I know what you and most of my friends say about the refugees, but it is not always quite the same for us. And Verwoerd is dangling bait for us, which stupid people might take. Besides, a British passport is nice to have, Kumar. The British have been a help to me too. Though not as much as I had hoped."

"You were trying to get some industry started. How did it go?"

"Well, nobody was interested. I had hoped, yes. I went to see people in offices with joy in my heart, believing that I would be able to help my people. But joy went out of me. And yet it had seemed so clear. For instance, we have cattle, and cattle have hides. Our people have bilharzia, which comes most certainly from going in dirty water without shoes. Also, those who have shoes can dig with the spade. But if there are shoes now they are kept for best or for the cold part of the winter, and for too many of my people and others in Bechuanaland they are too dear. I thought if we could have a small shoe factory that would make sense. I wanted the kind of machinery my people could learn to use: small, cheap machines. Old machines, even! No. All the ones in the offices want is to have big factories in the Republic, big markets all over, sell to us, wages to the Republic, profits to England. That makes no Bechuana sense."

"In India we get factories set up and our people are taught to run them. All sorts of large factories. Naturally that goes with stopping or taxing imports of things we can make ourselves. You could not do that till you were independent. It needs firmness, great moral firmness. Have you got that? I am not sure. We have plenty of iron ore and coal and that, so we can have great metal plants. Could your people learn to run even small factories, Letlotse?"

"I think so," Letlotse said a little uncertainly. "We never had a chance to try."

"You could get the Russians to come in," said Kumar. "As we did. And the Americans."

"What were the Russians like in India?"

"Well, they are like the Americans. Tidy suits, shoes, ties, sun-glasses. Those little smart cameras that dangle over their navels. The lot. And the poor English slop around in open shirts and sandals and their cameras have the cases mended with string. In fact they are our brothers now. Perhaps when they have entirely forgotten about being top people they will be your brothers too one day!"

"That would be nice," said Letlotse. "But I wondered about the Russians. Under the Communist system would I have got my shoe factory? Would they have seen that it made sense? Would they perhaps have not thought only about profit? That is something which makes me wonder about all they have been trying to teach me here. Free enterprise. Competition. Big business. London. The Western way of life."

"You had better not say that at the Colonial office, Letlotse! If you do they may not want you to go back as chief!"

Both of them laughed about this in the autumn sunshine among the dahlia beds and plane trees, with the river at high tide across the Embankment. But a few days later Letlotse was not laughing. He had been sent for and talked to, very politely to be sure, but very firmly. It all seemed to start with the indisputable fact that he had been in Russia when his father died and that this had involved him in an unseemly delay in sending the telegram. But it was further suggested that he had

Communist sympathies most unsuitable for someone in his position. If this was what he was learning at university —he came down the steps a bewildered and angry young man. Who had said what? His anger churned about in him. Could it have been Kumar? Yes, it must be Kumar! He was so angry that he took a taxi and found Kumar deep in torts, from which he was dragged extremely surprised to be accused of treachery, at having repeated things which his friend had said to the head people because he was jealous of Africa. He thought Letlotse was going to hit him and had visions of being stabbed by an undoubtedly African dagger. What a fool he had been ever to think one could make friends! He realised, however, that violence should not be met by violence. Letlotse crashed his fist on the table and a bottle of ink jumped and spilled between them like black blood. "Don't be stupid, Letlotse," said Kumar, pleased at being so calm. "Am I likely to do a thing like that? Is there anything I have ever said or done which would make it likely?"

"We were in Moscow together!" said Letlotse and his eyes were wide and bloodshot. "And you might have heard me say something—and that day when I was talking about industries—perhaps you do not want us to have industries! Perhaps you want Africans to be slaves, perhaps you are as bad as the whites!"

"Nonsense," said Kumar. "Sit down. You have offended me." Letlotse sat down suddenly. "Now let us think calmly. Perhaps it was one of the others who were with us in the Soviet Union. Or perhaps not that either. The officials could have heard that you had gone there.

Some of them only like you to do what has been officially planned for you. We made no secret of where we were going, any of us. Do you think it was any of the others? Are you yet able to think, Letlotse?"

Letlotse said nothing for a time; he seemed somehow to be sinking back into the hard upright chair. "When I can think," he said at last, "I remember that I thought we were all friends." He spoke with a curious desolation which touched Kumar, who had been thinking that he must get rid of Letlotse, possibly for ever; he had said to himself that Letlotse was a big mistake—Letlotse and all Africans.

"You may have other enemies," he said, carefully mopping up the ink with blotting paper.

Letlotse wished desperately that his sister was there; she might have had some sensible ideas. He thought also of a girl who had been one of the Russian party. Was someone jealous of him because of her? If not that, who could be trying to hurt him? To bewitch him. For suddenly it had come to him that this change that he could feel in his whole mind, this flooding of bewilderment and anger and helplessness had more to it than just being the result of a scolding or warning from the head ones. And then he thought, could it be Motswasele? Motswasele not wanting him to come back as heir. Speaking to the head ones in the Government pretending to be sad and ashamed of his nephew. Speaking to the Mission even! Saying, yes, he knew Communism was the same as the devil. If only, thought Letlotse, that man Motswasele knew how little I wanted to come back! And suddenly he threw back his head and laughed.

Extraordinary creature, thought Kumar; an Indian will stay in a melancholy for days, in a sad cloud, indeed I have done so myself, and will only come out of it slowly as the mist of unknowing thins. But this savage—"I am sorry about the ink," said Letlotse.

"Ah, well," said Kumar. "So long as it is nothing worse."

"They were nasty to me," said Letlotse reflectively. "Maybe they didn't mean. Could it be they didn't mean?"

"They are like that about this cold war often," said Kumar. "The idea of it blinds them. They just cannot like anything to do with Communism."

"I have heard you do not like the Chinese."

"The Chinese are different. But I think you must have an enemy, Letlotse. Perhaps he has libelled you. Perhaps you could find out and sue him."

"If he is the one I think he may be," said Letlotse, "suing will be not much use."

"What else would be of use?" said Kumar, curious.

"There is nothing like a good old assegai," said Letlotse and laughed. "Come out, Kumar, and we will have a drink on it. Perhaps I shall have to go back in the Christmas vac after all."

Chapter XI

KUATE STAYED WITH ISAAC AND TSELANE for the first two days, to help them move in. He was proud of the way he knew his way about in Craigs and took Isaac under his wing. With the letter and his knowledge of English, Isaac got a job in the repair shop; he hadn't liked to look in the letter, which was sealed. He might have steamed it, but no, he wouldn't do that with a friend. He had discovered and accepted that he counted the D.C. not as a white but as a friend, a rather distant friend no doubt, a kind of cousin's great-uncle, but still someone to be thought of warmly. What was it he said in the letter and who had asked him to write it? James? Ramodimo or Dithapo? He would never know. From what was said to him it sounded as though the letter had told that he was one of the Bamatsieng. If the D.C. had told what he must have known was lie for him, then certainly he was a friend.

Kuate shared a little room with them, but pulled his blanket over his head and pretended to be asleep so that Isaac and Tselane should enjoy one another fully; no more being careful since Tselane told him that his seed was strengthening the baby in her. He only half believed her because it was against the teaching he had heard, which, as he had been told, was modern and scientific: but what Tselane wanted she should have, and he stroked and nuzzled over the smooth mound beginning in her where his baby must be. This, then, was what she had demanded, speaking to her cousin Seneo so that she in turn should speak to the men.

By the second day Kuate had fixed with a friend of his from the tribe who had a little shop in Craigs that Isaac and Tselane should have space to build a hut and maybe keep half a dozen hens. He got hold of some straight branches from another friend, and one evening, working hard, he and Isaac got them dug in. He got rafters and roofing thatch and both worked on it while Tselane plastered. Here at Craigs it wasn't so easy to get cow dung to mix with the earth and water, but again Kuate found a friend and she got a couple of buckets full of good stuff. Kuate had to go back before the last coat of plaster was on; Tselane still had the floor to finish; but he knew that his friends had a home. It was only a little rondavel, smaller than most in Ditlabeng, scarcely larger than a granary, but Isaac and Tselane could be all night together, and together content at dawn. They barred the door because there were stray dogs and sometimes they became afraid of Motswasele. But they knew one another's bodies so well that darkness was a light.

For the first few weeks Isaac brought every penny of his wages back to Tselane, who kept the money in a purse. She bought him a new check shirt, carefully washing and mending his old one, and new shorts as befitted a P.W.D. worker. His shoes would do for a bit. The rest went on food and later three hens. It was odd having no land, but then, what is the use of land if there is no crop on it? Some food was dearer at Craigs, some cheaper, but Tselane had time to look about her and bargain. It did not seem to be a very big town, two main streets, but behind them, if you looked, were little dusty crooked streets going almost nowhere, but you could get lost among them and there would still be houses and tiny stalls and fag ends of markets. In the two main streets were the big stores where whites shopped as well as Africans; Tselane did not go into them though everyone was friendly enough. The only shop window where she hung about was one with books and records. They missed their music a little, but not much. Sometimes in the night Tselane would sing bits of the songs she had learnt when she was out with her *mophato*, but when Isaac asked what they meant, for the words often seemed to mean nothing or rather to mean something entirely else, she laughed and would not tell him or simply caught him tighter to her and said, they mean this, only this.

At first Isaac said little to his workmates; he got on well enough with them and with his foreman; it did not seem as if any of them were in a union or had even realised what one was, but he did find there were a few who were interested in politics, mostly in the People's Party, though in a rather casual way. They would go to a meeting, put something in the collection even, but not join. They would get one or two ideas in their heads that would stick fast, so fast nothing would move them and that would be that. They would also choose themselves favourite leaders and whatever that leader did was fine and any other leader was a traitor or a sell-out. The meetings, too, would give you a chance to loose off your mouth and shout great things. Yet perhaps there were one or two, thought Isaac, who had gone deeper, who might be persuaded to—but too soon to tell yet. Couldn't be too careful. Got to feel it with the fingertips.

At the end of the fourth week Tselane took twenty cents and closed his hand on it. He did not know what to say. All his life before he had earned and taken his pay. If he had taken a doll out, he'd paid for her sure, but he kept plenty in his pocket. When he had given all to Tselane his wife, he had broken with himself. It had been difficult —a pain withstood and conquered: to have earned and to have none of it. Now she had given him back twenty cents. For a moment it seemed an insult.

She saw that; suddenly she knelt at his feet and caught him by the knees and laid her cheek against them. "You should have all, my husband," she said. "It is your right and I am only your small sheep."

He was down beside her. "You are the woman of the house," he said. "The great wife. It is yours."

She grinned. "Twenty cents is too little even for a small wife!" she said.

He gave her the gentlest play slap. "You are all my wives, Tselane. Very well. I take it. Shall get newspapers. They are all I need."

"I like you to be able to give your friends a drink, my Isaac. You tell me you look at them. Looking is not enough. You need to talk. Talk goes better if something goes with it."

116

Perhaps, he thought, perhaps, and yet down on the floor of the hut with Tselane he did not think that there was anything else he needed. Anything in the world.

Yet the newspapers woke it up. The world came back into the hut, the world of injustice that had to be put right, the world of the sneering hurting whites who had taken everything. The world where a boy could get a ten year sentence for going to a meeting and perhaps singing "God Save Africa". And so he must do more than watch his workmates in the repair shop. He must try and see which were possible political comrades.

The funny thing was he hadn't much, indeed anything, against the two Englishmen he saw from time to time except that one of them had an unpleasant, smelly, snuffling dog which this man was always fondling. It was clearly old and useless. Isaac would have liked to kill it. Yet it remained that the two Englishmen were bosses; that was taken for granted. They gave the orders. Reasonable orders, right, but one day there would be Africans giving orders, people like himself. Only not unless they fought first. If they didn't fight, the accepted thing would go on happening here and everywhere.

He began very tentatively to speak to one or two of the others. There was a welder, Billy they called him, over six feet and broad. One day Isaac offered him the loan of a newspaper. "Ah, so you've started to read, man!" said Billy and suddenly Isaac realised that there was something in the pot already. Billy was serious, had read, thought. Isaac took a deep breath, stood straight, and told his other name. Billy nodded, "We thought somehow you could be—one of us."

"You—are you more than People's Party?" Isaac asked, feeling hot and cold.

"Oh, that. There are a few good ones in it. For that matter there are good ones in the Democratic Party. But they talk too much. Talk doesn't do. We know you, thought you were dead. That was what they said. Killed escaping from train."

"Good they thought so!" said Isaac. "I was lucky. Too lucky, me."

"You come with me after work," said Billy abruptly and turned his back, took up a casting and began to handle it.

For the rest of the day Isaac couldn't keep his thoughts straight. It was as though he had been hit on the head and was spinning but not with pain, with pure excitement and desire for action. Nothing else made sense. For the first time he made a bad mistake, the kind of thing a boy would do in his second week, putting a part in upside down, buggering up the whole insides of a new type of cement mixer. It was Billy who ticked him off even before his foreman did, saying he would throw him out on his neck. Equally Billy said that the strained parts could be welded and straightened, no bother, and offered to do it at once even if it meant staying on after work, "And tell that bastard he better stay on to help me. You leave me kick him, I wll!"

Isaac said nothing and felt himself shrink inside, but at least wasn't going to lose his job. At the end of the day he was turned over with some mockery to Billy,

118

who cursed him up and down and threw a spoiled casting in the direction of his bare foot. Isaac muttered a mixture of fear and anger and grovelling apology: the African thing, he thought at the back of his mind. When they were alone Billy said nothing, gave him sharp orders, made him sweat over the welding. It took them two hours and a bit to repair the damage Isaac had done and no words spoken of anything else.

Then it was over and Isaac suddenly felt scared in case Billy had it in for him, wanted to knock him about or, worse, was not going to take him back into a group. Billy drank deep out of the bucket of drinking water and motioned Isaac to do the same, then grinned and slapped him on the back: "Come on, man. That's over. Don't you slip up again. Not on that. Nor anything else."

Billy tightened his belt, threw his shirt over his shoulder, and went out. Isaac followed him. They got to a two-roomed tin-roofed house with a locked door which Billy opened; it was clearly his own make of lock and bars. They went in and Billy rummaged on a shelf and found a tin of beer, not too warm. "Here, man," he said, "make yourself easy, the others will be coming." But for a minute Isaac couldn't drink the beer. He dropped his head on the table, trying not to cry. He was back.

They talked till late on. It was the same words, the same hopes, the same news or absence of news. He had asked at once about Amos, but nobody knew for sure; some said he was in prison, some that he'd got away. At least there was no news that they had killed him, either before or after trial. So that was that. One of them

119

was a Xhosa-speaking chap with tribal scars, who had killed a policeman and escaped; he was hiding, not safe for him to be seen. They were going to get him away. Clearly a good deal of what they were doing was helping with escapes, more often from Angola and the south-west than from the Republic, though at the same time there was some passing back of useful news, and for that matter sabotage material, much of which might be hidden for months and years. Some day—yes, some day.

"Most of us, coming in, we test out," said Billy. "You, I'd say you've had your testing." The others nodded. "And me thinking you were a bloody tribesman. Well, if you can fool Billy——!"

"Your chum Josh, can we get him?" one of the others asked.

"Later, maybe. Not yet. He is all tied up, Josh." And then Isaac realised that the whole of the evening he had not once thought about Tselane. And now it was late on.

He left in a bit but yet he couldn't hurry. It had been good, using the old greetings and farewells. The words that had meant so much, that meant so much still. But once he got going he hurried back. When he got to his hut the door was unbarred, it was dark and empty inside; a horrible feeling caught him and then Tselane ran out of the night and her arms were around him, and her face wet with tears and sweat pressed into his neck. "I thought Motswasele had got you!" she said. "And if he came looking for me I had a knife for him." She dropped it clattering; he picked her up, took her back into the hut, nuzzled over her until she stopped crying, then went out for the knife. It was dangerously sharp. "One hour I took making it ready to kill," said Tselane. "Where were you, Isaac?"

Isaac did not at all want to speak of his stupidity, his mistake, his fear. "I was with my comrades," he said. "The old ones. We have found one another."

Tselane said nothing for quite a long time. She sat on the floor of the hut, one foot smoothing over the ground in front of her. "Not any from the People's Party?" she asked uncertainly.

"No," he said. "I think maybe they talk too much," and then, "Don't you talk, my wife! Say nothing. Not to the People's Party. Not to anyone, anywhere."

"I ask you nothing, my husband," Tselane said. "Only—if you must go back, back to the Republic, you take me?"

"I don't have to go back," he said, "but if I did I wouldn't take you. Wouldn't like to see you treated bad."

"Better than stay here," she said miserably. "Better than stay here with knife." He didn't know what to say, only stroked her. His mind was full of the evening. Then she said, "You hear about your friend? You hear about Amos?"

"Still we don't know for certain," said Isaac gloomily. "Dead. Prison. Nobody knows. Tselane, I said no questions!" He stood over her, for one moment wanting to hit her. In the days when he was a freedom fighter in the Republic there had been no woman to question him, no woman he would have answered!

She put her hand on his ankle. "Good. I don't speak."

121

And she wiped the tears off her face with her other hand, and then he remembered how he had come to her after the dream about Amos and how he had said to Dithapo that he would be good to her always, and now it was himself he hated.

Chapter XII

AFTER THAT Isaac spent a good deal of his time with the group. Once or twice they had a job for him. He would be told to go down to the station, take delivery of such and such a consignment, and then abstract just *that*. It would be covered in the shop, and not come to light until the next check-up, by which time it would not be traceable to anyone. Or again a few staples or bolts could go missing, and so long as it was not one person or one part of the shop they went from, nothing bad would come of it. So long, too, as none of it turned up in any of the stalls or street markets. But that was not what happened; everything was carefully kept. This was not thieving. At worst it was taking back something from the whites, even though in a way it was something belonging to their own country; but they barely thought of it like that.

Tselane tried to let Isaac have as much money as she could. She did this mostly by going short of food herself, making do with porridge and nothing to season it. Then she slept badly and sometimes woke crying. Isaac mostly slept too sound to notice, but at the same time he was aware that there was something wrong. Just when he wanted everything to be going right! Now and then he dreamed about Amos, and sometimes now Amos was not dead. Usually he woke Tselane when he had these dreams and she turned to him at once, but when she dreamed of Motswasele or sometimes of pythons or hyenas coming into her home, she did not wake Isaac.

Of course she had heard about Isaac's trouble in the repair shop and how he had been made to stay on and nearly lost his job. One of the other wives had told her while they were bargaining for soup bones; she pretended she knew. It was perhaps this that made her feel that she must have a little small life apart from Isaac. One evening she said, "You going to Billy's?" He nodded. "I go to People's Party meeting. O.K., Isaac?"

For a moment he was angry, he did not really know why. Then he said, "Fine, my wife. I pick you up after this meeting. By the market. Yes?" And then he put his hand in his pocket. "You take something for their collection. No. From me. You take it."

She took the five cents in her hand; on the way to the meeting she was terribly tempted to have a coffee-and-sandwich; she was hungry. The baby in her was making her hungry. But she said to herself first that she was a member of the People's Party and second that she was a royal and the two things mixing in her mind got her past the smell of coffee and bread. It was nice to be at the meeting, to hear speaking, to hear excitement. It was nicer when Isaac came and took her arm. Nicer still when Isaac took her to the exact same place and gave her coffee-and-sandwich. Nicest of all when she and Isaac came back to the hut and fell together on the blanket, she feeling fed and warm and full of the same word as he was. The big word freedom. Thanks to the People's Party for this!

The Democratic Party had meetings too. Again the words were freedom, democracy, independence and unity and in many ways this was a much more sensible and informed party. But Tselane did not really go for sense and information, and besides she felt somehow that it was the chiefs' party whatever it said and perhaps even the party of one family. She wished she could be in Isaac's group. Why would they not have women? Was it because women were supposed to be tender-hearted, more honest and so less good at hiding things? Not so clever? None of it was true. Sometimes she was angry with Isaac for telling her so little. There was not enough for her to do; she had no field, even, to think about here. Secretly she began to miss Kodunzwe the baby. Once when she saw Kuate turn his lorry, she ran over and asked and heard that all was well and wiped her eyes a little. Yes, said Kuate, Seneo was making arrangements to take out her regiment. This girl Josh was after, Dieledi, she would be in this regiment. And after that? Well, Motswasele was pressing her and so was the Council. Motswasele had killed one of the headmen who had refused to pay any more taxes, said he had paid already. "Killed? Himself?"

"The doctored rifles," whispered Kuate.

Billy's girl was called Gloria. She was a nice girl, good cook, two boy babies that looked just like Billy. They were not married, never got around to it. Maybe, thought Tselane, Billy wants to keep free. It could be that this is what Isaac wants in his heart. She was the

125

best friend Tselane had among the women of Craigs. They talked about little things, sure, but some day they might talk about big things and Gloria promised to come and help when Tselane's time came on her.

But then one day Isaac came back and it looked as if he was longing to speak. She did not ask at first. He had told her not to question him. Well, then——! He kept touching her as she brought him food, as though trying to speak without words. At last she had mercy and smiled and squatted down beside him as he ate. "Well?" she said.

He rubbed the side of his head against her. "I have news," he said.

"About—not from Ditlabeng?" He shook his head. "I thought maybe someone kills Motswasele. No. Isaac! Is it—is it your friend? Amos?" Then he turned his whole head round and buried his face in her and she knew she had guessed right. "He is alive? After all? After everything. Your friend is living. Glad I am. Glad, my husband! You hear this—how?"

He whispered, "A man has come to the group. From the Republic. He has messages. He wants us to help. Maybe even Amos will come! Tselane, I had not meant to speak of it, but now I think for Amos's sake we must hide this man here in our house."

"And the two of you will speak of Amos." Tselane looked round, shook her head a little, then smiled. There was no room, but there had to be room. "Bring him," she said.

He told them he was called Immanuel or mostly Big

126

Manuel. Not that he was very big. Scarcely as broad as Billy, but still big enough. He spoke of fights he had been in and he seemed to have been able to lay out a policeman easily enough. He laughed about that. Isaac could not stop questioning, getting more stories out of him and mostly about Amos. It looked from what he said that Amos had got away, even before Isaac and Josh, and made it, and had bravely gone back to the Republic. That was a wonderful thing to do. That was old Amos all over! But he'd had to be dodgy. He did not sleep more than a night in the same house. "But mostly with me," said Big Manuel proudly. "Knew I would look after him, see. But he was always speaking about you and Josh."

"What was he saying about us?"

"He'd say if only old Isaac was here with me——"

"Yes. He'd say that sure, sure he would. Was it for some special job?"

"There was a railway bridge. You heard about that?"

"Must have been when I wasn't seeing newspapers. Where? Tell me!"

"Maybe I better not," said Manuel, and he was right, sure enough, you couldn't be too careful, but Isaac was pleading with him to tell. At last he said, "You don't say one word. Not either of you. Not to anyone. I tell you because of Amos." It was a wonderful story, the railway bridge, made you go hot and cold, and when it blew up at last and the train crashed and the whites screaming and bleeding—Isaac was rocking about and showing all his teeth with pleasure, yet he was half crying too because he had not been there. "Oh, boy,

127

if I'd been with him!" he said. "Is there a plan coming up now?"

"There sure is. We want you all in on it. You got gelignite?" Isaac nodded. "I got money for tickets, see. Could you send a message, get Josh? Amos would give his ears to get you both again. And this Billy, we're needing him."

"Sure we'll have Billy! Tell me more about Amos, Manuel. How does he look now?"

"Better than ever, man, better than ever. But needing his friends."

So it went and Isaac was happy, happy. It looked as if something could be beginning and he might be part of it. Might be the beginning of the big crack-up that must be coming. The end of the Afrikaners. A railway bridge. He had always wanted to blow up a railway bridge. He danced a little with the pleasure of it. Them in the train, in the first-class carriages, thinking themselves above everyone, ordering everyone around, eating and drinking as they wafted along, and then crash! White bodies broken the way they had always broken black ones. How could he get a message to Josh? Maybe if he could see Kuate in the lorry. Tselane must look out. Get a message back. So Tselane said she would keep a watch for Kuate. Meanwhile she spread a blanket for Manuel. She washed his shirt and socks, they would dry overnight if he could wait until the sun was up a little. He went to sleep with his coat under his head for a pillow. He had given Tselane fifty cents; it must be made to last for a while, but she kept thinking what she would get—meat and sweet cane and a tin of sauce and shop

128

bread and meat. Thinking of meat she fell asleep, but Isaac stayed awake for a long time with everything going round and round in his head. Amos. Amos alive and in the same world. Amos whom he was going to see again.

At the meat stall, poking at the pieces, she met Gloria. Suddenly she said and it was beyond her not to say, "Did you ever hear of a bridge blowing up, a railway bridge in the Republic, train smashing up?"

"That's fairy tales. Who's been kidding you on, Tselane?"

"Maybe it was just a tale," said Tselane. She wished now she had not spoken at all. If Isaac knew she had spoken—what had she done? He would have had the right to beat her. She felt queer; the smell of the meat was making her feel sick. Not that she was giving anything away, but—maybe a man would have kept it to himself. This Manuel, she had not wanted him to sleep in the hut. A man not of the Bamatsieng, not even from Bechuanaland. This man who looked like taking Isaac away. Yes, she said to herself, he wants to take my husband. He means to, and I can't go with him, not to the Republic, not with this baby going to come so soon. This baby that's like a lion in me.

And then she saw Kuate's lorry. If she hurried—she dropped the piece of meat. Gloria said, "Maybe there was a bridge blown. Down south. Seems to me maybe I could have heard——" This was what Isaac wanted to do. Blow bridges. Get himself killed. Suddenly Tselane could not bear to stop the lorry. The lorry that was going to go back to Ditlabeng without her.

But was the railway bridge story true? Isaac believed every word of it. He had almost seen it, almost been there beside Amos carrying sticks of gelignite under his shirt. There were other stories, and Big Manuel, speaking of what he'd done himself, he and his friends.

A couple of evenings later Big Manuel went out. "I'll come, look after you," said Isaac. "You could lose yourself in Craigs."

"No," said Manuel. "You stay home. Look, I been here before." He laughed and it was all right. He went out into the night, quietly for such a big man.

"Seen Kuate yet?" said Isaac.

"No," said Tselane. "You believe—everything, my husband? Not test this man?"

"He comes from Amos," said Isaac. "That's test enough for me." And afterwards, grumbling at her: "You as bad as Billy!"

Big Manuel came back; he brought Tselane a bar of chocolate. She ate it, for she was hungry, but she kept thinking, you can't buy my Isaac from me for any bar of chocolate! And she began to wish dreadfully for Ditlabeng and her mother, and that baby Kodunzwe, which she had not wanted. If Isaac went back now, back to the Republic, he would forget his promise. He would not think of the tribe any more. Or else the police would get him the way they got the others. Her Isaac. In terror she saw the rope round his neck, the awful choking and twitching, the things she had seen in news photographs so they must be true, and she clung on to him that night for all her big belly and the jumping and squirming inside it. He had her, she felt him whole and alive, but some way it did not make her forget. Underneath she was scared. Dead scared the way she had not been since Motswasele had sent his men with their threats.

Isaac had a triumphant dream about Amos, in which they were together knocking over houses and big cattle, but Tselane slept badly again, waking every now and then and looking at the still dark bulk of Manuel that she could just see. He stayed in the hut while she cleared up and spoke now and then in a friendly joking kind of way. Not politics. He was the same as the rest, never trust a woman! Later she went out with a sad feeling in her, to get an onion and some rice, so they could finish the meat in a nice way. A tall young man put out his hand and caught at her, but not for badness, so she went with him to the back of a wall. And then he asked her why had the man from her house been speaking to the Special Branch man at night? Tselane leant hard against the wall. "You say this," she said. "You sure? Who are you, then?"

"People's Party," said the other man. "Saw you at a meeting. We know your husband. Could be danger to him, yes?"

"You sure?" said Tselane again stupidly.

"Dead sure," said the young man. "But, we watch again—if he goes there maybe we catch him. You say."

Chapter XIII

ISAAC CAME BACK LATE from work and a talk with
the group. He was feeling wonderful, everything was
going his way. One or two had been doubtful, but he
had told them about Amos. This man, this Big Manuel,
he came from Amos. What surer than that? And they
were all to go off, across in the Republic everything was
planned. This was the beginning of the big smash, of
the revolution! Yes, they could all go but more especially
himself and Billy. He would try to get Josh. Yes, he
would get Josh!

Billy had been worried. "Not everyone from the
Republic sure!" he said. "I can't anyways believe things
are as ready as he says. Conditions there not right. I been
reading Lenin——"

"A white!" said Isaac. "It's different here, we don't
need to build up that revolutionary proletariat, it's there
—we were fighting seventy, eighty years back, it's all
inside us. I tell you, Billy, they defeated us in battle,
but we never surrendered, never showed a white flag—
there is no truce, the war goes on!"

"Other workers won't side with us, not workers of
the world," said Billy. "Plenty to lose besides their chains
these days! Not even in Africa. Think, Isaac; Tangan-

132

yika, Ghana, Nigeria. Too much they got to do for themselves. Talk at conferences, yes, but won't help us. Can't help us. Don't kid yourself, Isaac. I say, all this you are dreaming up is too soon. We can't trust this guy, he runs our heads into a snare."

But Isaac had talked and talked and called on the magic words, this time the magic historic word revolution, and the rest were with him, and coming back it was not like walking through Craigs at all. Like walking as a prince in a new kingdom. But first he had to speak to Tselane and he meant to do that right away. He burst in. "My wife," he said. "I am going to the Republic to lead freedom fighters, take our country out of slavery——" And while he said it he knew he was talking too big but he couldn't stop it, couldn't look her in the eye. "You must go back, back to the tribe, have your baby, come join me later when we are all free——"

Tselane who had been squatting on the floor got heavily to her feet, the dress tight across her belly. "And your promise, Isaac? Your promise to the tribe?"

"What of it?" he said. "That's not mattering. This is. This is big, Tselane, big!"

"Bigger than your marriage promise? Maybe we aren't married."

"Don't you go saying that," he said worriedly, feeling his happiness getting spoiled. "Where's Big Manuel?"

"I got something to tell you, Isaac," said Tselane. "Big Manuel was a spy. For all his talk about Amos. A double-crosser. He meant to turn you all over to the police. The police of the Republic. They have their man here. He has got your names now. Yours, Billy's.

133

Everyone's. Maybe this Manuel never even seen Amos. All one lie."

For a moment Isaac had lifted his fists to hit her; she guarded her belly, not her face. His fists dropped. He leaned against the wall of the hut. He heard his own breath coming harsh and quick. "Where is he?" he whispered.

"We got him," said Tselane. "You want to see? Come." She walked in front of him not touching, then turned. "No danger yet. Maybe the police come in a day or two. Got to seem everything he said was lies. You and Billy just good P.W.D. workers, he maybe jealous. Some old quarrel; you make up a story. Everything got to be hidden. No papers, no stolen things." She said this with a curious dislike, and Isaac thought that perhaps she hated him for his stealing, even for a good cause, and he had never guessed it. Perhaps at first while they had been so happy together she had not hated it, only lately. And this thought was jagging and tearing him, for the moment getting on top of all his other terrible hurting, frightening thoughts and he walked very quietly behind his wife.

They went past the new telegraph pole and turned up. "Where we going?" he asked in a low voice.

"To Gloria's," she said, not looking back at him.

He came closer. "Tselane," he said pleading—but for what? He didn't know. He put out a hand and laid it gently on her hip. Under the cloth he felt something; he was almost sure it was the kitchen knife, the one she had sharpened against Motswasele. She jerked her hip away. He began to think what he might have done by

134

trusting this man. Should he go warn them now? Billy? But they were going to Gloria's. That meant Billy would know. And all this danger he had put his friends into was because of Amos. Because of the word Amos. If Tselane was right. As in a horrible way he knew she must be. The second time in his life he had trusted people wrongly. And all because of that one word Amos. Stronger word to him than security and unity. Even freedom. Too strong. And how had this man come by it? He must find out. He whispered again, "This man— Manuel—he alive?"

"Yes," she said. But the way she said it made him feel a little sick.

Gloria's house had a room and kitchen; the two little boys were sound asleep. Tselane squatted down beside one of them and laid her cheek for a moment against the delicate black crisp of his curls. Was one of the children moaning in his sleep? No. What then? There was also a man in the room whom Isaac didn't know though he felt he had seen him before: at a meeting maybe? People's Party? Gloria was ironing Billy's shirt; as they came in she spat on the iron and bent over it without looking at them. "Where——?" said Isaac uncertainly.

"Speak to him first," said Tselane over her shoulder looking at the young man, who reached out a hand, which Isaac took, thumb up.

"My brother is in B.P. Police Force," the young man said. "B.P. Police O.K. He tells me this Special Branch snake at Craigs. Comes in pretending to be trader, banker, big-shot. But our boys know. This man Manuel tells Special Branch everything. They wait at the border,

135

Mafeking maybe, get you all. See? Only waiting for Josh."

Inside himself Isaac squirmed with terror and misery. It could have been *that*. And he would have been the guilty one. "So—so it was all a lie? Lies to me? Using that name?"

"Lies," said the man simply. "You want to see him?"

"You got him?" asked Isaac. "Where he is?" He felt he hated this man more than anyone in his life, more than any possible white could ever be hated.

"Listen," said the young man, holding up his hand. And then Isaac heard quite clearly something which had been at the back of everything else, a kind of moaning rising and falling evenly as though it were a clock moaning, a piece of machinery. Gloria put the iron down on the ground and folded the shirt carefully. "Come," said the man and took the lamp off its hook.

They went through to the kitchen. It had a concrete floor easy to wash down. And there would be need. Big Manuel lay on the floor with his shirt pulled up and his trousers half down; where they should have met there was a dark and oozing mess. Isaac looked and smelt and felt very sick. One of Manuel's legs had been broken between knee and thigh, crushed by something heavy; bits of bone stuck out. His other leg had been broken at the knee. It could have been done with the blunt side of a chopper. People are easy to break, Isaac thought irrelevantly, too easy. You can't break a table so easy. One hand had been crushed, the other scrabbled about helplessly on the kitchen floor. The young man held the lamp over Big Manuel's head. One eye was shut with a

136

cut or bruise purplish red across an oddly swollen eyelid; the other was staring. "We left his tongue," said the young man, "for questions." The mouth was open; the moaning came out of it.

It was no use hating Big Manuel any more, Isaac thought. Hate has had its teeth in him already. No more from me. He spoke almost gently at the thing below him. "How you knew about me?" Big Manuel did not answer; there was no recognition in the one eye. Isaac forced himself to kneel beside him. "This is Isaac," he said. "Isaac. Isaac." Suddenly recognition came into the eye as an accentuation of fear. "I got to hear," said Isaac. "How you knew? Did you ever see Amos? Amos! Amos!" he cried at the face in front of him.

Slowly the lips came together. They only said, "Water." The young man spilled a little into the mouth opening out of a cup. Then the lips came together again, "Amos gave names—you—Josh——"

"When?"

"When he got questioned. Police."

"They caught him then! Ah, God. They hurt him bad?"

The lips said nothing for a minute then, "Not so bad you hurt me."

"Now—where is he? Where Amos? Amos! Amos! Tell."

"Prison. Life," said the lips, and then they began to quiver and the quiver turned into a shaking, a spasm that went from the lips into the nose and cheek muscles, tugging at the swollen eyelid, biting at the roots of the hair.

137

Isaac got to his feet quickly. "Kill him," he said.

Tselane and Gloria were standing together in the doorway of the living-room. "Not yet," whispered Tselane. "He cannot get away from us. Think Isaac, think close: what could have happened."

"And to my Billy," said Gloria. "That could have been your fault, Isaac. You owe us this death."

Isaac looked down at the horror, the stink, the dreadful lack at the man's middle. He held out his hands towards Tselane. "My wife. I beg of you. Kill him now."

Tselane said, "You want, my husband? Truly you want?" Isaac took a step over and knelt in front of her. "He could have died slower," she said, "in the old days. With a stake, as we did to enemies. Besides, it does not hurt him the way it did at first. He begins to be past it." Gloria went over and kicked him; he twitched and the moaning grew a little louder, but not much. Tselane stood with her head up and nostrils wide and it came to Isaac that she was indeed kin to Motswasele. She was indeed one of the Bamatsieng and he had almost betrayed her.

Isaac spoke with difficulty, trying to think the thoughts out clear and then the words. "We are civilised. We Africans. Africans must be better than whites. If they tortured Amos, if they could have tortured Billy and me and Josh: still no reason."

"You speaking like a Christian, Isaac," said Tselane and he could not tell if she was mocking him. "Forgive enemies, all that. You mean, Isaac, you forgive this— dirt?"

"Don't know," said Isaac, "don't know why. Only I

feel." He was crying now, his tears falling down on to Tselane's feet.

Suddenly she bent, touched him lightly on the shoulder and took the kitchen knife out from under her skirt band. Isaac put his hands over his ears, crouched down on the floor. Then Tselane was beside him, pulling his hands away. The moaning had stopped. The young man came into the room; he was carrying a pick and shovel. "Come on, Isaac. You help me. Get him into the ground. Give the women a chance to wash the floor." They went out together and prodded with the pick until they found a decent bit of ground where they could get down beyond where the dogs would hunt anything out. Then they dug. They took no light, better not. Nor did they speak, except an occasional grunt and murmur. Isaac wanted nothing less than to speak or even to think. When they had dug deep enough they went in and fetched out the body. The young man had something wrapped in layers of newspaper so that the blood wasn't getting through. He chucked this in with the rest. "Best he takes this too," he said and then, "Isaac, all finished now. No police trouble. Only—you and Billy, you better maybe keep quiet, hide everything. Not be seen talking. Good P.W.D. boys. If you good boys, your white bosses won't let anyone take you. Same for the rest. Careful, see, go careful. Just in case."

Isaac said, "We have to thank you, I think. Thank you plenty."

"Oh, don't mention it," said the young man, "all poison snakes got to go. One day we have a country."

The two women were scrubbing out the kitchen.

Tselane's big belly was down almost on the floor between her knees. "You give me that brush," said Isaac.

"Not man's work," said Tselane, and suddenly she looked round and grinned at him, and he knew that whatever devil had come between them was away now.

Then Gloria said, "O.K., you Isaac, you scrub. You get down on floor now. You be woman!" She took the scrubbing brush from Tselane and handed it to him; he got down on the floor and began clumsily. "Quicker, you, get quicker!" said Gloria and swashed another bucket of water over the floor. Tselane held the lamp low. There were still bloodstains. He worked at them. The young man had gone. "When the rains come," said Gloria, "I plant mealies out there. Mealie roots they eat him. All finished." The rhythm that Isaac's scrubbing had got into broke for a moment; he had found himself thinking of what they had buried out there, not as an enemy, a traitor, a piece of filth, but as Big Manuel his new friend. Then he caught himself together and went at it hard. In a little the bloodstains were all away.

"I wonder," said Tselane, "will we get rain this year? Good rain?" She was thinking about her field far off by Ditlabeng. Would her mother be able to cultivate it? Perhaps Josh would. Yes, Josh might plough for them. If she could get a message to him. She had meant to put in some beans this year. She looked down at herself. Yes, it was getting lower; Gloria had said it looked like soon. And now Isaac would not be leaving her.

Chapter XIV

BEFORE DAWN someone whispered softly at the door of the men's rondavel, "Josh, oh Josh," but a sleeper awakes to his own name and Josh stepped over bodies that didn't stir. Was it a message from Isaac? But mostly Kuate brought these. What then? He couldn't see who it was, only not a full grown man and he was carrying something big in his arms. "Take it!" he whispered. "Hide—quick! My uncle in the chief's regiment—he give me."

"What is it?" whispered Josh, reaching out and suddenly feeling a weight in his arms.

"Kodunzwe out of Agnes Mookodi," the boy whispered back.

"Dead?"

"No, no, my uncle not want kill him for medicine. We give him what makes him sleep."

"His grandmother?"

"Chief kill her," said the boy. "Take—take." And ran, his bare feet almost soundless.

Josh woke Murphy and unwrapped the child heavily asleep, making a kind of unbabyish snoring noise. "He all right?" asked Josh doubtfully.

Murphy looked. "We get Sarah." He went quietly to James Mookami's mother's window, leant in, woke her and told her. Sarah came bustling out in a long red shawl with fringes, looked at the child, guessed at the drug, told Murphy to heat some milk, then went for Seneo and for her son.

James, rumpled from sleep, watched how Seneo and Sarah made the baby vomit and then drink milk, but he was still only half awake. "I think," said James, "Seneo better not marry that one. Wonder what he will say about the old woman. There will be someone worked out to blame and no-one will witness against the Regent. If there is good rain he will be little enough blamed. Not after two dry years."

"My brother would never have done this," said Sarah. "It was bad enough when he went to the hole."

"We all followed him then," said Murphy. "We would not have followed him to murder. Also Motswasele did it not only for rain medicine, but out of spite against Tselane."

"To kill his own child!" said Seneo. "That I cannot understand. That is work of the devil."

"He does not kill himself," said Murphy, "only gives orders. Looks another way. But makes use."

"I wonder what kind of flesh will go into the medicine?" said James reflectively.

"Perhaps a lamb," said Murphy. "The liver would look about the same. Think it's liver they use. Kid or lamb."

"A lamb on the altar—as it once was," said Sarah.

Seneo had her finger on the pulse of the small drooping wrist, her eye on her own watch. Now she looked up, satisfied: "He'll do."

The little boy, half waking and recognising Josh, began to smile and babble a little talk at him.

"We'd better get him to Craigs," said James suddenly. "I'll get the car before it's light enough for them to see."

Josh picked up the baby. "Tselane will be near her time."

"She will need to hear about her mother. And that nothing can be done—yet."

"When Letlotse comes——"

"Yes," said James.

Tselane knew the car at once and hurried heavily out of the house. They told her while Kodunzwe, now fully awake and hungry, held on to her with arms and legs. "I promised I would protect them," said Josh, "but there was no warning."

"That's Motswasele's way," said Tselane, "but this little wicked one is safe"—she was stroking her chin into the folds of his neck—"and perhaps but for you——"

"I think so," said James. "Now, my cousin, try to hide that you have this child. Say maybe he is not yours——"

"I understand," said Tselane. "Will you see Isaac?"

"Josh can stay, come back with the lorry, maybe. I will go. There are certain ones I must see. Also I must write a letter to Letlotse and post it here, not Ditlabeng. No, Tselane, I have airmail form all ready. Give me a table and chair."

Tselane said nothing to Josh about what had been happening at Craigs. If Isaac wanted to that was between him and his friends. For herself it was over; she said nothing when Josh accidentally nicked his finger on the sharp kitchen knife, only that he must put it high up where Kodunzwe could not reach it. Nor did Isaac say anything the first evening. They talked about Ditlabeng, the look of the land and the cattle, a new brick house that someone had built, the crate of soft drinks that had been stolen from the trader's. Isaac talked about his work at the repair shop, about how he had been doing some typewriter repairs and his white boss thought this was very clever of him, not knowing how much he'd used typewriters in the old days! He hadn't let on. And then he began talking about the local football team; they were going to play Mahalapye and it was just not too hopeful. No class, their forwards. It was time they got a pitch going at Ditlabeng! But Tselane thought the other thing was going to come up the second evening. Isaac would begin to speak as though to come round to it, but always somehow shied away, ashamed. And then the police came.

It was simple enough. Isaac pretended stupid, let on he was a tribal, he was one of the Bamatsieng. He knew nothing. He had told Tselane he would do just that, and she played his game. So, after a minute or two, did Josh, and much change the white policemen could get out of them! When they left Josh said, "Why was that?"

Isaac said nothing for a long time: he sat with his head down. At last he said, "I've been a fool, Josh. Worse than I've ever been. Nearly got us all into it. You, too. But for her——"

Josh turned round and stared at Tselane; she had Kodunzwe on her knee and was rocking him, his head between her big breasts, his legs round her big belly. "Her?"

"She found out. I was blind. I thought Amos had sent him. The spy. Josh man, Amos is in prison. Life."

"Ah, hell! Life. But it won't last that long. Can't. We know that. He'll come out. We'll see him again."

"Wish I could be sure. Ah, Christ, it's like a great spider spinning webs farther and farther out. Trying to get us here. And all the time sucking blood, strengthening itself. I hear about things, Josh. Armoured cars. Gas. Planes ready to bomb us. And the laws like traps, like the ant-lions in under the sand and everywhere we little black ants scuttling round and falling into their pits, the sand in our eyes, the jaws open to get us. No chance, no bloody chance we got!"

"Ah, come on, Isaac, we've had bad luck before. Never lost hope. Why d'you lose hope now?"

"I think the whites win always. Use us always. Same way they use that Manuel. Scare us, buy us. Make us lie. Make us bits of their things. Like bits of a machine. Whites drive the machine. Be the bosses always."

"No, Isaac, no! Don't you say that. This thing just got you down. What do you do with this man nearly fools you?"

Isaac said nothing, only covered his face again. Tselane said gently, "We killed him, Josh. All finished now."

Josh wasn't sure what to say to that. A last he said, "I tell you one white that's not on top. That District Commissioner, he was friend of our chief. Now Motswasele does everything to make him feel small, put him wrong with the head ones. We are sorry for him. A great deal sorry."

"Him, an Englishman, you are sorry for him?"

"Yes, Isaac, I am sorry and sad. He has tried to help us. But can we say? Can we tell him? How? I don't know. Only his office clerk always sticks to him."

"What about the Mission, then?" Isaac asked.

"Oh, them. They know nothing. Not even the doctored rifles, they don't know!"

"The D.C. knows?"

"James tells him. The D.C. says he is not afraid."

"Good. Good. Better still to say he is not afraid if he is afraid, even a little bit afraid."

"His clerk afraid, much afraid I think, but goes to the office. He has a bicycle now. He sings hymns on his bicycle in case someone shoots at the tyres."

"That is very scientific, Josh! That is tribal scientific. Hymns on bicycles!" Isaac began to laugh and Tselane was glad, for Isaac had not laughed at all since the night of the knife.

But Josh had to go back with Kuate's lorry and Isaac fell into gloom again. He would hardly speak to Billy for the guilt which he felt like a red cloth between them. He kept out of Gloria's way because she had made him scrub the floor. He scurried obediently for his white bosses, and hated them as he had never done before. He knew they had done nothing bad to him and yet he hated them. As though the hate was something outside himself. But none of it could turn into action. When he read the papers, instead of seeing signs of a crack-up, the beginning of the end of the Republic, all he saw was signs of their power, of the impossibility of ever doing anything.

146

Rain came two days running, hard rain drumming on the roof of the repair shop. Had there been rain too in Ditlabeng? People said it was all over the middle of the country, good rain. Gloria planted her mealies. Tselane with only a little patch, planted a few melons and pumpkins and a little square of beans. Josh promised to plough and look after her land. She told her neighbours that she had taken in her dead sister's child; they took it for granted. One of the hens began to scratch up the seeds she had planted; anyhow it was not laying, so she killed it and they had a chicken dinner. The next day Isaac came back from work and found that he and Tselane had a son.

Gloria said everything had gone fine. Tselane had wept a little for her mother but that was over. She had barely cried out at the worst part of her labour. "She is a fighter, that one," said Gloria. "She should have many, many sons."

Isaac held the tiny one in his arms and touched him gently, gently, with his lips and tongue, so new, so little, and would grow to a man. "What do we call him, Tselane?" he said. He felt she would want to call him for something wild, some strong swift beast.

But she said, "You want to call him for Josh?" He looked at the little soft creature in his arms, the little pale palms, the fingers with delicate pinkish nails; difficult to believe in him. Gloria had put a ticky into his palm for luck, but his fingers uncurled from the silver—he won't take their money, thought Isaac. Not my son! Tselane spoke again. "You want to call him for Amos?" And then he found himself clutching the baby to him defensively. He nodded. He couldn't just speak. Tselane from the floor said, "You bring me little Amos, let me love him too, Isaac."

In a way it was queer for Tselane to have Isaac about so much. This was a woman's time; men should keep away. Often the wife would still be with her own people. The baby was a joining up of past and future in her family. His family would no doubt be glad, but it was her own that she would feel close to; but now in the town it was different and perhaps, she thought, for many other mothers. When Isaac came back from work she felt close, close to him. For a day or two he would not let her get up to look after him as a wife should, but fed her porridge or soup out of his own bowl till she laughed and spilled it all. He took Kodunzwe on his knee and fed him and played with him. And Kodunzwe turned and snuggled into Isaac's coat. It seemed to Tselane, looking up from the floor, that Isaac had his arms round them all.

But in a few days she was about again and weeding her garden. Gloria came with Billy. "You got a fine son, Isaac man," said Billy. "You feel better?" Isaac wriggled his shoulders uncomfortably. "Think we could start up the group again pretty soon. Special Branch been and gone. Found nothing. If they make that report they get it wrong. Thank God, police are stupid!"

"Wish I thought that," Isaac said. "Police too clever. Those Special Branch men, they know, they wait, they come back. Too clever for us always."

"You speak like you're afraid, Isaac man. What are you afraid of?"

148

Isaac did not answer. Tselane answered for him. "Himself. My Isaac afraid of himself."

Gloria turned round from the baby, her hands on her hips. "Bewitched maybe. Who bewitched you, Isaac?"

"Look, man," said Billy, "we can't do nothing if we are afraid. We can only hate. Right? Well, hating's no use. I don't hate whites. Waste of time. Look, there are whites wanting to help us, true there are. Not much good, maybe, but there are some lose their jobs for us, damn' near lose their lives. Will do just that before they're done. That makes them our brothers, I think. They're not afraid of the police. You going to let them do better than you, Isaac? Better than us?"

Isaac said, "When I think what I did. Myself. That plumb scares me."

"You won't do that again," said Billy. "And it didn't happen, see? You're scared of shadows. Scared of dreams. Stand up, man!"

"You sure the group's wanting me back?"

"Sure true! Come Isaac, we find them. Have a small celebration. I leave Gloria. Good example to her!"

"Good example you get married to Gloria, Billy!" said Tselane. But Billy only laughed and put his big arm round Isaac's shoulders and took him out.

149

Chapter XV

ALL WENT WELL. There was more rain. Tselane had plenty of milk for the little Amos. Her pumpkins and melons began to grow fast. She was always chasing Kodunzwe off them, but she never smacked him hard. Kuate brought back a message that he and Josh had ploughed her field; his wife would hoe it and maybe the girl that Josh was after. James Mookami had given seed. It was said that the D.C. was leaving and a new man coming instead. Which meant a win for Motswasele. Too bad, that.

One evening Isaac had worked late; he would get a bit of overtime. Billy had taken him on as an apprentice welder. It would be better money in time, and he had a good character apart from that one lapse. Funny that! One of the Englishmen had been heard saying to the other that it showed just how much better chaps these tribesmen were than the town boys.

When he got back he found Tselane ladling out porridge and a drop of milk to two boys; twelve to fourteen years old they might have been. The younger one seemed to have been crying. His face was streaked, and his shoulders shook a bit still. Tselane put her finger to her lips, then took him out into the evening. "What kids these?" Isaac asked.

150

Tselane said low, "Those Big Manuel's kids. Came to look for him."

"But how? Why?"

"This my notion," said Tselane, "what he meant, that snake. Meant to take you all into his trap, then meant to come back himself, money in pocket, thirty pieces silver, more. Meant he'd settle here, get his kids over. The mother dead, see. Meant to get them educated here."

"You mean," said Isaac, "Big Manuel's kids refugees from Bantu Education Act?"

"Just that."

"Paid for out of me getting hanged. Billy getting hanged——" His lips began to curl back from his teeth.

Tselane put a hand over his mouth. "Hush up, Isaac! The kids don't know that. Got out at the station, asked for him. Someone told them he'd been with us. They never knew they'd a snake for a father."

"But they had!"

"Maybe he wasn't bad all through," said Tselane. "No, Isaac, you leave me say that. I killed him, me. I cut him up before he died, me. For me to say it. Those two children as much refugees from the Republic as you and Josh."

"His children!"

"My children, now, Isaac. I have said. Told them their father died of bad illness. Fed them. My children. Your children, Isaac." She stood close to him, the milky smell coming from her, the stars beginning to come clear in the evening sky behind her. She put her arms round his neck; she could feel him struggling inside himself.

At last he said, "More for the tribe. Do they know they are boys of the Barnatsieng now?" And he felt Tselane warm and yielding under him, only just kept off her. It was too soon, could hurt his baby. "Four boys!" he said.

"Next time we have a girl," said Tselane, "you like that, Isaac?"

Isaac made the two boys help him to build another hut for them to live in. By the time it was finished he had got very fond of Jim and Moses. He invented a quite different kind of father for them, but explained that they must never talk about him except to their new mother and father, since the illness he had died of had been thought to be very unlucky. No, it was not painful. Somehow he had lost all wish for further revenge on Manuel. But it was two more mouths to be fed, and now there were school fees to be found. Funny the way Africans have to build their own schools, but white children's schools get paid for by the Government— buildings, teachers, pencils, jotters and all. And the same their white fathers have to pay as Africans: just the same. But who are the richest?

Tselane took the whole family off to church. She chose the Catholic Sisters, as their Christmas Party for the children was said to be the best. Good toys, sweets and cakes. Almost Christmas! A year since Isaac and Josh first came to Ditlabeng. A long year. Tselane found out from other women what she should do at this church, different from the Mission at Ditlabeng, but easy to learn. She showed Jim and Moses what to do. But Isaac didn't want to come; if it had been their Mission

152

at Lady Selborne, perhaps; but he was not going to sham and beg even for the children. In the end he came once, but did not care much for the singing nor the smell of the Sisters.

Luckily the two boys had brought a suitcase, so there was no bother yet about school shoes and clothes. For a boy must not be shamed before his school mates and teachers. They were quite good at reading and writing, but they had been taught some queer history and scripture. Isaac began carefully to try and explain to the two of them what the Bantu Education Act was for; how it was thought out to make them look backward into Verwoerd's idea of their past, to make them think that they were for ever a slave people, children of Ham, unable to do skilled and privileged work, for ever unable to be the equals in mind and morals, in civilisation, of the stupidest and cruellest Boer farmer. It seemed to Isaac that Jim, the older boy, had an idea of this; but they were muddled. After the Bantu Education Act started, there had been the same school buildings, many of the same teachers—what was the difference then? Again and carefully Isaac explained, telling the two boys how they were not slaves, how they might by hard work and perhaps luck become as skilled as any white, how they were entitled as human beings to sit for an examination, just as they were entitled to travel on the same seats of buses. And as he talked to them, he began to feel himself building up again and all that he cared about coming back strongly into his mind.

It was hot again now, too hot. The rain stopped, but the crops had got off to a good start. A day came when

Seneo walked up to the house, handsome and trim in an enviable cotton dress, the colours still clear and bright, not washed out as all Tselane's were. Nor were her shoes cracked or even dusty. "Well, Tselane," she said, "James has gone up the line to fetch Letlotse."

"He is coming then! But why not meet him here?"

"Because," said Seneo.

"Motswasele? You mean to get at Letlotse first. I understand. Good."

"James will bring him here. I want that he should see you and I both. I think he has some foolish ideas."

"Isaac and I, we have foolish ideas sometimes," said Tselane. "Should he not see the elders?"

"He may not want to see the elders. He is feeling—how shall I say?—not altogether of the Bamatsieng. That one can understand."

"But Isaac and I are only poor people now. Letlotse may think our ideas are stupid."

"Not as stupid as his. Not the same class of stupid! Tselane, he thinks he can talk reason to Motswasele, and to Motswasele's creature Dikgang, the one who told the new D.C. he was a Communist! Oh, yes, I know. Poor me, only a woman. Letlotse is the man, the leopard, thinks he can talk reason to everyone. Sees himself as head of a Batswana National Political Party. Programme: reason, sweet reason! Oh, he is crazy."

Tselane was rather shocked at this talk about the prince. But also, as another woman, a little pleased. She changed the subject.

"And you, Seneo, you have raised your regiment?"

"Yes, I have raised the women's Magwasa. I have

154

learned the songs, taken the tests, answered the questions, as though it all made sense. Maybe it was sense once. At least it has more sense even now than films and jazz songs. It was not the same kind of lies. The songs of my *mophato* I like."

"I liked the songs of my own *mophato*. I sing them when I am sad, alone. But what is said now in Ditlabeng?"

"It is said I must agree to marry Motswasele."

"But you will not?"

"I will not by any means. And also if Letlotse comes back, and if it is decided that he is to be made chief——"

"——and if Motswasele does not manage to kill him," said Tselane, looking straight at Seneo.

Seneo nodded. "I know. Letlotse will have to be very careful. I do not know how many people can be entirely trusted. Many can be half trusted, but that is not enough. And Letlotse has not learned to be careful yet. That, I hope, is what James will talk to him about in the car all the way. It is a pity there was all this good rain. People are beginning to say that Motswasele is lucky, that he has good ways of bringing rain. Tselane, I am sorry about your mother. A time will come. At least the little one is safe. And the new baby, the little Amos? I have not seen him."

Tselane picked him out of the blanket nest and handed him over to Seneo, who handled him professionally, then said, "Tselane, is it true you have taken in two refugee children?"

"We have," said Tselane. "Jim and Moses; they are good boys."

"That is a fine thing to do. Sometimes I think educa-

155

tion is the only thing that matters in Africa. More than all this politics. Are the children orphans, then?"

"Their father was killed," said Tselane.

"Ah, these politics! Death, death, death. You will not let your Isaac run his head into too much danger, Tselane? You need a man to look after this big family!" They talked for a while of babies, then about the clinic at Ditlabeng and the new ideas Seneo had for it. She would need to go carefully against custom, sometimes, but it could be that the women would accept more from the chief's sister then they would, say, from the Mission. But all the same the Mission doctor must be constantly consulted, and with deference, or he might become angry.

While they were talking, Tselane made tea. Then James came up to the house with Letlotse beside him, looking very smart in his London clothes he had started the journey in, but his coat over his arm and patches of sweat already staining his shirt. He was looking worried, as well he might be with all his cousin James had been telling him as he drove along the straight dust road with the dry browned bush that he remembered so well on both sides of it. He and Seneo kissed one another Western fashion. To Tselane he seemed even more different than he had been other times, but also not grown up, a half-formed man still not thickened out, a big and clever boy. She gave him tea too, wishing she had fresh milk instead of the tin of condensed, and biscuits, yes, it would have looked better to have biscuits. But the children had finished all the few remains that she'd had.

Letlotse said, "I have been hearing bad things, Cousin Agnes—or do you like to be Tselane now?"

"I am Tselane," she said. "The other was my teacher's name, and now I suppose I shall never be a teacher. You heard, for instance, about my mother?"

"I could not believe," said Letlotse—they were speaking English—"I had thought all that was away back in the past."

"So did we all," said James. "At least all who have had education."

Letlotse said musingly, "I think it was like this in Europe for my friends' fathers and mothers when the Nazis started. That is the way they have told me. They also could not believe. Perhaps we all have beasts inside us."

While they were talking Isaac came back from work. He was embarrassed to find his house so full of the great ones of the Bamatsieng, but at the same time he said to himself, "Equality, Democracy". When James told him it was Letlotse the Prince, and Letlotse held out his hand, Isaac took it and muttered. He was not going to say My Lord, not going to show any mark of respect to this one who had had all the luck and all the money! But he wished he was not in working clothes, wished he had known so he could have had a wash before coming in. He scowled at Tselane and Seneo who had brought this on to him. "Let's go out and have a drink," said Letlotse, feeling the embarrassment and wanting to shake it away. "All right," said Seneo, "but bring us back a couple of Cokes."

In the course of two or three beers a threshold of

embarrassment was crossed, but they couldn't talk seriously in the bar, finally came back with sandwiches and Cokes. Tselane was nursing the baby, and Letlotse looked away, though she did not mind. Her heavy breasts were dropping into a woman's pattern. It was odd for Letlotse, the smell of the hut, the smell of Africa, it was beginning to affect him, he wasn't sure how. They all ate the sandwiches but Tselane kept half her Coke for Jim and Moses. Letlotse asked about the refugees coming through. "Do many of them stay?" he asked.

"Some of the Angolans have stayed and planted ground and put up houses. We of the Bamatsieng, we have let them have some land," said James.

"They don't want to go on?"

"The poor farmers stay wherever they see a piece of land where they can make gardens, grow crops," said Isaac. "In the Republic things are bad for all Africans who think. In Angola things are bad for all Africans. It is like that."

"And the ones who want to go on? Are they let through on the railway into Rhodesia?"

"If they have papers," Isaac said.

"And if not?"

This was not something Isaac was going to speak to Letlotse about—not yet anyway. Nor did he like thinking about it. When he thought about that frontier he also thought about himself and Josh and Amos and the men they had trusted. He looked away and his face went blank. To fill the gap Tselane said, "We thank God often that there is also Zambia."

158

"You aren't in either of the political parties yourself?" Letlotse asked Isaac.

"No," said Isaac, "they are fine if you want to be in a political party. If you want the enjoyment of it. Myself, I am only interested in action. Naturally we have contacts; you will know I am from the Republic. I was part of an organisation there."

"You will not tell me what? No, you are quite right. Why should you trust me?"

"I would like to trust you," said Isaac, and looked from him to Tselane and back. "After all"—and he swung one foot about—"I suppose you will be my chief, and my children's chief."

"Oh, never mind, never mind," said Letlotse, smiling, a little embarrassed himself. "Tell me some more about things in this country. For instance, there is no Communist Party here?"

"There are some who call themselves Communists. But it makes no sense in Africa."

"Under a Communist economy——"

"*That*, yes. But it will not happen through having a little Communist Party. Of course, I would like to see all trade, all industry, run by the State, no bosses, no private profits. But for that matter I work in the Public Works Department. And there *are* bosses!"

"There is Management. There will always be Management. There is Management in the Soviet Union."

"And all of it white?"

"Well, where I was, Isaac, the Russians were all white. Very fair people, blue eyes. I suppose Management is national in the other Republics of the Soviet Union, and some of them at least are dark-skinned."

"Lucky, lucky whites, to have no Africa!" Isaac was beginning to be able to talk freely. James sat and listened and sometimes looked at Seneo.

"So you think one need not bother about the Communists one way or the other?"

"They are not"—Isaac frowned and hunted for the word—"not relevant in our situation."

"Would people accept a multi-racial party? Multi-racial society?"

Isaac thought. "In time, in a hundred years. Fifty years, perhaps. When we have forgotten."

"Is there so much to forget? I can very easily see Bechuanaland as a multi-racial state. Happy. The whites sending their children to school with ours, whites who were born here and mean to leave their bones here. True Batswana. Of course, the whites who do not feel that way must go—You are laughing at me, Isaac!"

"Remember, I come from the Republic. We shall have to win before we accept it. We shall have to have won the war—for it is a war—and felt ourselves to be the winners for a time. For a year, even! After that, perhaps, we might start to forget. I cannot see any multi-racial society until after that."

"That could take a long time."

"I know," he glanced at the baby in Tselane's arms, "in that one's children's time."

"But meanwhile?"

"You mean would I work politically with whites? I don't know, because I haven't tried. Have not been asked! You are a chief, or nearly. You could be asked. I, no."

"I wonder. You have never had a white friend?" Isaac shook his head. He couldn't count the D.C.

"I have had many white friends. I have been, can I say, multi-racial?"

His sister laughed and whispered to Tselane, "In bed." Letlotse glared at her. James smiled with half his face.

"I am thinking," said Letlotse, "that if we could start a serious new party, a Liberal party——"

"There is a Liberal party already. So big." Isaac held his two hands a palm's width apart.

"My poor little brother," said Seneo. "It is difficult to think of a new name for a party!" Letlotse jumped across and shook her. James looked away and giggled.

Tselane said rather formally, "Our Prince will have more to think about than political parties."

"Prince, Prince! Even my cousin Tselane says these things," said Letlotse. "I shall never get used to it."

"Oh, yes, you will," said Seneo. "You will have to."

Chapter XVI

LETLOTSE CAME BACK and threw himself into one
of the big chairs at James Mookami's house; he took
off his sandals and wriggled his long toes, which were
pleased not to be in shoes. He was much less tidy, he
was cross, he was worried. He felt he had been snubbed
by the new D.C., and he wondered just why; for that
matter, he wondered why the old one had been replaced.
Did this tie up with his interview at the Colonial Office?
He had no proof yet that it had anything to do with
Motswasele but proof would not be easy. Was he to
believe what James said? Especially about Dikgang. It
seemed uncommonly likely: there was this and that thing
which had been said, a conversation with the new D.C.
overheard. Letlamma had said something different, but
then Letlamma had been drinking, and besides—oh, it
was difficult! And himself, what did they think of him
now? Had he said the right thing to the headmen?
Hard to tell. He longed for a cool drink. James had an
ancient oil fridge, but it didn't work well. He couldn't
bear the enlarged and tinted family photographs on the
walls. One was his and James's grandfather, looking very
stern. Letlotse made a face at it. Was James going to
grow up into someone like that, stern and respectable? For
that matter was he himself? There was a Mission

wedding photograph that he didn't like either. It was not like his English friends' weddings with the bride laughing and the little bridesmaids with their skirts like butterflies. For that matter, he didn't care for his Aunt Sarah's artificial flowers and embroidered table-cloths. Nor for his cousin James's taste in best ties.

The day before he had had a letter from his tutor, a little anxious it seemed. He had written back at once, assuring him that he was working hard. But was he? He had brought some text books with him, yes; he had read in the plane and the train, but since then the number of pages he had got through were alarmingly small. It was hopeless trying to work at night, the lamps weren't good enough, besides it was then that people turned up and wanted to see him. He had a feeling that they preferred to come after dark. Would it make any difference to them what kind of degree he got? Probably not, it was all much too far away. An invitation to a Royal Garden Party would be more their cup of tea! His father would have cared. He knew now that right down underneath he missed his father dreadfully, much more than Seneo did. His father who used to tell him what it meant being the heir, the one born to be chief, how he would have to lead and yet be at the beck and call of every tribesman who had a grievance, who wanted justice or help. How he would have absolute significance for the Bamatsieng and absolute responsibility which he must always be prepared to share with, or justify to the Protectorate Government. How he must be all his life an inspanned ox—no! He dropped his head in his hands and began to think about two or three girls, about

163

Patsy who had been so delicious to get one's arm round and pinch, but whose father had been so unreasonable, and also about another more recent girl friend with whom he had wandered round in the Russian white nights when one had to stay up and talk because everything was so exciting. He thought she must be more what Seneo meant by class; her father was some kind of Sir. It had been a near thing, but as it happened they were both sharing rooms with others in the party. And now—oh, it was far away! He would never be able to explain to someone like her what was tearing at him now; she might try to understand, but she wouldn't be able.

Did Motswasele feel any of these things about being acting chief? It didn't seem so, but he had not had it dinned into his head when he was a boy. Letlotse thought of his father now telling him all he had to learn, telling him about the history of the Bamatsieng, most of which he had now forgotten. Not that his father was perfect. He remembered times, especially just after his mother died, when his father had behaved far from perfectly. But at least he had tried. Especially later in life when his temper had cooled down, and he had stopped being interested in women. I suppose they'll want to marry me to someone, he thought, but I won't, I won't! James came in, "Lepedi and Dithapo want to see you."

"What about? Must I?"

"Of course. They will be the fathers of your own *mophato*. Lepedi is the leader of Mantwane, but after the time he had his face clawed and lost one eye, he has become old and he depends much on Dithapo. But as he is the leader, you must greet him first."

164

"They want me to do this? To raise my regiment? I do not at all want to do it. No! No! You yourself think I should do it, James?" He looked eagerly at his cousin for surely James, who had been to secondary school, was—civilised?

"Of course," said James again. Letlotse gave it up, got to his feet and shook himself, shook away thoughts of those two white girls and also about what raising his regiment might mean. They would not spare him, his fathers, for all he was Prince. "Well, Lepedi? Well, Dithapo?" he said after the greetings.

Dithapo came to the point. "We could have everything arranged for you to take out your *mophato* next week. There are certain things you will need to do. One of the erosion dykes which Magwasa built is not on a good line. When the heavy rains came, it was useless. Another is too short."

"I understand. That shall be done."

"The Regent will say you must make him a new fence for the great cattle kraal which will be yours one day. The old uncle agrees with him. As he does about everything. But we have decided that the dykes must be finished, and that this would have been your father's wish."

"Do I get a lorry for the stones?"

"No, they are on the ground. Rollers you can have. And your hands."

"And after that?"

"We shall be your fathers. There is nothing to fear, Letlotse."

"Nothing to fear," echoed Lepedi.

165

"Why should I fear?" answered Letlotse, in the properly casual way. It might, after all, be rather fun, in a way. But it mustn't take too long. "You know," he said, "I must be back for the beginning of term?"

"If you go back," said Dithapo.

"I have only two terms more, and then my degree. Motswasele has agreed not to press my sister to marry him."

"Why do you believe him, Prince?" asked Dithapo. James had come back into the room and was listening.

"Why not? It is not to his interest to lie to me."

"If you believe him you will go back. He could say then that the Council and the headmen have said that this marriage must be made. He could say that Seneo herself had come to him. There are plenty who want to believe him. They feel that he is making them into something they want to be, something to make people fear. When they themselves fear their chief others will fear them. Also the rain——"

"Oh, the rain, the rain, I am tired hearing of the rain!" Suddenly he saw that he had shocked both Dithapo and James. Lepedi had not taken it in. Yes, well, he must be more careful.

James said, "I would like to marry Seneo myself. If Motswasele were out of the way it would be thought suitable. I am the same relation to her."

"And what does *she* say?" Letlotse asked a little jealously. It was one thing having one's sister not wanting to marry someone, but if perhaps she wants to marry someone else, why had she not said?

166

"Of course," said James with his nose in the air, "I have said nothing to her."

Letlotse got up. "Very well, I will raise my regiment. I will do everything in order. But I must have another talk with Motswasele. I know you are all against him—and I see another reason why *you* are," he added sharply to James. "But perhaps he is more reasonable than you think."

"Certainly you can talk, Prince Letlotse," said Dithapo. "But if you go to his house take care of what you eat and drink."

Letlotse didn't much like sitting in front of his father's desk with Motswasele on the far side of it where his father used to sit. But Motswasele appeared in a friendly and reasonable enough mood, very ready to talk, almost sympathetic. Nobody could have agreed more readily that what was needed was a united Bechuanaland, but that neither of the present political parties could do the uniting. "A new party altogether," said Motswasele and shoved a tumbler and a bottle of South African brandy across the desk for Letlotse. It didn't seem likely that there was a catch, but Letlotse waited until Motswasele had poured for himself out of the same bottle before drinking. "A party with new ideas," said Motswasele, "Oh, yes, you'll find the tribe backing you with that party. I see what you have in your mind." It was strong brandy, good, not cheap stuff. Also I have a good head, Letlotse said to himself, listening to Motswasele, disparaging both the Democratic and the People's Party, then talking about the danger from refugees who had no respect and no morals, would stop at nothing, brought in

167

the Special Branch after them, upset everything, were criminals as often as not—Letlotse nodded, but at the same time thought of this Isaac who had married his cousin Tselane and this Josh whom James was protecting. That didn't fit. He sipped at the brandy. Motswasele was talking very reasonably about another kind of political party, how it could be started by the right people. "And now much more modern," Motswasele went on, "than anything here! We in this tribe are out of date." He shook his head. "As you know, Letlotse, I had to agree to be Regent, no stopping them, but how much work! It has put many years on to my back. The doing of justice! The settling of disputes!"

"The arrangements for murder!" said Letlotse, and suddenly found himself laughing. Come, come, this wouldn't do. Or would it? Did Motswasele now trust him?

"You should not believe everything you hear," said Motswasele, half smiling. "But still, I think you are a realist. A man of the world."

That is just what I am, Letlotse thought, but I will not drink any more of this good brandy. It is making me speak what I intended to keep in my head. And I think I see where Motswasele is leading. "Yes," he said, "you will be glad to give it all up."

Motswasele put his elbows squarely on the table and looked across at Letlotse. "Is that what we want?" he asked, and suddenly he was speaking like a hammer talking to a nut.

"I think it may be what the Bamatsieng want," said

168

Letlotse very reasonably, careful to smile. "But I am prepared to discuss anything."

"And you, my cousin, what do you want? Your political party, the modern party? I do not think you can do both. No. You must think very carefully what you want. I too must think what you want. And what I want."

"If I were to think of being a political leader——" said Letlotse slowly, and without noticing took another sip of brandy.

"You would want some compensation, Cousin Letlotse", said Motswasele, leaning forward, a big smile creasing his face. "Naturally. You are entitled to it. That would be the expected thing. A big help to your party's funds. And perhaps you could persuade your sister——"

"Not possible."

"Pity. For it would be possible, you know, Letlotse. Very possible. She might even get to like me. To like me much. Women change, you know, and if her son is to be chief——"

The room was swirling a little. "Stop!" said Letlotse. "We are going too far, too fast."

"No, no, we are agreeing. We are two people of sense, and we can come to agreement, is that not so, Letlotse? We can agree that you go back, finish this fine English education, that you get a good start for your party, get yourself an office, typewriters, perhaps a party news-paper——"

"I agree to nothing," said Letlotse, and held on to the edge of the table.

"Now, let us talk about the programme of your

169

political party," said Motswasele. "It will be for unity so everyone will join it. And independence, of course. Tell me, Letlotse, when you were in Russia I suppose you spoke to them about helping us? Industries, money? You will have seen the big ones, the heads? What did you say to them, Letlotse? You told them about us, yes?"

A vision had come quickly and enticingly into Letlotse's mind of himself talking, talking—to Kruschev, no less —speaking about the Batswana. It could have been— should have been! It almost was! This would put Motswasele in his place. And then—then—he would escape—no more nonsense about raising a regiment. He would be modern again! If only the brandy hadn't so thickened his tongue! And then as he started to speak of it the vision walked out of his mind, just in time. Instead he felt a little sick and shook his head. "What makes you think that?"

"You are right to say nothing," said Motswasele amiably, and filled his glass again. "But I am sure you did what was best. And gave promises as well as got them. Unity, independence and voting with ballot boxes, plenty of aid, plenty of prosperity, yes, everything! I see your party, Letlotse, yes indeed, I see it!"

But Letlotse, looking down on the floor, listening to the noise of Motswasele's confident voice, suddenly saw his party shrivel up and die like a fly in a flame, and knew it had never been real, never been anything but words. And knew that Motswasele had been trying to make him boast of what he had said and done in the Soviet Union. And knew that if he had done it Motswasele would have

170

repeated it all to the new District Officer. Probably there was someone else overhearing to confirm it if necessary. Perhaps the old uncle. He looked round, thought he heard a soft step, wasn't sure, got to his feet and felt the floor swaying. He wished he could remember exactly what had been said.

"Sit down," said Motswasele. "You don't want to argue, Letlotse, don't want to talk. We just drink, O.K.?"

"No," said Letlotse, "I've had enough."

Motswasele leant over the desk and put a heavy hand on his shoulder, so that he sat down suddenly. "Never say you've had enough," said Motswasele genially. "Drink, man!"

"I think I feel sick," said Letlotse. "Get outside——"

"You be sick here," said Motswasele in a man to man way. "Plenty of women, clean everything up——"

"No," said Letlotse thickly and desperately, and made a shambling dash over the heaving floor and fell down the steps, arriving at the bottom rather more sober and with his cousin James holding his arm.

"Told you not to drink," said James. "Damn' fool, you, Letlotse!"

"It was only brandy," said Letlotse. "Not poison." He leant against the wall and was very sick.

James looked on unsympathetically. "Motswasele has a stronger head than you. Or me. Too strong. What did he say?"

"Was trying to make me agree he was to stay chief, I to have political party," said Letlotse, fumbling back in his mind for what had been said, feeling a good solid ache beginning in his head.

"I thought that was what you said you wanted," said James.

"That was what I wanted," agreed Letlotse. "Until I saw it."

James took him by the arm and began to walk away. After a bit he whispered, "And now you have seen it?"

"Let me be," said Letlotse. "Let me be. After I have taken over my regiment I will think. James, I promise, I promise I will think hard."

"You will raise your regiment?" said James shaking him. "You are sure? We have been afraid——"

"I have said," Letlotse answered and looked hard at James and saw James take it in the eyes and look away, look down, as was proper when stared at by a leopard.

Chapter XVII

IT HAD BEEN a difficult and discouraging week for
the group. First there had been the couple from
Angola, the woman supporting the man somehow or
another; he had been beaten with the usual wooden
paddle that is slammed down from the punisher's
shoulder on to the punished's hands, or his feet if he is
held upside down, crushing and fracturing small bones.
These were not politicals, just members of a small religious
sect, unorthodox, no doubt, since it had no Portuguese
in charge, in fact no white. They had heard of the little
settlement of Angola farmers in the Bamatsieng Reserve;
that was where they were making for slowly, slowly, more
slowly each day as the man's feet became more inflamed
and infected, more desperately painful. He died at
Craigs, and the woman knew neither Tswana nor
English. Suffering is bad enough when there is com-
munication, but without it—you almost wanted the
woman to die too. Tselane had tried to look after her,
but she had run away, nobody knew where.

Then there was the political from Johannesburg about
whom they couldn't make up their minds; he had no
documents; Isaac was strongly against him. He seemed
very frightened, desperate to get to the escape route, and
yet—if he was double-crossing that's just how he would

need to seem. Essential to keep the escape route secret. They decided not to tell him, avoided him, pretended to know nothing. And then. Then he was arrested and marched to the station, not like a double-crosser, but marched with his arms twisted to hurt. The way Isaac knew it. And on him the look you get when everything is over except the final humiliations, the final choking, the knowledge that evil has got you for ever. All night Isaac could not sleep, thinking of that one's journey back into hell, and realising how easily they could have helped him. But that was the kind of thing that happened. In a bad situation, it is impossible not to make some mistakes.

It was the next day that a young white came to the repair shop at the end of the day with a typewriter, and asked if it could be repaired. Asked in a half-whisper as if he hadn't the right. Isaac didn't want to look at him or any other white. He couldn't get what had happened out of his mind; instead he looked at the typewriter, a battered portable, could have been got second-hand. He started doing the repair, and the young white seemed surprised and pleased and began talking to him haltingly. After a little Isaac suddenly caught himself feeling sorry for this young white with freckles and kind of orange-coloured hair, who wasn't much more than a boy. He looked up from the type-writer and found the boy was actually going red in the cheeks the funny way whites do. "Where are you from?" Isaac said, putting no respect in his voice

"I'm V.S.O.," said the boy.

"What's that?"

174

"Voluntary Service Overseas," said the boy. "I've come out for a year after school to try to give a hand. I know I'm not just qualified as I should be, but I'm teaching——"

"You it is, at the school where my Jim and Moses go!" said Isaac. "They call you——"

"Oh, what?"

"I'll tell you one day. It's not meant bad. Why are you doing it?"

"Well just—you're a bitty short of teachers."

"How much you get?" said Isaac. "Who's paying you?"

"Voluntary Service Overseas pays our fares," said the young man, only too obviously speaking the truth, speaking the truth immediately to a complete stranger! "Here I get food and lodging and a bit of pocket money."

"How much?"

"Och, about a pound a week. Two *rands*—I can't get used to this money!"

"That's not white man's pay," said Isaac. "Still I don't know why you do it." But again he stared at the boy until he went red. "Maybe you do want to help," said Isaac. "Look, there's your typewriter. It wasn't much of a repair. But it's going to go wrong again— see? The ratchet's worn. I'll put a string round the lid. Old, this typewriter."

"I know," said the boy. "My dad gave it me before I came out. Thank you very much. How much do I owe you?"

"Out of your two *rands*? Nothing." It was suddenly as sweet as ripe grapes to be able to say this to a white.

"Oh, but——" said the boy. "Well, come away out and have a drink anyway. My name's Dugal."

"Dugal, that's a funny name."

"It means black stranger," said the boy. "In Gaelic—that's the old language in Scotland."

"Black stranger!" said Isaac. "That's something I never heard. So you're a Scotch boy! My name's Isaac."

"Are you from round here?"

Isaac said nothing for a minute, put his tools away, looked round and spoke very quietly. "If I said I was from Pretoria—now mind, Dugal, I may be lying—what would you say?"

"I don't understand." The boy stared at him, then suddenly reddened again. "Yes, I think I do! Gosh, Isaac, I think it's just awful, you know, the treason trials and Apartheid and everything!"

"Don't speak so loud," said Isaac, "and don't say a word. Let's go and have a drink. Sure you want to come with me?"

"Sure!" said the boy.

They went along the road, but passed the bar; Isaac steered him to a fizzy drink counter, and they both had an orange, Dugal paying. He could afford that much, Isaac thought. As they drank the sweat jumped out on them; Dugal mopped his face hopelessly with a squashed handkerchief. In a while the boy left clutching his typewriter. "See you soon?" he said.

"If you like," Isaac answered.

"Day after to-morrow? Here?"

"All right," said Isaac, amused, and took the boy's hand when he held it out.

It was two days later when Kuate came to the Public Works Department repair shop where he was quite well known. In a minute he saw Billy and Isaac with him holding the other end of a strip which was being welded. When it was finished, and Isaac was taking it over into the store, Kuate said, "The prince wants you for his *mophato*. You can come with me."

"How long do we go for?"

"Don't know. But Tselane will be safe. Motswasele won't dare while Letlotse is at Ditlabeng."

"Besides," said Isaac, "I have two big sons now! Can I finish this job?"

"Pick you up at home," Kuate said.

So now it was on him. His promise to the Bamatsieng. He had thought it might be coming now that Letlotse had come back but he had shied away from thinking about it. He would have to say something to Billy. He wondered if they were depending on him for anything special during the next two or three weeks. Couldn't be helped if they were. He was going to go through with this, his payment for Tselane.

He held down the next strip, and while he worked said to Billy, "I must go to Ditlabeng. You tell the boss, Billy. Say my sister gets married, say something. Be away maybe a week, maybe three weeks."

"Why, man?"

It seemed oddly difficult to tell Billy. He looked at the welding arc and away. "I have to go back to the tribe, just have to," he said.

"Why, man? You're not one of them!"

"I will be," said Isaac.

"For Christ's sake," said Billy, "you mad?"

"Never saner," said Isaac. "When I come back I think I come back—strong."

"But," said Billy, "surely to God what we're against is the past, the tribes, the chiefs, the whole bloody set-up. You, Isaac, you try to go back to the past—you, you play Verwoerd's game, turn your back on freedom and progress——"

"It's not that," said Isaac soberly. "It's not any wickedness this, we don't go into the past I think, or only a little, just to drink at old wells, to find our fathers and come back strengthened."

"Well, Isaac, one thing sure, we need strengthening. Don't you get staying with your tribe."

"I'll come back," said Isaac, "never you fear. My tribe is Africa."

He was hurrying home when he thought of Dugal, the white boy, waiting at the fizzy drink stall. Well, let him wait! Then he thought what whites always said about Africans, couldn't trust them, no notion of time, never did what they said; and besides the boy was so young and a stranger. A black stranger—Isaac laughed to himself inside. Wouldn't take a minute to go past. Yes, there was the boy, a bit to one side, glum-looking, waiting. "Hi, Dugal!" he said, knowing well enough that it was as hard for a white to tell one African from another at first as it is for one African to pick out one white from a crowd. The boy brightened and came over. "Look," said Isaac, "I can't stop. Not this time. Got to be away. Maybe two, three weeks."

"Oh," said the boy, disappointed, and then suddenly blushing again; "Oh, I see—well, good luck!" and squeezed his hand, then went off. Why did he say that, thought Isaac, and then it came to him that Dugal thought he was going off as a freedom fighter—and had wished him luck.

Tselane was feeding porridge to Jim and Moses. "You boys," said Isaac, "you got to look after your mother! I'm going to be away for a while." He turned to Tselane, "Letlotse has sent."

"You go to his *mophato*? Isaac, you are not sorry you go?"

"It is for you," said Isaac, "instead of cows. Then after this we are properly married." Both of them laughed. Tselane gave him a bowl of porridge, and while he ate it she kept touching him, his face, his shoulders, everywhere.

"I shan't change," said Isaac.

She picked up little Amos and put him for a moment into Isaac's arms. "Good when his father is one of us," she said.

Jim said, "I been thinking. I could be delivery boy after school. Think I know a shop would take me on. A little money——"

"Knew I could trust you, Jim," said Isaac, and then the lorry was round. Kuate would want to get over most of the road before dark. Isaac got in beside him, leaning down to say stay safe to all his family, then they were away and the thoughts in his mind began to turn to

179

Ditlabeng, to Josh, to Letlotse, to whatever was going to happen, something, he thought, which had pain in it but not the kind of pain which hurts.

After a while Kuate said, "You know that village, poor devils from Angola. Rasemonje is chief down there, small chief under Motswasele. But his family always chiefs. He was good to the Angola boys, helped with seed, roots, houses. Everyone helps. The crops were beginning to come. Then Motswasele suddenly sends, says he wants extra taxes. Heavy taxes, too. And these Angolans have no money. Now Rasemonje comes to Ditlabeng and tells Motswasele, but Motswasele don't care. Says he must have taxes or else complain to Government and those ones from Angola sent back. Back to Angola!"

"God!" said Isaac. "What happened?"

"Well, Rasemonje thinks a bit, says he will see to it, goes back, finds the tax money himself. You see the ones from Angola were crying so much, too much for any persons with good hearts. But next year?"

"Next year," said Isaac, "we got to have Letlotse."

"I think that too," said Kuate, "but—Motswasele likes power, likes to be able to kill, to do magic—we all get afraid."

"No good being afraid," said Isaac, "most of all not afraid of magic. You, driving a lorry, you can't be scared of magic, Kuate." But Kuate said nothing.

After the rain things looked better; there was a more varied green among the thick-set bushes, more grass below them; the golden flowers of the *motswake* trees swung lightly. A couple of monkeys lolloped from one

180

tree to another, looking disparagingly at the lorry. He looked and looked as they drove along the dust road bumping and swaying. He began to see it all freshly, this flat country where the thatch of the houses rose easily among the bush like something growing there. He saw the grass and herbage sparse above the red sand, but enough to feed a herd of cattle. How many different trees and bushes, the separate shapes and shinings of their leaves, even of their thorns! Rows of small birds sat on the telegraph wires or chirred and skimmed in and out of the branches, flashes of grey and bright.

All these years, thought Isaac, I have taken all this for granted, have never used my eyes, have never thought of my own wild Africa as beautiful. He went on speaking to Kuate, "When Letlotse is chief, everything gets cleared up. The light comes in. That will be good."

"Letlotse is small," said Kuate.

"The tribe will make him great. He begins now. With his *mophato*."

"I hope he will grow. I hope Motswasele will let him grow."

"When he has his *mophato*, we will see to that," said Isaac, and suddenly felt extraordinarily happy that he had been chosen for this. That things had worked out the way they had.

Kuate took him round to James Mookami's without going through the middle of Ditlabeng. "Best if you are not seen," said Kuate "still." But had there been something special to scare Kuate? He didn't say.

James Mookami's courtyard was full of men, and all of them seemed to be talking at once. When Isaac walked in they smacked him on the back or took his hand, or simply shouted at him; there was something going on, but he slipped through them quickly and at last found Josh. They went out at the back, and sat down under a morula tree at the foot of the kopje. "What's up here, Josh?" Isaac asked. "What got into Kuate to scare him?"

"Oh, that," said Josh. "Well, it's something he saw. Motswasele had got hold of one of the old witch doctors. He had his things and all that. Nasty, but it didn't scare me."

"How many did it scare?" Josh shrugged his shoulders. A procession of big ants was moving across the red dust in front of them; Isaac put his foot on them and squashed a few; the rest went on. "Look, does the D.C. know?"

"Not him. He thinks Motswasele's a great chap. They've gone out shooting together. He thinks Motswasele's a kind of Englishman."

"The old D.C. would have known. Nobody tell the Mission?"

"Could be dangerous to tell. Mission's job to find out."

"Letlotse know?"

Josh looked round, not that there was anyone there, and the noise in the courtyard drowned everything. "Letlotse has wanted not to believe. Until now."

"Tselane says Seneo tells her Letlotse is not wanting to be chief. Only wanting to lead some political party."

"That may be. He will have to think otherwise. It is not only for himself he must think. It is for all the Bamatsieng."

"Yes," said Isaac, "all of us."

182

"There is something else," said Josh, "and it's real bad. We don't know yet, not for sure, but it's said that Motswasele means to send all James's regiment off to the mines. Someone got that out of the Native Recruiting Officer——"

"Ah, I hate that word!" said Isaac.

"Seems Motswasele would be due a little present over that. Big present, maybe. Let alone he'd weaken James. I think, too, he has not quite forgotten you and me, Isaac. Not a forgetter, him. This would get rid of me."

Isaac clutched his hand: "You sure about this? Surely it can't be done these days? Surely not legal?"

"A chief can do plenty. A bad chief. And make it seem good to top Government people. But what I don't see is him doing it while Letlotse is at Ditlabeng."

"What does James Mookami say?"

"James swears he won't let us go. James says if need we shall fight. But then, what does the D.C. do?"

"The D.C.," said Isaac, "can go to hell."

Chapter XVIII

"PRINCE, PRINCE, you are breaking the rules!"
Isaac whispered agonisedly, trying to get Letlotse to
stop. They were not allowed much sleep, and after
yesterday he longed for it, and here Letlotse had lain
down beside him and suddenly dragged him up out of
a deep bore-hole of sleep to ask, "What do you really
think about Marx?" It was only in a low whisper, but
they were supposed not to speak at all except in certain
set forms, and about certain subjects only, of which
economics was not one. The dried white clay patterned
on half his body started itching the moment he awoke,
and Letlotse was pinching him to wake him further. "It
doesn't apply, don't think about it!" he whispered almost
into Letlotse's ear, and then, "They've heard us. You'll be
punished. And me." There was a rustling at the far
end of the grass hut where the old men of the Mantwane,
the father *mophato*, sat round the glow of a small fire
listening, listening.

"Damn," said Letlotse, and then very quickly into
Isaac's face, "If we're caught we're caught. Tell me one
thing. Shall we kill Motswasele?"

"Yes," said Isaac, and then there were the dark
shadows of two old men standing above them.

"Who spoke?" one of them said in a hissing whisper.

184

The rest of the men lying on the floor flat out in a sleep of exhaustion barely moved or lifted an eyelid. After a moment Letlotse said, "I did, my father."

"And I," whispered Isaac. Down came the cane on their bare shoulders. Isaac wondered if it was his special father Dithapo. Whoever it was hit hard twice, three times. Both Letlotse and Isaac turned on to their faces where they could bite their hands and so appear not even to wince. It felt as if the third cut coming across the other two had drawn blood. Someone stooped and rubbed something roughly on to this; it hurt more than the cane. They went away; in the dark Letlotse's hand reached out and clutched Isaac's. The two live communicating hands kept tight hold of one another even when the two brains had fallen again into exhaustion and blankness.

Another day of early rising and no food until they had tracked and hunted it down, the younger *mophato* running. Letlotse had to lead, and he found his back was unaccountably sore. Surely three strokes of a cane wouldn't do that? Nor did he find himself able to eat much when at last the buck was half roasted and they were allowed to drink a little. By now both of them were beginning to notice a bit of pain in their armpits as well. One of the group was a young man who worked in the Mission Hospital as a dresser; he was another far-out royal cousin. He took care not to be overheard, but while the meat was being eaten there was always a good deal of noise which covered everything. "What happened?" he said with a glance at Letlotse's back.

"Punished for talking," said Letlotse.

"Looks more like a bad sting to me. Or an abscess coming. Watch it, Letlotse."

"Can't watch it," said Letlotse.

"I will," said the young man.

"Look at Isaac's too," said Letlotse. He wasn't feeling at all well, and this was odd, for the tough five days before had at least made him feel marvellously alive and well. So alive that all his thoughts had started stirring in him, not only to quick learning of the songs and riddles, but reaching out everywhere, back to the books he had read and half read in England, and so it came that he had to speak to the only one who was likely to share his knowledge and his questions. Now he felt sick and shivery, and it looked very much as if Isaac was feeling the same. The whole thing was ridiculous anyhow —raising a regiment! Why had he agreed to this? Looking back at himself at lectures, in the Underground, in the Red Square in Moscow, at British Council At Homes, he couldn't imagine he was even the same person. But he supposed he was. Oh, he knew he shouldn't have agreed, he should have fought against custom! Now— it served him right. Oh, God, how his back hurt, and under his arms, and horrible achings shooting out all over him!

Isaac exhausted, dropped asleep, but had a dreadful dream in which the police had got him, were working their will on him, and he woke to find himself in the same pain and cried out with surprise and hurt before he was properly awake. A minute afterwards there was someone beside him; was he to be punished again? He held his fist ready to bite on. But the man whispered, "It is your father, Dithapo. There is something wrong. I think someone put bad medicine into your cut. And Letlotse's." Isaac felt a hand on his back, kind, but it made him wince; he could tell without looking there was a great lump out of which the pain was streaming; he held hard on to Dithapo's knees. "There were two who were trying to catch Letlotse all the time. Both of you if they could. We have got them. It was treason to the Mantwane, your fathers. And treason to the prince. Come!"

He was helped on to his feet, and realised that he was in a fever, that no bit of him felt as it should. He tried to speak, but Dithapo hushed him while they stumbled over to the fire; someone had thrown on some dry sticks so that it gave a bright light. A few of the older men were standing whispering to one another. Isaac wished desperately that Josh was there; somehow he had got it into his head that he was in some kind of political situation, that the right answers would have to be given and he himself was too tired and muddled with pain. Then he saw Letlotse held up by two of the father group in the same state as himself. Someone brought a half gourd of water and held it up for him, but he had the idea he must not drink and shook his head. "No," said Dithapo, "you are given leave—drink!"

The cousin who was a dresser at the hospital, George Senyele, was examining Letlotse who was lying at the far side of the fire as limp as a dead snake, his long arms flopping back as they were moved, his eyes half shut, only a slit of white showing. George Senyele came over to Isaac, and he was looking desperately worried, tears hanging in his eyes. Why, thought Isaac dizzily, we

187

can only die and what of it? And then he remembered Tselane and how he was going back to her and suddenly came more awake. George Senyele was pressing on his armpits and groins asking if it hurt, as indeed it did. He fell into pain and woke to hear Dithapo say, "Will they live?" and then the answer coming not from George Senyele, but from a man who was tied up on the floor wrists to ankles, doubled up. "They will not live," the man said, "but Motswasele the Chief will live and so will his friends. And it will be slow death to those that hurt his friends."

Dithapo stood over the man, "What did you put in the medicine?" The man said nothing. Dithapo began to work a knife blade into the man's face. "What was it? What was it?" Lepedi, the leader of the Mantwane, was twisting the man's ears slowly. He was perhaps not very bright, but this was something he could understand.

The man simply said, "I warn you not to do this, Lepedi and Dithapo. It will be so much the worse for you when Letlotse is dead."

Then George Senyele said, "It doesn't matter what filth was put in the medicine. There is only one chance now. I go to the hospital and get penicillin."

"Will they give it to you?"

"I shall take it. It will still be night. If I wait it will not be given to me in time. Now I want three to run with me."

By this time more and more of the Matsosa were awake, and had come to listen. Immediately half a dozen came forward. George Senyele chose three, flicking his eyes at them. All drank a little water. The rules meant

188

nothing now. Dithapo said, "Tell James. Get Seneo. Get the car."

"Horses," said George Senyele, and then to one of the older men, "Your little gun," and belted the revolver which was handed to him with no question. Then all four started out of the shelter into the night at a quick trot.

Letlotse had come to a little and was drinking gulps of water. "What happened?" he whispered, seeing a face upside down above him, its eyes blurred with tears, feeling himself supported by hands that kept clear of the sorest part of his back. The chirring of the grasshoppers hurt his mind; he was not too certain where he was.

Lepedi, the leader, said, "George Senyele has run for European medicine. Our chief must have courage, all will be well."

"I took too long making up my mind to kill Motswasele," whispered Letlotse with a ghost of a smile; it was expected of him that he should show courage.

"That will be done," said Dithapo, "and we shall see the leopard skin on our right chief's shoulders yet."

They were trying to build him up, and he was accepting it, was being carried along towards being chief. If he lived. But he did not entirely think he would live, and the pain and confusion was such by now that he could not even feel anger or resentment at the prospect of dying and never even taking his exams.

Isaac began to see shapes behind the people who were holding him, and could be presumed to be real. Once he saw Tselane pass and not notice him, and he cried out

189

to her. But often they were police shapes and they looked at him sideways smiling as though to say he would be theirs soon. Was that then hell? Was he going there? He tried to ask this of Dithapo, his father, but the words muddled themselves and jumbled in his mouth. Dithapo wiped his face and body with a damp cloth that cooled a little the throbbing that was going on inside him like a generator out of control. He heard whispering, and after a time a mud poultice was put on to his back, but did not seem to help. He heard dimly that they were whispering old praise words at Letlotse, the chief, the young leopard who would yet leap on his enemies. But how would Letlotse like that?

George Senyele and his friends trotted through the night, keeping a course on the stars; there was a three-quarter moon, enough to see by. They knew there were two deep, and one less deep dry water courses between them and Ditlabeng. They crossed the first one throwing stones ahead of them to scare any snakes there might be out of the close, prickly undercover. It was going to take them almost all night; they said nothing, only occasionally touched one another on the narrow cattle paths. All the time they kept a lookout for hobbled horses which were often left out, at any rate near houses; though no animals big enough to attack them were likely to be about. George himself was a believing Christian, his friends less so, but when he occasionally prayed aloud they listened and seemed to feel refreshed. Then they crossed the second water course, and George began to visualise the store at the hospital and the locked cupboard. Everything would have to be broken into, perhaps the watchman and the night nurse forcibly held. He would lose his job of course; the Mission doctor wouldn't possibly understand, would think he should have been asked. But there was no time. No time. He had seen it done often enough, had prepared the syringes. Perhaps if the sick ones were cured he might be taken back to the hospital. But not if they died. And he thought they looked very ill. Also, whatever happened, there would be Motswasele's anger. He patted the revolver comfortingly, not that he had ever fired one.

They came to the third ravine, and now there was an occasional cock-crow showing that dawn was not too far off. Here they found two hobbled horses with rope bridles. George took one, a friend—the best rider—the second, the other two ran quicker. After ten minutes they changed over: it certainly got them over the ground, though not so fast as if they'd had saddles. By now they were all very tired, but had their second wind. Now George turned off towards the hospital, which stood a little way from the main village, with its own compound where there were always a few flowers and trees. They tied the horses and went on cautiously. George led the way along the veranda passage, past the ward doors, keeping an eye open for the watchman. The store-room was locked, the windows shut; either way there would be a noise. But he knew it was not a very thick door. All four got a good place for a shoulder and gave one sharp push, and the door gave from round the lock. They had decided that two of them would tackle the watchman who was an oldish man and unarmed except with a stick, frightening off the occasional marauding boy by his mere presence. They would hold him down and explain why they had come; if he did not agree, gag and tie him.

George knew where the big electric torch was and turned it on to the drug cupboard—just a chance. No, it was locked. Nothing on the desk; key drawer locked too. Best chance to prise open the drug cupboard. It was terrible to do this, against all he had been taught and taken in so eagerly with his loyalties to the Mission Hospital. It was as bad as betraying his chief. No, not as bad as it would have been not to help Letlotse, the leader of his *mophato*. He had to do it. He gritted his teeth and went on carefully, working first with a wire and knife blade, and then a broken bone-chisel that had been left on the table for mending. He worked so intently and fiercely that he didn't even hear his comrades of Matsosa seize the night watchman, stuffing a shirt in his mouth, explaining what they had come for, and then when he nodded vigorously taking out the shirt. "Tie me up," the night watchman whispered, "they must see I have done my duty."

That was fair enough. They did it and left him on the ground in a reasonably comfortable position. They got into the store in time to see the door of the drug cupboard swinging ajar. George whispered to them, and they went off to try and find saddles for the horses. The other one held the torch. George took two syringes, needles, surgical spirit, cotton wool, and a tin box of the precious ampoules of penicillin, twenty million units, enough for two people for five days. If they lived. One million units in each ampoule. Then he took a lancet and a tube

192

of antibiotic ointment. He put the whole thing inside his shirt. As they tip-toed along the corridor, past the tied up watchman who whispered good luck to them, the night nurse opened the door of the ward, scared looking. Luckily it was another cousin, George's kin sister; he told her quickly what had happened and left her to make up a story.

The horses were just being saddled in the beginnings of dawn. Whose saddles? Bad and broken ones, but better than nothing. George didn't even know whose horses. When the owner found out he would perhaps be proud. All was moving to a climax. He told the two who had got the saddles to run to James's house, tell him and Seneo, try to give them a direction; the car might even by daylight cross the first ravine lower down, meanwhile he would ride.

By the time they got to the first ravine it was light; they led the horses down the difficult path and across, then mounted again; they could trot most of the time, sometimes even canter, but they could not possibly gallop without proper bridles. It was getting hot. The broken piece in his saddle was beginning to run into George's leg; he couldn't do anything about it without stopping. The second ravine. The third. And at last they sighted the grass hut and George became intensely anxious. If it had all been for nothing—— The others came running out. "Is he alive?"

"Yes, both, but sick men." They held the horses while George Senyele dismounted, went over and knelt by Letlotse, rubbed a clean place on his skin with surgical spirit, broke the ampoule, filled the syringe and plunged it into the gluteal muscles. As the stuff went in he prayed. He did the same thing for Isaac. Then he went back to Letlotse, looked at his back and pressed on the place, finally decided to lance. He had done this often enough himself to out-patients. "This will hurt," he said, "and I must have it steady for the cut. Hold him down." But Letlotse murmured, "Don't hold me. I can keep still." Only when it came to lancing Isaac they had to hold him still because he had got it into his head that George had something to do with the police. At the end of it all the stuff that came out was wiped up with cotton wool and very carefully put into the heart of the fire. It must have been bad medicine right enough, and George was not grudged any of the precious water to wash his hands over and over. After that he saw to boiling up his things over the fire, and then, blindly tired, fell asleep beside Letlotse, his cousin.

Chapter XIX

AFTER THE NIGHT OF WATCHING and misery many had fallen asleep, exhausted in their hearts, sprawled out as they had fallen on their backs or faces. Those who watched over the sick men spoke low. But Letlotse reacted better and more quickly to the penicillin than had been possible to hope. By the time George Senyele woke, well into the afternoon, the swellings in his armpits and groin were softer and less painful; he seemed to be in less of a fever. But Isaac looked as if there had been little change. Perhaps it was not going to work with him; yet probably the infecting organism was the same. George wished he had brought a thermometer, but at the same time thought that his hands were as well aware of fever coming and going as the little silver thread under the glass. He decided to give them both a second dose. At least they were having no symptoms which could make him think that the stuff was harmful. Each of them in turn was turned over by friendly hands, and the other buttock got its million units. George rubbed over them softly to ease it in. Isaac moaned a little, but Letlotse managed a little joke.

Some of the rest of the *mophato* had gone to hunt, but two had been sent to the nearest cattle post to get some milk. They must manage this without saying a word about what had happened. Discipline had broken up, and yet the Matsosa had never felt themselves so fully at one. The two evil ones from the older group were still tied, but those who were frightened of what might happen had given them water. Then out of the hot breath of the afternoon a runner came. He was the one of George's comrades who had been sent to James Mookami's house. He was gasping and tired, but had made a last minute sprint. He saw that Letlotse was alive, had his eyes open, was watching him, flung himself down in front of him and gasped, "Motswasele is dead!" And then he put his head against Letlotse's bare feet. He was the chief.

Letlotse looked round slowly. It was not now for him to speak. It was for his fathers and uncles, for the Mantwane to greet him; if they chose to. As they did, coming forward one after another standing or kneeling, calling him by the ancient names and attributes. Lepedi was first, and longest, then the others. After a time he began to get very tired, his eyelids flickered; where pain had kept him awake, now its comparative absence was leaving him free to sleep. George signalled to them to let him be, and now the older men asked the runner for more news and more. "I saw him dead," the man said, "most certainly dead, and I ran before I was held for evidence. It was at James Mookami's house, and I do not know just what happened. It was about calling up his men for the mines, perhaps other things. I think they will come soon and tell you all." They gave him water and meat, and made him go through it again, telling everything he knew, trying to add it up into a story. But there were still big uncertainties.

Letlotse slept for a couple of hours, but it was still light when he woke. The first thing he said was, "Where is Isaac? Is he too coming out of the badness?"

George said, "I think he may be beginning to react to the penicillin, Letlotse, but he is still a very sick man."

"Will he live?"

"I cannot say yet."

"Bring him here," said Letlotse, "I have strength for two."

He drank a little milk while they carried Isaac over carefully, turning him to face Letlotse. Isaac moaned: his eyes were shut. "He does not know us," said George Senyele. "He is in a nightmare. Perhaps that was mixed in the bad medicine. He speaks names we do not know. He speaks of Manuel and much of Amos. If we could get him free of those names——"

"I will bring him clear of the nightmare," said Letlotse, and laid his hands on Isaac's shoulders and whispered, "Isaac, it is I, Letlotse. Your brother, Letlotse. I am the chief now, I am protecting you. Come into Letlotse's protection, Isaac. Come, I am the leopard, I can kill your enemies. Come, come, this is Letlotse holding you, Letlotse. Come to me, come to your chief, Isaac. Come to Letlotse." He spoke like this over and over in Tswana and English, and changed his hands so that one was on Isaac's forehead, the other over his heart. Everyone else was in a deep hush waiting and watching. Suddenly Isaac opened his eyes and looked at Letlotse as though searching for something; then recognition came and a very slight smile, a slight relaxing all over his body. There was a sound of indrawing breath, a murmur from all round, a purring movement of approval. Isaac's left hand, which was uppermost, wavered towards Letlotse. George helped him a little, and Letlotse took and held the groping fingers. George felt in the armpit for the swollen glands; yes, they were softer. Isaac was definitely beginning to react—to something.

As it became darker the two men both went to sleep, Letlotse still holding Isaac's hands in a loose grip. The fire was kept burning; there would be a reassuring light if either of them woke, and in it the presence of their friends to frighten away any badness. Some of the older men had gone back to teaching the songs and sayings to the Matsosa, so secure they were that the bad medicine had been conquered, and so certain they were also of the power and strengthening which God and his ancestors had given to the chief. But they did this quietly at the far end of the shelter.

The elders, especially those who were most closely related, had watched with great interest Letlotse's methods on Isaac. They spoke to one another softly behind the thin curtain of smoke from the fire; they spoke on and off through the night and into the dawn. "This is not something he learned while he was away." "Not English education." "No, it was put into him; it has been brought out by the need." "From whom does it come?" "I have heard it said that his mother's grandfather had also this power. He could have worked through Letlotse when Letlotse was himself open."

"Open and also strengthened. But it is now known to the old ones that he is chief and we are his people." "Who have made him what he has become." "The leopard has sprung and scattered his enemies." "See them now; they sleep like small children. It is at such times that strengthening can come." "Through dreams and also not through dreams." "They are having good dreams now, both of them. The spirits have been close to them." "We should give a new name to this Isaac." "Letlotse will say what name shall be given. It is his right." "Since he has taken him out of the jaws of the lion." "Let them breathe strength all night." It was fully light when they woke, Letlotse first yawning and stretching a little, moving his arms and legs like a live man, Isaac after him, weak and in pain but clearly himself. George Senyele hovered, uncertain about the next dose, feeling dreadfully his guilt of breaking in at the hospital, although he had prayed about it; but he could almost feel the anger of the doctor already overwhelming him. Yet his patients looked like recovering, certainly Letlotse, who was the one that mattered, probably the refugee. And perhaps, thought George, he matters too, because my chief seems to love him like a brother, and he is now my brother of the *mophato* and also, of course, because to God a refugee matters as much as a chief.

Letlotse said, "I could almost eat now. Is it allowed?"

"All is allowed, Chief," said Lepedi, kneeling in front of him. "Mantwane says to Matsosa that all is allowed."

"It is finished then?"

"For you to say on your own *mophato*. We think they

have learned much. Should go back strong, strongest of
all the tribe."

"They do not need to be beaten?"

"They have been beaten in your body, leader of the
spears."

"The milk should be boiled, boiled!" said George,
dancing about in a frenzy of responsibility. "To kill the
bad germs!"

"I shall never forget what I have learned, my fathers,
nor I think will my comrades." Letlotse raised himself
a little; the cut on his back was almost healed. One of
his *mophato*, a mine boy who had come back, was
fanning him with a bunch of leaves; another one killed
a fly that came near him. He looked across at Isaac,
"And he?"

"Two more injections to-day, to-morrow again," said
George. "Then who knows? And you, Letlotse, you,
I should say, Chief, I think you should have one more at
least, perhaps two. The—the septicaemia"—he had
remembered the word at last!—"must not be allowed to
return."

"There is no place for you to put it!" said Letlotse,
and rubbed himself behind in a way which made everyone
laugh. But George jabbed another million units in a
little lower down; Letlotse joked again, but then looked
across a little anxiously, "But Isaac will do?"

"Yes, I think," said George.

"You see," said Letlotse. "I could not have faced my
cousin Tselane otherwise. And besides—I think we need
Isaac." He took his hand. "Be very brave now, the
needle comes again!"

200

Dithapo came over and coughed and said very carefully so that attention should be paid to what he said. "Kgosi Letlotse, what is the name of that one now, that one that was snatched like a lamb out of the jaws of a lion?" Everybody had stopped talking, were now listening only. Letlotse realised that this was something important, and could take his time. And with one part of him he was thinking that in changing Isaac's name he would also break any bad magic which was still holding on to him, and also tie him into the Bamatsieng and in a sense into his own possession, and with the other part of his mind he was thinking what nonsense it all was, but in a friendly way since nothing but good was being done. At last he said, "His name shall be Koboatau."

Dithapo raised his voice, speaking to Isaac, "My son, your name now is Koboatau."

"My name is Koboatau, my father," repeated Isaac dazedly; he was still full of pains, and yet he knew he was somehow going to get well as surely as earlier on he had known he was going to die. He knew also what he had become with the new name, someone small who had been put into the skin of the great lion, so that now he was safe against his enemies.

"Leave your sickness with your old name, my son," said Dithapo, and turned back satisfied to Letlotse. He was now sitting up and eating slices of buck's liver grilled on the fire. Liver, thought George, is full of vitamins—or is it something else? But he mustn't eat too much—not yet. He caught Letlotse's eye and shook his head a little; sensible Letlotse stopped eating, drank some more of the boiled milk. There was a phrase the doctor used:

201

Vis medicatrix naturae. He had explained: the healing way of nature. Oh, the doctor. If only he had been able to stay on at school, take matric and learn Latin! He would have been able to face the doctor now.

The young man fanning with the leaves changed hands, but would not let any of the others take it over. Letlotse looked round and noticed something was not there. "And the two who made the bad medicine are where?"

"We judged them in Council," said Lepedi, the head of the Mantwane, "but it is for you to say if we were right."

Letlotse frowned. "You judged them?"

"We did not know, Kgosi, if you——"

"Would live. But I have lived. What did you do?"

"They are outside."

"Alive?"

"Yes. But judged to die. It is for you to tell us if we were right, leader of the war axes."

"Bring me to them." They lifted him carefully; he seemed to himself to be getting farther and farther from anything he had ever been or even thought of being; he felt their skins hot and slippery with sweat against his own. Would his university friends know him now? Would Kumar? They carried him half-sitting with arms under his thighs and shoulders. Outside the shelter the sun struck blazing. In a minute or two he came to where he could see. The two men were pegged down so that they could not move. It was a question whether insects or vultures would get them first. They might even attract the rare hyena. He was carried close and looked down at them. They did not ask for mercy; they kept their lips shut. Only they looked at him. But they were men he

202

had known, who had once been respected. He said to them, "You have been judged. It is death. But I can make it a quick death. Do you ask for mercy?"

Again neither of them spoke. But this time another man spoke, the half-brother of one of them, "I ask it, Chief, in their name. They have nothing now, only their pride. They cannot ask. So it is for me. And I thank you." He knelt in front of Letlotse and put his head to the ground.

Letlotse said, "Tell them that if their sons are proved innocent I shall not take their cattle. Has someone a revolver?" The man who had lent his to George Senyele took it out of the holster and held it muzzle-end to Letlotse. "I would do this if I were whole again, but my fingers have no strength yet. I am long enough in the sun." The men who were carrying him turned; he did not want to see the pegged-out ones again. After a minute there was a revolver shot and then another. The man who had accepted mercy on behalf of the condemned tried to speak to Letlotse to thank him again, and there were tears in his eyes, but Letlotse suddenly felt very tired, too tired to do more than move his head slightly. It was not going to be easy to be chief. If George wanted to give him another shot of penicillin that was all right by him.

He slept for a little. When he woke he said, "Bring me Koboatau." They carried him over and laid him beside Letlotse. "Better?" said Letlotse. Isaac-Koboatau reached out both his hands and murmured, "Yes." "That was not something that came into Mr. Marx," Letlotse said in English, grinning. Then he became aware that all round them in a solid circle his *mophato* was forming up and beginning to sing, beginning one of the great praise songs, and as they sang they began to dance in a close circle, their bodies smelling of sweat and wood smoke, moving from one shuffling foot to the other, the movements spreading upwards through their bodies, through their shoulders, their hands holding upright in the air the white peeled fighting sticks that danced with them, through the proud set of their necks into their heads, showing in their faces as delight, as utter happiness in the shape of their new chief, the leader of the Matsosa, even before he was leader of the Bamatsieng.

Chapter XX

IN THE HEAT AND STILLNESS there were small noises from far off, the rustlings of large birds moving among dry leaves and branches, hornbills and guinea fowl mostly. Little birds were stilled by the strike of the sun, would only move again in the evening. And that? No, perhaps only cattle moving or being driven far off. Letlotse was restless, more sore from the injections than anything, didn't want to have another, but George Senyele had insisted. Isaac-Koboatau was still very weak, but the fever was down and he was eating a little. Letlotse saw that some of the group were listening beyond the natural noises of the outside, what was it? Then he too picked it up, a car. After a bit it stopped, and then there were distant shouts. Several people went running down to where the car was.

Seneo was running ahead. She ran straight to Letlotse, knelt and took him in her arms. "My little, little brother," she cooed at him, "what would Father have said!"

"But I am alive!" said Letlotse, "and almost well."

"And Chief, after all. That isn't what you intended, Letlotse, my pet, my little leopard."

"Well, it happened. But you—Motswasele—I know nothing, nothing! How was he killed?" He watched her. "Seneo—my sister—what did he do to you?"

205

"Well, yes," she said low, her cheek against his, "he raped me. But it was worth it because he is dead. Besides, perhaps James—ah, Letlotse, my little one, do not be so troubled. All can be made new. We shall forget him. Do you want to hear it? Wait then till James comes."

James Mookami was coming at a sedate pace, discussing gravely and at length with the elders of the Mantwane, using with them certain forms of avoiding saying what should not be said. But Josh had been with them in the back of the car and he had run to Isaac, only limping a little, had half picked him up, was rubbing his head against Isaac and, "You do this with Josh not there!" he said. "Isaac, you old bloody fool!"

"Something I got to tell you, Josh, I'm not Isaac, not any more. I got a new name."

"How?"

"My chief gives it. Letlotse. I am called Koboatau now. I have been put into the lion's skin."

"That's not good, Isaac. Your name, your own name, that's a name of honour wherever there's fighting for freedom. You can't just lose that name!"

"I thought of that but it didn't seem to mean much against how I got this. You won't maybe think I'm telling true, Josh. I am. I was damn' near dead. He pulled me out of it himself. Letlotse, my chief. Funniest thing, first his father saves my life, then he does. But I was dying right enough and getting in among ghosts. Police ghosts catching at me, dragging me, putting the cuffs on like I was being dragged off to the cells and there they'd get me, do what they wanted—ah, Josh,
206

it was worse than anything ever happened, for I lost my courage. All gone." He held tight on to Josh and the memories of his fever bobbed their filthy heads out of his mind, and Josh murmured to him. Then he went on, "Then I began to hear Letlotse speaking, calling me out from the ghosts, putting me under protection. His protection. I began to be able to fight them a little, began to have a little courage. Seemed to me he was strong, so strong, clever and strong as a leopard, could keep back my ghosts, stick his claws in them. Stop me from going dead. That was what he did for me, Josh. But I know now he was only just out of death danger himself. First thing he does is to help me. Me, nothing. Giving me all the strength of his own body. So I take the new name he gives me. Take anything from him, don't guard myself. I'm his, Josh."

"You can't say that," said Josh gently and firmly. "You belong to Africa, not to any one man, even your chief, even the head of your regiment. Even this Letlotse. Africa, Isaac, Africa, all this that we haven't seen but we know it's there once we get free. Africa." But Isaac did not brighten at the old magic word. Josh went on anxiously, "I think all the same our Letlotse is a part of Africa that we never knew, we in the Republic, we city guys. We're lucky to have him for our new chief, but me, I didn't think he'd turn out like that. Seems he's changed in eight days."

"All of us have changed. All in the Matsosa."

Josh looked at him curiously, "So that's how it seems to you, Isaac. No, I can't get to saying this new name. Doesn't mean a thing to me. You're thinking purely tribal. Gone back, back. One day I think you wake up." He took his friend's hand and swung it gently. noticing how weak he still was.

Isaac-Koboatau was suddenly aware of something. "Bandage round your leg, Josh—what is it?"

"Doctored rifles," said Josh and grinned, "but don't work on me. Aimed to kill, but bullet goes through my leg, just nicks the muscle. Nothing. Look, Isaac, here is James. We shall hear all well told. Lean up against me, Isaac, or whatever you say you are."

James Mookami had now greeted his cousin Letlotse in the formal terms that were expected by all who had gathered to listen to him. Letlotse was impatient to hear. He kept hold of Seneo's hand, every now and then squeezing it violently. Then James began, "Motswasele had made his evil plans. He thought, you see, that you were certainly dead, but that is not a sensible thing when one deals with a strong young leopard."

"No!" said the Matsosa and the Mantwane, "that was folly! The leopard was strong. Was cunning. As quickfire a destroyer. His claws were knives. The leopard has a body of strength!"

"So he came to my house with the demand that the Magwasa, my regiment, should all go off to the mines, should pay more taxes. He accused us of not paying taxes, had made out a false tax book. Those in the office had been made so afraid that they had done this."

"That they must pay for," Dithapo said, "and heavily!"

"They have paid," said James grimly. "My men were ready to fight, most of them, yet we had not expected it would come to this. We had thought no, these days have passed. And there was fear of the doctored rifles. I said to Motswasele to come into the house, we would talk it over. Yes, Letlotse, I too tried to be reasonable, modern, all that. He came, but also some of his men came, all armed. We talked for a few minutes, I tried to argue, he said you were dead, he was no longer Regent but full Chief. Suddenly his men got me, tied a towel across my mouth, twisted my hands behind my back, tied me into a chair. Tight. It was not nice, that. No." He shook his head.

"And Seneo, what were you doing?" Letlotse asked low.

"I had just time to take certain tablets out of my bag, sleeping tablets, told Aunt Sarah to get brandy, put them in. Then he was on to me. That was not nice either. I fought him very hard, but he was strong, he began to tear off my clothes. James could see this, see through into the room."

"They put me," said James, "where I was made to see. And Motswasele laughed and I wished very much to kill him. Seneo screamed very much, and he slapped her across the mouth. The men who had tied me also wanted to see but Motswasele ordered them out. That, thank God, was his mistake, but he thought he was master. Then my mother runs in and she carries glasses of brandy and cries to Motswasele to stop, have mercy. She puts the brandy down on the table and tries to pull him off your sister, but all he does is to shove her back so that she falls against the wall, and then he reaches out a hand for the brandy and drinks."

"But it did not work?" Letlotse asked painfully.

"Not quick enough," said Seneo low, "but—it could perhaps have been worse. He fell out of me, off me, and his mouth was open and he was snoring, and my Aunt Sarah put a cushion over his mouth and sat on it to hold it down. Then I loosed James, cut him loose with the big scissors. He had been tied so tight that at first he could not stand on his feet; I had to rub them. Then we all held the cushion down so that we should share what had to be done. I had thought he might struggle but he did not. It was like killing a dead man. It was a pity we could not hurt him."

"Then," said James, "I ran out and shouted to the Magwasa that Motswasele was dead and we must fight. So there was a small fight, but most of Motswasele's *mophato* were too frightened. They had thought he was strong, would live for ever, do whatever he chose, lead them always to victory. I took two of them in, Notshe and Disele, showed them the body, showed them Seneo with her clothes torn and weeping much."

"It was only—reaction," said Seneo in English, and then she turned her head away from those who were looking at her, and after a time she began to cry. She had no handkerchief, but George Senyele passed her a piece of cotton wool and she dabbed her eyes.

"All thought I had killed Motswasele. I wished it had been so. I wished my eyes had not been made to see what they had seen: the shaming of your sister. The fighting stopped, a few hurt, nobody killed; most had fought with sticks, not rifles. But one of them had known that Motswasele had a special hate against

Josh; he fired. But the doctoring had gone out of the rifle!"

"When Motswasele died," said the head of the Mantwane.

"Then two things happened. First the D.C. came with the police and the doctor and a nurse from the hospital who spoke to Seneo and my mother. The doctor also very angry about what had been done at the hospital. Indeed his anger was such that he paid little attention to the body of Motswasele. In fact, I do not think anything will be said about what was in the brandy, the —the——"

"Phenobarbiturates," said Seneo in precise English. George nodded.

"But much was being said by everyone, and there was great bustle and shouting and the police making arrests, and then protests and the arrested one freed, and the doctor puts on dressings, sends wounded to the hospital, but all the time talking, talking about his robbery."

"What did he say?" asked George, "has he been told it was me?"

"Your friend came up to me, whispered. That was the second thing that happened," James said. "I had quick thoughts. First thought I should tell the doctor at once, then thought, no, wait. Then I told your friend to hurry back, since otherwise he might be held for evidence on this matter of the hospital. Meanwhile the D.C. was in a great fluster and awkwardness since so much had suddenly changed and most of all his own idea of Motswasele as an English gentleman. I wished very much that the old D.C. were there; he would have been less surprised. After a long time and much arresting and un-arresting, it was said that Letlotse must be found at once. Now I knew from your comrade, George, whereabouts the Matsosa was camped, but by now it was getting late, and I did not like so much to drive across land without roads after dark, so I said I must wait until the morning. Meanwhile the D.C. had first arrested my mother, who had told them very fiercely that it was she who had held the cushion over Motswasele's head, but then said she could be let out on bail, and there was much talk and much noise and the fool Dikgang has entirely run away, and my cousin, your sister, was most unhappy, although the wicked one was dead, so that no man could point a finger at her or her family."

He stopped and looked about him. All the time people had been making noises of encouragement and excitement, of anger and pity, of hate and mockery and relief. But Letlotse was looking terribly tired and drawn about the face. James Mookami turned to the rest. "There is more to tell, my fathers and brothers. But our chief must rest and get strength for killing. There are still snakes in the bushes." All the men moved out of the shelter with him and found patches of shade here and there, rocks and bushes, near enough to him for question and answer. Only Josh was left holding Isaac-Koboatau against his knees, his head down whispering to him.

Letlotse said low to Seneo, "And then?"

"So you think there was a then, little brother," said Seneo and raised her head. Tears dropped out of her splendid eyes, but in a little she smiled. "You are right. We know one another too well, you and I." She held a half gourd of boiled milk to his mouth, and when he had drunk it she began to speak in English, half to him and half to herself. "All the night I was crying, and not sleeping at all. I was altogether full of shame and anger, the thought that I could have fought better, above all the thought that James had seen, been made to see. I think he has forgotten, indeed I hope he has, but once while it was happening he yelled with his own pain like a beast. Through the towel over his mouth. Besides, I had been hurt and bruised in all the parts where a woman can be hurt most. Plenty to make me cry, Letlotse. Then James was kneeling beside me and he too was crying, though perhaps that also is something he has forgotten. He said my name many times, and he wiped my tears with his fingers until at last I said his name. Then he said to me, "I have been mad inside since I saw that being done to you. I have wild beasts clawing inside me." "I too," I said, and then I whispered to him that I knew the pain would go, but perhaps Motswasele had left a shameful thing inside me and this was the worst. James said, "But if one comes stronger than he—for he had already death in him—would that not put out the fear and the shame, beautiful daughter of our house?" And then it seemed to me that this was perhaps the healing that I needed, and I said, "One that is welcome may go through the innermost doors of a house." So James came on to the bed beside me and he was gentle, gentle. You do not mind that I speak of this, Letlotse?"

"No," said Letlotse, making an effort because he was a little tired and some way torn with pity for his sister who had always been the strong one, and also feeling

213

in two minds about James, yet knowing that James had been right about this. "I am glad it was like that."

"It was so strange that he did what the other had done and that it was altogether different. I hope it has done for me what he said it would. Also I think if it had not been done James would have been wounded in his mind for ever. In the end James and I slept in each other's arms with healing coming to us, and Aunt Sarah brought coffee in the morning, and then we got the car out and drove. And poor Aunt Sarah is, I suppose, still half arrested for murder!"

George Senyele came quietly and said, "I think he should have his second injection. What do you think yourself? This will be six million units of penicillin. He is reacting well."

"No rash? Nothing?"

"I do not think so. Perhaps you should look, too, Seneo. You will have more knowledge than mine."

"Better give him the full five days."

"Oh, no!" said Letlotse.

"But yes," said Seneo, "and I have brought some sweets, very plain, for a sick boy. If you are good, my little Chief, you shall have one to suck while George jabs you, and your friend shall have one too."

214

Chapter XXI

IT WAS DECIDED that Letlotse's Installation should take place in three weeks. It would take him that time to get well. All had been explained to the doctor, money paid for a new cupboard and new door. But naturally the doctor had to take over the patients, and for the sake of his own dignity give them treatment of a different kind, although after being scolded George Senyele was congratulated. A thing had also begun to take shape in George's head, that he might start education again, and perhaps in many years himself become a doctor. Letlotse had said he would pay.

There were also many head people from the Government who came in white uniforms and large cars, and there was much talk. And after a little, the Bamatsieng were aware that the old District Commissioner had come back and that he was in and out of James Mookami's house and seeing Letlotse. There was also talk of marriage between James Mookami and Seneo. Those who knew what Motswasele had done held their tongues. It seemed that no more would be said about the murder charge against Sarah.

Dikgang crept back into Ditlabeng like a beaten dog, with many people saying that he had nothing at all to do with any of it, had broken with Motswasele, but other people waiting to see him thrown down. Letlotse sent for him, and Dikgang immediately confessed only too much; it was like someone being sick after over-eating; at last Letlotse stopped him in the middle of a sentence, said he would hear no more. Not that Dikgang had done anything except talk. Now he would certainly talk the other way. For the moment, Letlotse decided, this Dikgang had better be left in Legco. The man could just as well be his mouthpiece as Motswasele's. And he thought it would look well—for the moment. The change would come at some time which he would decide himself, and which might be a surprise for Dikgang.

As soon as he was well enough, Letlotse went down to Kgotla every morning to listen to the doing of justice. All deferred to him, asked for his opinion; but as was proper he said that he followed the advice of his fathers. Everyone helped him and told him of past things which he ought to be aware of so as to appear knowledgeable. Kuate, for instance, told him about Rasemonje and the Angolans so that when Rasemonje himself appeared in Kgotla with a story about taxes which would otherwise have been very confusing, Letlotse was able to praise him and find a suitable gift for him. Those who had supported Motswasele had either gone away or become very repentant. Two were handed over to the British courts. They could be charged with nice strong crimes under British law which would keep them in prison for a long time during which they could be made powerless. Several were heavily fined and some of the younger ones who could have been implicated in murder and oppression but had perhaps been constrained by their elders were beaten in Kgotla. The old great-uncle fussed around demonstrating his loyalty and Letlotse had to be very polite since he was two generations back. Letlamma was as bad, tried to give presents or recommend wives or warn Letlotse against other people.

There was one odd thing which Letlotse, when he had time, noticed about himself. Among the men in Kgotla were, naturally, his fathers of the Mantwane including several who had done various unpleasant and undignified things to him. Men who had hurt him. And yet he had no shadow of feeling of resentment against them; it was not they as individuals who had done what had been done. Both he and they had been part of a pattern which had been fulfilled.

Sometimes he thought, this is of course nonsense, and half tried to break away. But everything was too strong for him. And when he went back to his Aunt Sarah's house the family atmosphere caught at him until he no longer even disliked the photographs; they were all part of the same thing. Various other families produced suitable candidates for marriage, but nobody Letlotse fancied. And in the middle of it all, he suddenly remembered that he ought to send a cable to his tutor: "Regret unable return. Being installed Chief. Writing." But the days went by and he didn't write.

Three weeks before the installation would give time for Ditlabeng to be cleaned up, the fat cattle to be chosen and driven in, and for all the invitations to be decided on and sent out. Letlotse and the elders had several sessions with the tribal treasurer, trying to disentangle public from private monies, since it seemed that Motswasele

217

had dipped into the treasury. The treasurer was not a bad man himself, but he had been frightened; it was those who had frightened him who were due for punishment. At last the whole tangle was brought into Kgotla; there was much talk; everyone seemed to want to speak. Letlotse got furiously bored and tired. Suddenly it all broke up in the shouting of their own tribal word, when it had been decided on to confiscate all Motswasele's goods and put them at Prince Letlotse's disposal.

He had not quite expected this, had thought that it would all drag on, that there would be claimants. But perhaps they did not care to speak. He had to say something suddenly, and what he said was that with the advice and encouragement of his elders, he would found a secondary school. In his present formal position as heir, it was proper that he should only speak shortly and modestly; he wondered if there was really enough money for this project, but above all he was saying to himself that if it came off, he might find a few people to talk to —he might even teach there himself, a good excuse for not going to Kgotla every day—and suddenly he thought, here is something I can tell my tutor and be proud of it! And indeed the next day he actually got down to writing a letter.

Everyone congratulated him on his decision. Now with the secondary school the Bamatsieng would be as good as the Bakgatla, even as good as the big Bamangwato with Moeng College! Letlotse was quite sure that there would not be enough money for a school the size of Moeng College, but he did not say so. Perhaps more money would come. And then he thought I shall also write to Kumar. And perhaps—no, Patsy wouldn't be interested, but the other—if only he could get her out to his Installation! But no, no, what would she think of him, wearing a great savage leopard skin and carrying an assegai and a kerrie! But when the new school was opened then he would wear his good London suit, the expensive one that Seneo had scolded him about. And make a speech. He would not even be allowed to make a speech at his Installation. He would just have to listen to the elders all over again!

Kuate and Josh went over to Craigs to tell Tselane what had happened, to help her to pack and come back. All was well there, but the elder boy Jim became more and more gloomy, and even made a half-hearted effort not to come with them. Josh found out that this was because Jim was hoping to move on into a secondary school; it was not certain, but there was a possibility that the Mission school at Craigs might have taken him; going back to tribal country looked like it was ending his education. He whispered in English to Josh, "They have been good to me, my new mummy and daddy; but they don't have the money to send me to boarding school. I know that. Looks like I've got to give it up. My education: what I wanted."

Josh answered carefully, "Could be, things might be better for them now. The new chief——"

"What good a new chief to me?"

"More than you think, maybe," said Josh. "Might one day be secondary school at Ditlabeng. Now plenty of fun. Plenty to eat, your mummy a big lady here. Everything coming all right, Jim."

And indeed it was fun. Indeed it was feasting! Best of all for the Matsosa, the lucky ones, the chief's regiment. It was close and singing and joy and excitement. It was the happy ending now to go on for ever. Everything done or imagined had value beyond itself. Everything was shared. Eyes spoke to eyes, hands to hands. In the evening Letlotse went down from James's house and danced and sang with the Matsosa. Songs and dances all had layer upon layer of hidden meanings, uncoiling and weaving in again among the close comradeship of bodies, the thudding of feet, the delight and laughter. From the edges of the dancing, the women cried in encouragement to them, tongue-shrilling and sometimes dancing among themselves to the same beat. Or a man would run out of the crowd and shout a rapid and intense, a manic praise verse, at Prince Letlotse, who stood and received it smiling as if it were a garland. And perhaps their praises were also incitements to anger, perhaps they were a kind of hate which would burst on the chief and dissipate itself as a wave bursting into spray against a hard rock.

During the heat and dust of the day Letlotse worried and fussed about the arrangements, the invitations, the food, the leopard skin, the order of speeches, what the Mission should be allowed to do. But at night all was healed again in the dancing and he slept late and awoke stronger. But Isaac-Koboatau was taking his time getting well, even now that Tselane was nursing him. The doctor had taken him into the hospital for three days and given him a different treatment because the place on his back did not heal as it should. It was odd to be treated as someone of importance by the Mission people. He wondered whether if they had known what he had been doing before he came to Ditlabeng, they would have been the same.

But once the place had healed up and he had felt better, during the last week, he too sang and danced with his initiation comrades, and it was only afterwards that he felt tired, only afterwards that he said to himself, what am I doing? Why am I doing it? Who am I? And gradually began to think of himself again as Isaac. The others all called him by his new name Koboatau, laughed in an embarrassed way if they forgot. Tselane took his new name seriously, and happily, cooing over it, and made the boys address him by it, formally and with increased respect. She was back in her old house; at first it had been bare. Motswasele's men had taken everything, but gradually and quietly almost all the things came back including the record player and most of the records. But not her mother. Jim and Moses found that she was now a person of some consequence, only they were still puzzled about their daddy. Just what was he? People treated him respectfully, as of course they did. But where did he fit in? It didn't really matter. They would know some time. Then one day Letlotse, coming back from Kgotla to James's house, picked Isaac-Koboatau up from the roadside where he was sitting in the dust suddenly overwhelmed with the tiredness that still got him now and then. James was driving. "Shall I leave him at Tselane's house?" he asked, but Letlotse said, "No, bring him back, I have not spoken to him for days." And leaned over from the front seat to look at Isaac slumped bonelessly and small looking in the back.

Josh came over inquiringly. He was still living in the men's rondavel, but he had asked for and been given a piece of land to cultivate and had acquired a yoke of oxen, always a beginning. But Letlotse shook his head, "No, I want Isaac," and sat down with him on the bench in the long shadow of the house; it was getting on for evening. "Are you too tired to talk?" he asked, speaking in English.

Isaac shook himself, "No, Kgosi," he said, "what is biting you now?"

"You are the one that can see that I am being bitten," said Letlotse, "Look, Isaac—or which name would you rather be?"

"It is for you to say," said Isaac. "I am yours."

"Nonsense," said Letlotse, "you must not say such things, Isaac—it—it shocks me. I shall call you Isaac again because that name has nothing to do with me, and really I want your help."

Isaac looked round and he was seeing Letlotse suddenly, not as the chief, the leader of the Matsosa, the man who had taken him in his two hands out of the pit of death, but as someone younger than himself and troubled, the kind of young man who comes into politics perhaps out of a mission school with all his old assumptions and values cracking under him and the new ones not yet found. "Is it difficult, then," said Isaac, "becoming Chief of the Bamatsieng?"

"Yes," said Letlotse, "very difficult. And I have had to give up much. I wanted to finish my education,

222

Isaac. I—I liked being educated, though I was lazy sometimes. I would have liked to get a degree, very much indeed. Now I have had to go back in time. They made this happen when I raised the Magwasa; you too, you went back in time. I have to go back to all this at my Installation, to the leopard skin and the assegai, but I can only do it with half of me. The other half wants to be civilised."

"It is possible to be a chief and civilised. I think, for instance, of Khama. He was of his time, but he had great ideas. But for him, perhaps our country would have been given away, given to Rhodes and the adventurers. If that happened, we of the Batswana would have been a bit of Rhodesia, perhaps even a bit of the Republic. But Khama stopped it."

"I am not that sort of person. I am not, so to say, a heavyweight. All the same, I would like to do good. But I also want a little freedom, not to be always tied by the old men, by precedents, by this thick smothering blanket of past!"

"You did not punish the sons of the two men who tried to kill us. Although many wanted you to do it. That, I think, was civilised, Letlotse."

"It was not civilised. It was only clever," Letlotse giggled. "If I had punished them, they would have told the British Government what had happened to their fathers. Then all would have been dragged up in the High Court at Lobatsi, and perhaps we would all have been accused of murder and one of us might have been hanged as an example to the rest. Me, I think. It would have been more democratic. Now it is a secret that will be kept among the Bamatsieng."

"For ever?"

"What is ever? For long enough. If anything is said, first it will be denied. There will be no evidence. The hyenas will have taken even the thigh bones. Also, if anything were to be said, it will be known that something not nice will happen to that one who spoke." And suddenly he showed his teeth, shining like a lion's.

I would have been afraid once, Isaac thought, a little afraid. Now I am not. He said gently and lightly, "I am sure you could be just like your cousin Motswasele, if you choose. But something stops you choosing. What? Your white education?"

Letlotse's mouth and eyes became gentle again. He said, "Perhaps you are right, Isaac. When those men whom I did not punish knelt in front of me I felt stupid. Half of me said one thing, half another. It is, I think, not so good that one man should kneel in front of another, waiting to be punished."

"Others in Kgotla thought it was good. They thought it fitting. Perhaps the young men wanted to kneel themselves. They were saying to themselves, we belong entirely to the Chief of the Bamatsieng."

"As you said to yourself."

"As I said to myself." Isaac lifted his eyes to Letlotse and smiled, and suddenly Letlotse knew why Tselane had so much wanted to marry him. "Do not be anxious, Letlotse. This will not last. It is because of what has happened, because there was a bad chief whom they feared and now they have one they can love, one whom

224

they hope will be wholly good. I am sure you will soon do something bad, Letlotse."

Letlotse smacked him lightly. "No doubt I shall spear and eat one of the elders. But it is frightening now. It was most frightening when you, who are a political, gave yourself up to me. But though now you have escaped, Isaac, now I have chased you away and you do not belong to me any more, do you still like me?"

"More," said Isaac, "I accept you as my Chief. Remember there was a time when I thought that all this about tribes and chiefs was nonsense, was wrong, was taking us back into the bad past, as surely as Verwoerd and Vorster would put us there. I thought a tribe was utterly against progress. Against freedom and democracy. As they try to make them in the Republic. In the Bantustans. I thought it was another kind of slavery."

"And now you think——?" said Letlotse softly.

Isaac's hand gripped the edge of the bench; the sun was almost down now and in the longer, softer shadow that stretched right across the *lapa*, you could see the small pale flames of the stick fire that shows there is life in the house. "What I think now is harder to say," said Isaac. "Because I do not believe it has been said before. But it could be that our tribes are the kind of coming together, the kind of society, which we all want in our hearts. Not always, perhaps, but now, this month, among your people, the Bamatsieng, who are my people also, while every man and woman is in a common purpose. And the purpose is you, Letlotse, you, the heir, the chosen one. And you have to act so that this common purpose is worth the whole of life."

Letlotse made a face; for a moment he was tired and angry and above all impatient. "Yes. I am their sacrifice. I am their ox. I am not free any longer. If I was a political leader at least I could go away to conferences and enjoy myself. I could make policies and change them. Now—it is not enough to have praises shouted at one! I am tired hearing them."

"Yes," said Isaac. "I can see it would be easier to be a political leader. Then also you would believe you had a common purpose with your party. Economics. Plenty of fine words. Unity. Independence." He saw Letlotse wince a little, and wondered what he had hit. He had not wanted to hurt Letlotse, only to get something clear which was in both their minds. Something which must be caught and tied down before it ran away. There was singing now, a pulse of singing somewhere all the time, somewhere in Ditlabeng, a building up of joy and strength. He went on softly, "You could have had the common purpose of a political party. For what it is. Perhaps you could have had the common purpose of all Africa." Letlotse turned round and looked at him. "If there is such a thing. I don't know. It is very hard to think of. But you would have lost the common purpose which is in the heart. Which is happiness. The thing which is in the Bamatsieng now. Listen, Letlotse, for I think I have it! Most kinds of society are too big for this. It is only for war that they come together. Never for anything good. Or that might be good. And because they are big, some things do not get done. I know, because I have read, and you, I suppose, Letlotse, because you have seen, that in the democracies, children and old

226

people must be collected like thrown-out roots and looked after by the State. It could never be so here."

"But if we unite, we of the Batswana, in one country?"

"As we must. I agree entirely, Letlotse, my Chief. But we can still keep the warmth of the separate tribes. Which is a different kind of warmth from that of the whole country. Just as it is a different kind from the warmth between husband and wife. That is not all. There in the democracies, in what they call the free world, what matters is to be rich. To be successful, to have trodden on the faces of others. Here—but you are rich, Letlotse——"

"I have more cattle," said Letlotse. "And more clothes. And I shall have a bigger house. As my cousin James Mookami has a bigger house. But he used his house to shelter you and Josh. I do not think I shall ever be rich enough to—to——"

"Exploit," said Isaac.

"Just that! I took off my shirt like the rest and split my nails building erosion dykes. But I want us all to be richer. I have been thinking, Isaac. We could do something about these miserable cattle! We could get modern tools, perhaps a tractor, not mine, it would belong to the tribe. We could have an agricultural committee."

"Who would be on it?"

"Well, there I am caught, I don't know yet. Perhaps James. He could at least add up the mileage of the tractor! But we want people educated in agricultural science. People who have been to school. You know this school I am going to start, Isaac. But we have only two primaries. One with no roof. Too many children never go to school at all. We have so few teachers and books. I see myself soon with very little money! Will you teach in my school, Isaac? Will you teach them electricity and using tools and all that?"

"I'm no teacher," said Isaac. But he felt warm inside to have been asked. "But perhaps I could get you one. If you did not mind having a white. But his name, he said, means Black Stranger!"

"I would have a white," said Letlotse. "I would have anyone who would help me, black, brown, yellow, bright green! But do you really think this about the tribe, Isaac? After all they followed Motswasele. They thought he was lucky. They thought he brought the rain. When he murdered people they only said he was strong."

"Yes," said Isaac. "Yes. The same thing that can make them good will also make them evil and there is plenty left from the days that are not so far back when all that mattered was fighting. When a man, to be a man, must have killed. It is difficult to move from that kind of order into another."

The two of them sat there, thinking about it, their thoughts going different ways. By now it would be almost dark inside the house; Aunt Sarah would be lighting the oil lamps, taking them from room to room, moving squares of pale light. But outside, though the sun had set, there was still a luminousness in the air, diffused and golden, that strangely cast shadows of small things on the floor of the *lapa*, faint and different from their hard day-time shadows. But the luminousness

228

streamed away, far up, and now the horizon glowed with a deep orange against which the shade trees showed heavy and noble, more beautiful even than by day.

Isaac was trying to think about the moral order and how here in Bechuanaland it could be entirely an order for peace and prosperity, for progress and education and happiness. But back in the Republic it could be none of these things. It was still an order of fighting and perhaps, before one could think of such things as happiness, one had to think of courage and steadfastness, the virtues of war, of the old moral order of the tribes. The war that was still there, out in the Republic, that must go on happening.

But Letlotse, watching the glow in the sky, fading by now into the gentleness of night, was thinking of his own immediate difficulties. He did not think there would be enough money for a secondary school, after all, and besides, nowadays a chief is not allowed to do what he thinks right for his people. All must go through Government. Even the old D.C., friendly as he was, had not been as hopeful as Letlotse had wanted him to be, was pulling him down just when he needed most to be strengthened, as his own people, at least, knew. Letlotse thought of his ancestors, men who would not have let themselves be pulled down, men who were quick with the spear, proud, angry—and then he drew back from his own thought in a kind of horror. Why, then, was it wrong for him now? Stupid, yes, you could see that quite plainly, stupid to think in terms of spears and axes in a world of H-bombs and all that. But wrong? Was it wrong? Why was it wrong? What had come between him and his ancestors?

"I suppose the Mission people think they have changed us," Letlotse said.

"It may be," said Isaac. "My Mission at Lady Selborne, I remember one of them saying, he that loseth his life shall find it, and also Greater love hath no man than this——"

"I know," said Letlotse. "We have said this in other words, we of the Batswana."

"The Christian words are very strong. I used to think of them when we were working together, Josh and Amos and I. And the rest of the group. They helped us not to be afraid. He that loseth his life——" Isaac's voice had dropped to a sad kind of whisper; he was thinking that there were two ways of losing one's life. Either one can be killed or one can be alone in a prison cell for always. Life sentence. That is losing one's real life.

But Letlotse did not want him to begin again living in those days. He said, "But supposing the tribe shifts from an order based on war to an order based on peace —and co-operation and all that—is it still what we ought to want? You and I, Isaac? I mean—democracy——"

"It is a funny word, democracy," said Isaac. "I have thought about it. I thought while I was ill. Perhaps it is not only voting, not only having a parliament; government and opposition and all that. Perhaps it is deeper. Perhaps it is a kind of sharing. Power. Responsibility." He sounded tired; Letlotse put one arm round him. Two or three bats came out from under the eaves and flickered away, quick and uncatchable like thoughts.

230

Someone threw more sticks on to the fire; the flames danced into sparkles. Thin smoke wavered in front of the stars.

"I shall take you back to Tselane," said Letlotse. "And tell her you are a free man. Not mine any longer. I know she is against chiefs!" Isaac said nothing, but put his hand up to cover Letlotse's which rested on his shoulder. There was no need to speak.

Chapter XXII

THERE WAS GREAT GIGGLING in the back room of James's house. This was Seneo fitting Tselane out with a Marks & Spencer outfit for the Installation. There would have to be a safety-pin in the skirt, but that could be covered up by a frill—so! This little pink wreath with a scrap of veil—"I meant to give you this for your wedding," said Seneo, "but you were wearing the handkerchief Isaac gave you."

But there was more to it than that. Tselane had asked a certain question, and Seneo had answered joyfully: "No, nothing happened in me. Perhaps there was a fight! Or perhaps—no, Tselane, here I am not sure if I am a nurse at Thomas's with a scientific training, or a woman of the tribe. But now I am quickly forgetting the evil thing."

"And that is good," said Tselane.

During the last week before the Installation, there were showers, good heavy reviving showers on all the land. They did not last long, but they cooled the air a little, and it was lucky they had come for there were those among the Bamatsieng who had been anxious in case Motswasele's rain might have turned its back. Now it seemed that a new chief might be as good. Tselane was pleased with the crop that Josh and Kuate had planted for her; almost the first thing she had done was to hoe her beans. She told Josh she was going to speak to the mother of Dikeledi, the girl he fancied.

Letlotse had began to get a good deal worried during the last day or two before the Installation. It did not seem to him that all the necessary things could possibly be ready in time. His Aunt Sarah soothed him and cooked him meat meals which he could barely get through, and told him slightly scandalous stories about his father and grandfather. The fat cattle for the feast were driven in, shot and skinned, the man who killed getting the skin. Tselane's regiment was carrying water, filling up every available container with pails from the bore holes. Tselane enjoyed this, being with all the others again and carrying little Amos on her back, the son begotten in marriage, the wanted and admired. It was only now that she let herself think how lonely she had been at Craigs. But Billy and Gloria had been asked over for the Installation and would stay with them; Tselane was glad to get back home her own good karosses, beautiful soft skins, not like the rough shop things at Craigs! They were cool and smooth to sleep on, cooler than blankets.

Seneo's regiment was crushing the corn for the great brewing, everyone at it, singing and laughing, swinging the five-foot wooden pestles, two or three at a time in rhythm, round each of the tall white-wood mortars, so that the millet was continually crushed instead of spurting out. When they were tired they sat on the ground and talked and sang, but they did not tire easily. If a man came near, even to look on, they shouted small insults at him pleasurably. Then the crushed corn was put to ferment in splendid earthenware pots, each safely bedded on to an old car tyre; this part was being looked after by Sarah's regiment, experienced brewers, most of them. Here all bubbled darkly and softly under the shade of cut *morula* branches. Now and again one of the brewers would ladle out half a gourd full of the mild, pleasant drink, look at it, perhaps sip it, make sure that all was going as it should.

By now the *morula* trees everywhere, through and around Ditlabeng, were dropping their fruit, tough skins, big stones, but a roll under the hand against a rock and then the spurt and nibble of juice between. "Do you remember," said Josh to Isaac, "the way we used to gather them up last year, glad of anything at all to eat? And now meat for the taking. Told you I liked this place, Isaac."

"Going to stay, Josh? For always?"

"Always is a long time. I want to get married. Have kids. Not all of us starts off with four boys! After that— still a freedom fighter, Isaac."

"I too."

"But you"—said Josh—"you got a good place here. Your wife with good land. You could get more land, cows, everything. The chief would give you anything you asked, Isaac. If you asked him now."

"While I'm still tied up with him? But he loosed me, Josh."

"Can't loose you. Not by saying."

"He offered me a job. Teaching in the new school. Technical Instructor! How's that, Josh?"

234

"Better than P.W.D. You taking it, Isaac?"

"No, Josh, I can't. Not while Amos is still in. Not *till we're all free. All Africa, Rhodesia, Angola, Mozam*bique, the South West, our neighbours."

"The Republic most of all. I know, Isaac. But still——"

"All our leaders are caught: Mandela, Sobukwe, Sisulu, Luthuli. Doesn't matter what letters they put on their party. If not in prison in detention. That means the rest of us have got to do what they can't do."

"I know," said Josh sadly. "Maybe we must be more clever. Hate more. Perhaps they did not hate enough."

"I don't want to think like that," said Isaac, "but perhaps I shall have to."

"I know," said Josh again.

Tselane also knew, or half knew. Isaac had told her about Letlotse's offer, and then said, "You, my wife, you could be teacher."

"I have forgotten," said Tselane. "Don't even speak English too good now."

"Could go back to teacher training."

"With all these?" She was suckling and playing with Amos; this one she would suckle long. Isaac had Kodunzwe on his knee. The two big boys were out playing a whole set of new games with their new friends, learning to drive oxen and ride on them, learning songs and riddles, telling about town life, laughing, running, eating.

"Plenty to help look after them," said Isaac. "All the Bamatsieng. Then you could be Agnes again. Teacher name. It is fine for kids to have a teacher mother."

"And a father—what?" Isaac didn't answer; by now she knew what he was thinking.

Billy and Gloria came. So did other guests. Most of the head ones, especially those who were going to speak at the Installation, stayed either at James's house or at the chief's house, into which Letlotse would move when he was married. There were Leapetswe, Seretse and Ruth Khama of the Bamangwato and their cousin Lenyeletse; there were several members of Legco, among them Tsheko Tscheko from Maun of the Batawana. There was Chief Bathoeng; there was Chief Neal of the Bakwena, and indeed most of the others: for it was an occasion. The only one near Letlotse's own age was Linchwe, Paramount Chief of the Bakgatla, and they had plenty to talk about, but little enough time for talking.

Before the ceremony, various things were done to Letlotse which he disapproved of but had very little say in. Well, his fathers could have their own way for this, it would be different once he got going with progress! He thought of a number of things which could shock them, and which he would much like to do. Meanwhile, the Matsosa were all gathering so as to be opposite him in Kgotla. A good many of them had rifles, including Isaac; this rifle had been one of the doctored ones, but it had been put overnight into the Mission church, though the Mission heads were not told of this, so that all evil should go out of it. He was carrying it when he saw the old District Commissioner, and suddenly felt he had to speak. He stepped out of the ranks: "Do you remember me, sir?" He hadn't meant to say sir, but out it had slipped!—and then to avoid embarrassing the good D.C. who clearly didn't remember. "I was a refugee from the Republic—you and the old chief saved me——"

"Of course!" said the D.C. "But there were two of you?"

"My friend is here too."

"I am glad," said the D.C. simply. "And you are both men of the Bamatsieng now? I remember I was asked to write a recommendation for you—that was in the bad days—and you got the job, I hope?"

"Thanks to you, sir." There, he'd said it again!

"But now if I am not making a mistake, you're one of the chief's own regiment?" Isaac nodded and laid a hand on the rifle butt. "Splendid, splendid, and no politics—sensible chap. I am sure Chief Letlotse will be able to make good use of you with all the skills you're bound to have. And the old chief—if he's anywhere he can see us—he'll know he did the right thing."

"I hope so," said Isaac quietly, stepping back into the ranks of his comrades. Yes, the D.C. was a friend, a kind of friend. But if he knew what politics still went on—but he need never know. They were not against him or his like.

Letlotse sat on a chair covered with leopard skins, the weapons hot and slippery in his hands, the leopard skin, which had been the symbol of authority and absolute significance, hot and hard over his shoulders. Sweat dripped down him in long trickles. With one bit of himself he was thinking how much nicer it would have been to have a modern nylon leopard skin, light and cool, and not smelling as this one still, a little, did of leopards

237

and killings. He looked down most of the time as became one who was listening diligently to his elders, and to the representatives of the British Government. If he looked up he might pick out faces without recognition, since now at this moment he was infinitely far from them. Separated by something invisible. There were the Matsosa in front of him. George Senyele, Isaac, all of them. The mine boy who had fanned him, whose face he knew so well, but who had never spoken. Others. Chief Rasemonje, and with him, in their oddly different dress, a few of the Angolans. There was the Mission in force. There was the doctor. James and Seneo and his Aunt Sarah were behind him, as was the District Commissioner and the Resident Commissioner.

The speeches went on and on, all of them saying exactly the same thing: that he must listen to the Council of his elders, follow precedent, not be led astray by the young men (and who is that—James?—respectable James?), consult the older chiefs—for now he would be in the House of Chiefs—honour the protecting flag, and over and over again, that he must always consult and be advised by the elders. Lepedi made the worst speech, though one or two of Motswasele's old supporters were bad and lengthy. He realised with a certain pleasure, that he was not the only one who was bored with all this. There was no reverent hush, but a very great deal of talking and laughing. The speeches were to give pleasure and importance to their makers, not to any audience. But the poor chief had to listen. Or appear to listen. In the middle there was a new voice, one he didn't know and so really listened to, Linchwe of the Bakgatla.

"Make up your mind," the new voice said, "on what you know is right. Be a leader for good and you will be followed." Perhaps, thought Letlotse, perhaps it will not be so bad being chief. Perhaps there are ideas floating about among the Batswana and they may be caught and made into something. Perhaps I can get into the future after all. Perhaps there are other ways than through that poor political party of mine that I used to dream about. Other ways for my country and for my tribe, which will be part of it and of which I am now, so strangely, part. Because I have given myself and it is for ever.

At the end all broke up into shouting and dancing, praises and acceptance and the tribal word that meant so much more than any translation would show. Seneo beckoned to Tselane and half a dozen of the women crowded on to the back seat of James's car, sitting on one another's knees. Both babies had been left behind, with Tselane's old aunt, who had, for many purposes, taken her mother's place. But the boys had been tremendously impressed with everything, especially the fact that the important whites with the swords and feathers had saluted Letlotse, their new mother's kinsman.

Seneo whispered to Tselane, "Are you still a member of the People's Party?"

"Yes, certainly I am," said Tselane. "Did we not club together and give Letlotse a tea-set for his Installation present?"

"Pink roses," said Seneo. "Does the People's Party think of him as a pink rose? Pink, but certainly not red."

"They did not ask me to choose. But at least it shows Letlotse that we exist as a party."

"And are against chiefs."

"Well, we are the opposition, I think. Somebody must be the opposition."

All evening the party went on, eating of beef and drinking of beer, singing, dancing, talking. Great happy crowds flowing through Ditlabeng and Letlotse the centre of it. Isaac and Josh and Billy and Kuate and Murphy rolled around meeting one another and all their friends, slapping one another on the back, laughing, holding hands, having just one more beer. They saw George Senyele almost arrogantly sober, and occasionally they saw the older ones, Ramodimo and Dithapo and so on, cosily getting together and amiably greeting their juniors. The British guests at the Installation had all left long ago, their swords and feathers neatly packed into their cars. The D.C.'s head clerk and the rest of his old office staff walked back with him to his house, occasionally dancing a little. They lighted his lamp before they left him to go down again towards Kgotla and join their friends.

Somewhere in the small hours Isaac and Josh and Billy found themselves sitting with their backs against a rock, still comfortably warm from the day; they had been asleep, at least they thought they had, but the world had been spinning and rocking rather too much to stand in. Now they had woken and stretched and the stars were splendid, though some were blotted out in the light-haze around the moon, which had seemed suddenly to have risen while they were not looking. But farther down in the sky how many, how bright, the great single stars and like fingerprints in the sky Tlala and Kgora, smudges of light, stars everywhere to stare at! "I have things to say to you," said Billy quietly. "A message came through —and we are sure it is no trap this time—but it is now being said that you are dead. So it is safe for you to go back. With a new name."

"I have been thinking this myself," said Isaac. "But I will not go for always. Not now that I have all these children to care for. I will go for—for a certain time that will have an ending. And I want Josh stays here, gets a son as I have done, before he goes."

"If you go," said Josh, "I must."

"No. No, I say. We do not both go from Letlotse, from the Bamatsieng. I think something will happen here, a tree grow from a small seed. But nothing can come utterly right for the Batswana unless it is also right in the Republic."

"And in Southern Rhodesia."

"And also in Southern Rhodesia. In all our own Africa. And there is another thing. I do not think you will understand, Billy, but I want to leave Letlotse, my chief, while he still thinks well of me, while he perhaps still wants me to stay. I think I could stay too long."

"You are crazy," said Billy. "Perhaps after all you should not go. Let me unsay the message. You were always a little crazy, Isaac. Now more than ever."

"I understand," said Josh. "It is because you and Letlotse have become too close, and that can mean that love turns inside out and becomes hate."

"Hate?" said Billy. "You are both crazy! Is it by any chance—class?"

Isaac shook his head, "I know my mother's people and my father's people three generations back. They were—respected. Known. But that does not signify, except that there were fighters among them. I cut myself off from all that when I become a freedom fighter, as I cut myself off now." He got to his feet. "Come. There will be a day very soon when I have no house. No wife. When I am afraid to look round. Now and here we are friends. Come."

Chapter XXIII

IN TSELANE'S HOUSE all woke late and it seemed to Isaac that there had been a dream which he did not wish to think about. The rugs and skins were rolled up neatly, Gloria admiring the handsome new kaross which one of her uncles, seeing how the wind blew, had given to Tselane. There was much laughter while the two women cooked meat from the good share Tselane had got when the fat cattle were cut up and divided. Isaac and Billy drank milk and then drank beer and spoke about the visitors who had come from other tribes and even from the Republic, to do honour to the Bamatsieng. And so long as this was all that was spoken about, so long, Isaac knew, the dream would stay hidden.

Billy spoke knowingly about certain ones, why they had come, whom they had been seen speaking with. Some were plainly jealous, knowing they would never do as well themselves. Billy had a good idea of the way the political cats were jumping in Bechuanaland, not only those who had been at the Constitutional talks, but those who had looked on critically. Isaac was throwing in talk and yet he only half listened. He was looking at his wife and the four boys, laughing softly and decorously, their bones well covered, obedient to him, their provider

243

and lord! Yet he knew also that this was an old thought and perhaps he should not have it, but because not having it was mixed with the dream, he wanted to keep the old thought and the old pride, and he drank beer again and tried only to hear a song in the back of his mind. But Billy would not let him, Billy pulled at him, about the official documents which had been going the rounds in Bechuanaland, and what the papers had said: "Listen, man! Once this Constitution goes through and this development plan, what will be left of the tribes?" He dug Isaac in the ribs: "You and your tribe! You will forget all this that is nonsense, that is part of the things we need to finish with. You will become modern again!"

"You cannot say that," said Isaac, "not with your mouth full of my tribe's beer and your guts full of our meat. This Constitution! This development plan! They are only there to look at, for the English to say they are helping us greatly. Why should they want to kill the tribes? Good and well in Kenya, but it was the English settlers who made the tribes there hate one another so that they could profit by it. Here in our country we do not hate one another. It is a long time since we even poked one another with spears. Do I hate a Mokwena or a Mongwato? No, we are brothers."

"You are not brothers in the songs," said Billy, and quoted one.

"Oh, that! The songs are funning. Does anyone say it is true-true when a jazz song croons you are my only baby? Not true either when we of the Magwasa sing that we eat small tribes. Nor are the small tribes afraid of us. They liked to hear such a song well sung. It was good yesterday, good for all of us. Why should it be killed?"

"Mad," said Billy. "Knew this would make you mad. Told you not to come!" And now Tselane and Gloria brought the meat, hot, salty, ready to have the juices chewed well out of it. Eating that meat, mixing it with beer in his stomach, Isaac forced the dream back from his mind. Not yet. Tselane was making Gloria a present of some baskets, close woven, elegantly patterned, good for any kind of food, more alive, nicer in the hand, than ever plastic or enamel could be. Both the men looked at their women proudly and with stirring towards them, which the women could feel as a pleasing and teasing and Tselane as a full flooding of pride. For it had been a great thing for her to pay back Gloria with the full hospitality of the feast, the chief's cattle. I know myself again, Tselane thought, I have been lost and now I am found.

A weaver bird perched for a moment on the low wall of the *lapa*. The nests swung on the ends of the branches of the big thorn between them and Small Snakes Rock. So upright the bird stood, yellow and bright black, little against the world. And then Josh was coming along the path. And Isaac began to know he had to remember the dream which was not a dream, the light-haze round the moon, Billy giving him the message and what he had said to Josh. The weavers scurried and chattered round their nests, but he himself was a man with a certain necessity laid on him. And perhaps it was the same necessity which had lain on Chaka and on many others. But, for

245

Isaac, no man would forge the new weapon, as the stabbing spear had been forged for the young Chaka. He would have comrades, but none by his side, none shouting with him. He must go alone and unarmed. He must tell Tselane.

"Eat," he said to Josh, "you have come at the right time." He would not be the first to speak of other matters. Nor would Josh. After he had picked out a good piece of meat and was holding it by the bone, eating at it, he said to Isaac, "James Mookami has given me a heifer in calf."

"So you will get married!" Tselane said. "Oh, well, my man did not give even a goat for me. I am shamed in front of your wife, Josh." And she giggled, never looking less shamed. But, Isaac thought, I gave no cattle, I gave myself, have I the right to take myself away? And it seemed for a moment that a door had opened on to a way of safety which was also a way of honour.

Tselane was telling Gloria about Josh's girl, Dikeledi, disparaging her enough to make Josh a little angry; then praising her enough to make him embarrassed. Dikeledi would do nicely for Josh; she was hard-working, sweet-tempered, came from a family that was not rich, would not expect too big a *bogani* for her. She had got to Standard IV, so she would know how to keep house nicely, would be able to follow instructions on baby-care and dressmaking. Her parents should be glad to have her married to a man like Josh who would do skilled work and be paid for it. They would have a Mission wedding and Dikeledi would wear a white dress and a veil;

her little sisters would be bridesmaids; then she would settle down and be a good wife and bear plenty of children. The Mission ladies had pointed out to Tselane that she too could have a Mission wedding now, it was not at all too late. But Tselane had put it off; she had not been entirely certain that she wanted the blessing of the Mission God. Though the wedding party would have been a nice time. However she had taken the baby there for christening and the Mission ladies were pleased that the parents had chosen a Bible name like Amos, instead of one of these African names which could not be allowed. Christening would not hurt little Amos; the more protection the better. The message of Amos, the Mission had said, was that God is just. Tselane had bowed her head in silent assent, turning this justice in her own mind into justice for Africa.

For a while the men had not spoken much; they had finished piece after piece of good filling meat. Josh signed with his head to the others. They went up to the top of Small Snakes Rock, which was really a little kopje made up of many rocks, watching carefully in case any of the small snakes were slithering out into the heat. It was a place where one could not be overheard.

Isaac was seeing things he did not, mostly, see or think about. There were so many different kinds of plant and flower, even now, long mauve flowers, little yellow and pink ones, and silky pale golden flowers with a dark blotch in the throat. He had never thought of asking their names: perhaps Tselane would know. A green-flowered, low creeper fingered and tied up other plants. As he, unawares, had been caught and tied up. Beetles and grasshoppers and ants moved ceaselessly through everything in their busy dust world, as they would if he was dead, far-off, forgotten by Ditlabeng. No, he would not be forgotten. He was part of it now for ever.

They settled down under the shadow of a rock, a great rock foursquare in a thirsty land. Josh said abruptly, speaking in English, "You will try for one of the contacts —first?"

"If he goes," said Billy, "but he does not mean to go—no. He is bewitched."

"Isaac, man—you will not go?" said Josh eagerly.

He too—he wants me to go through that other door, Isaac thought—but if I go, perhaps it is only the door to the past. Tribalism with freedom—yes. Tribalism without freedom—no. The Bamatsieng must work out their future in a free world, my tribe. That is what I must be willing to die for; that is the real meaning of what happened out with the Magwasa when I became truly a man. "I will try to see——" said Isaac and wrote a name in the dust with a stick and rubbed it out with his foot.

"That is safe," said Billy, "but you had better not stay in the township; the police have too many of their friends around. Also we have heard that so-and-so is in for his second ninety days."

"Poor bastard," said Josh, taking a deep breath of Ditlabeng, of easiness and love and not being afraid. Birds scuffled in a small tree, a lizard moved jerkily across the rock. Somewhere below there was singing, a dozen men who had eaten meat and drunk beer, as they themselves had, and their women shrilling round them. It would have been nice to be doing just that, but—"Isaac, man, I got to come with you!" he said.

"No," said Isaac once more, "the thing is not on you. Not yet. Marry. Take care of Tselane." And his face crumpled a little, for he had still to tell Tselane. Perhaps at night, to soften it, perhaps to leave with her the daughter they had sometimes spoken of.

"Don't suppose you can get any message to Amos," said Josh staring in front of him. It was not possible, of course, he only said it because, somehow, some way, Amos was still one of them. His name had to come in. But Isaac shook his head.

"How will you go?" asked Billy. "Coming back to P.W.D. for a spell? They ask me, where my apprentice gone? My boss, he asks me. I say, back to the Reserve, bloody tribal!"

"No," said Isaac, "I have thought of another way." And it seemed to him that his mind had been working on its own, underneath the level of knowing about. That must be it, since it was all plain to him, as plain as though he had done it already. He told them and they agreed that it was a good plan, the best.

It gave him, perhaps, a fortnight. By that time Ditlabeng would be itself again. The tribe would be settling back to work and talk and sleep; cooking; wood gathering, going back to the work on the lands, most of them; deciding what cattle to send in for sale, quarrelling, laughing, snatches of singing still going on. But the guests would be gone, the feasting over. Letlotse would perhaps be wondering how to do any of the things he was intending to do, beginning to see all the forces, ancient and modern, from ballot boxes to witch doctors, which would stop him, if they could, from being the kind of chief he wanted to be. Unless he had help from friends. But what friends? Not whites, not even if they had money or power to help him, not even the good D.C. who had helped his father. Not the Mission. Who then? Only his tribe, only the Bamatsieng who were shaping him as he was shaping them. The only certain help would come from what he could call up in their minds and actions, which would be on his side, showing him ways round and forward and showing them how things could be for good as between tribe and chief.

Chapter XXIV

"YOU HAVE GOT YOURSELF a mines pass. How?
Why?" said Letlotse, angry and anxious. Isaac
had been dodging him, and he himself had been hours
in Kgotla over an elaborate quarrel which appeared to
go back a couple of generations at least. No evidence
was barred. Speeches of remarkable irrelevance had
been made and applauded. Beer had been brought in
and drunk from the old yellow gourds. It could have
gone on another week, he thought, and he had been
somewhat frowned on for trying to hurry it. Kgotla
was fine for the sudden flare up, the misbehaviour which
could be punished summarily and which everyone could
agree should not have happened. Better for a man to get
a quick public thrashing and the knowledge that everyone
thought it was just and only what he deserved, than to go
through all the length and fear and formality of a police
court, a night in the cells at least—he had been to see a
police court at work when he was in London and felt
that it was inappropriate, and also, rightly or wrongly, that
those with money could pay fines instead of going to
prison and no more said and nobody caring. But anyhow
European justice was to do mostly with property, Tswana
justice mostly with people and their rights and with the

251

restoration of order and decency in the community. "Why?" he said again. "Why have you taken out this pass?"

Isaac said nothing but walked beside him. At last he said low, "I had to."

"Had to? What have you done?" It suddenly occurred to Letlotse that Isaac had been guilty of something—but what? Where?

"Must I have done—something wicked? I have only taken out a mines pass."

"But why, Isaac, why?"

"Well, I have a family. Must pay my taxes, educate my children."

"You are lying. I would pay your taxes, educate your children. You are mine, Isaac!"

"Am I, Kgosi?"

Letlotse said nothing, felt the rebuke, at last said, "You are quite right, Isaac. I should not have said that. But I do not believe you all the same. You cannot want to leave Tselane and your own little child."

"I do not want to leave Tselane," said Isaac. He was looking straight in front of him, keeping his voice steady. Then he fumbled under his shirt. "I ask you to look at my pass, Kgosi Letlotse."

Letlotse took it and looked, "So you have taken *that* name. My name that I gave you."

"Because," said Isaac, "if I am caught I am not a citizen of the Republic. I am one of the Batswana. One of the Bamatsieng. And I appeal to my chief. Who will perhaps be able to help me."

Letlotse said nothing for a moment, then, "I see. Your

252

chief will try to protect you again. Doubtless you will have fallen into bad company, my poor tribesman."

"I hope I shall not get you into trouble," said Isaac. "I very much hope so. Perhaps I shall not be caught. Or perhaps if they catch me I shall be smashed up before I have time to show my pass. Or they will take it away, tear it up. I am going into a war, and the Sabotage Act is part of it. And there are no rules about prisoners and no Red Cross. Or any such nonsense."

"Isaac," said Letlotse, "don't go!"

"Don't say that," said Isaac. "Wish me good luck, Letlotse, my Chief. In the end it is your war too." And again he knelt as he had once done to Letlotse's father.

As it grew light Tselane watched the bundle on the floor take shape, become inescapable. He was still asleep, turned to her, breathing slow, his fingers relaxed and curled like a child's. Like Kodunzwe's. She touched one of his hands; it came half awake, negligently, then slept again. She began to count his breathing; if she could make him sleep on and on in her house on the kaross where there had been such delight, if she could keep him—he woke and looked at her, deep, deep through the heart. His breathing quietened. His fingers alerted. For a moment he laid his head in between her milk-deep breasts, then, lightly, got to his feet, and put on the shirt and shorts she had bought him in Craigs. He stroked one finger gently over the sleeping baby's head. "Take care of my little Amos."

"You will find him fat when you come back, my husband. And also I will take care of your Josh. You will find him married."

"The worst thing was saying good-bye to Josh," said Isaac, and then: "No. This is worse."

"This is good," said Tselane, but her lips were not quite steady. "You go to war, my husband." And then she said suddenly, "I wish you were armed. Oh, oh, I wish that!"

"No, no," he said. "You have it wrong, Tselane my wife, I do not go to kill. I go to make things difficult for them. Only difficult. So that slowly they begin to know that their days of easiness are over. That they must go or come to terms if it is not too late. Perhaps even that some of them may become ashamed. That is why many people have to do this work." He picked up the bundle.

"I wish I could come with you," said Tselane.

"I must go light," he said. "And you will care for my house and my children and my honour. I will think of you doing that if they kill me. It is the last thing I shall think of, my wife, and then perhaps if what my Mission said has any truth in it, we shall be together again somehow. But I do not think I shall die. I will try very hard not to die. And I may be able to send a message back to Craigs. But if I do not send, there is no need to despair. And if I am caught, I will try to make out that I am a Batswana tribesman and my chief will help me."

"So I have been some use to you," said Tselane, with a kind of smile that covered up the working of her mouth. She took the bundle from Isaac, and told the boys to stay and see to the baby. They said good-bye and go safe to their father, low and respectfully. Both were upset. Both trying hard to be brave and worthy of him. Not to show it.

He said to Tselane, "I am an altogether different person because of you and because of the Bamatsieng. There are things I am not afraid of any longer."

They walked down to join the lorry and the group of other men from the tribe who were going to the mines. There were two or three from the Matsosa. But none of them knew that Isaac would slip away somewhere at some station beyond the border, that he would no longer be with them. Other women had come. And there was Josh who could not trust himself to speak. They climbed into the lorry. The lorry started up. Some women cried, but not, not Tselane. Go safe, Isaac. Go safe.

Printed in the United Kingdom by
Lightning Source UK Ltd., Milton Keynes
137665UK00001B/41/P